THE SKULL KEEPER

A PSYCHOLOGICAL THILLER

MARIËTTE WHITCOMB

WWW.MARIETTEWHITCOMB.COM

This novel is a work of fiction. Names, characters, places, and incidents are the product of the author's imagination. Any resemblance to real persons, living or dead, events, or locales is entirely coincidental.

Copyright © 2023 Mariëtte Whitcomb

All rights reserved. No reproduction is permitted without written permission from the author except for the use of quotations in a book review.

ISBN Paperback: 978-0-620-97819-4
ISBN eBook: 978-0-620-97820-0

I dedicate this novel to the victims who never made it home. To their families and loved ones who grieve without answers.

Also, to the police officers and everyone else working tirelessly to solve cold cases to apprehend and convict the perpetrators.

Prologue

15 years earlier

The victim didn't fit; the crime scene similar to the other seventeen, but different.

Detective Boyle turned to the medical examiner standing next to him. They focused on the victim's remains. Seventeen times and they still struggled to comprehend the carnage.

He didn't ask if this was the work of the serial killer he'd spent the past five years trying to identify and apprehend. Every night he fell asleep staring at photos of the crime scenes. And every morning he woke up to the same images. Death and destruction haunted his dreams. The mutilated bodies called out to him from his subconscious.

No matter what the killer did, Detective Boyle knew every victim's face. Their faces before. And after.

"Your guess is as good as mine, Will." Doctor Jessica Linetti shrugged before squatting down next to the body. "He left us everything; the same as with the other victims. Something doesn't add up with this one. Despite the obvious."

After the discovery of the fifth victim's body, Boyle no longer had to swallow the bile back down as he stared at what the killer left of his victims.

Why this one?

Doctor Linetti pulled the victim's wallet from the right pocket of his faded jeans and read the name on the driver's license. She handed it to one of her team members.

Boyle took it from the crime scene investigator and studied the photo through the plastic evidence bag. "He was at the top of our suspect list. No way he did *this* to himself."

"No, he didn't." Doctor Linetti turned her focus to the lump of skin which used to be the victim's face. She spread it out next to the body. "Unless high on drugs, he wouldn't have been capable of mutilating himself. Not to this extent."

Detective Boyle looked at what the ME pointed towards with a gloved finger. She pushed herself up to standing and shook her head.

Boyle spoke before Jessica could. "Unlike the female victims, he was alive when he was decapitated."

One

Allysa

She exited the elevator and made her way through the hotel lobby. Morgan Wright didn't walk the way most women did. She demanded attention, but at the same time, people were often intimidated by her mere presence and glanced away as soon as their eyes landed on her. Morgan winked at me as people stepped out of her way. I still couldn't believe she had dropped everything and came.

"How do you do that?" I asked once she slid into the booth across from me in the restaurant.

Morgan signalled a waiter. "Good morning to you too, Allysa. How did you sleep? Does it also feel strange to you being here together? What's on our itinerary for today, other than the reason we're here? For the first time, you're not wearing a tank top. You clean up well. Did it take a team of professionals to make you this presentable, or did you manage on your own?"

"Wow, that's a lot of questions for someone who hasn't had her second cup of coffee yet." I smiled.

"You haven't answered me."

"I asked a question first, which you answered with more questions. Why do we do that?"

Morgan's laughter filled the restaurant. Once the waiter arrived, she stopped, ordered her coffee and one for me – without asking. "So, Mrs Ross, we've been friends for close to a year, and instead of doing what normal long-distance friends do and meet up for a cruise or something, you asked me to fly across the globe to be your plus-one at a funeral. If anyone else had asked, I would've declined, and not politely. But coming from you, there's a reason behind it. Spill."

"You're the only person I know who is always dressed for a funeral. Every. Single. Day. Do you even own any clothing that isn't black?" I had never thought Morgan would put her life on hold and fly to Marcel. She hadn't asked why or who'd died when I told her the real reason for us meeting. "You came without asking a single question."

Morgan reached across the table and covered my hand with hers. "You said you needed me." She shrugged, letting go of my hand and thanking the waiter for our coffees. "Liquid breakfast. I'll need two to go if I'm to remain upright until they lower the coffin into the ground."

"Rachel was cremated. It's a memorial service."

Morgan leaned back in her seat and ran her fingers through her short blonde hair, tucking it behind her ears. I'd never asked whether she was a natural blonde. "Who was Rachel to you? Did you invite your new best friend to your previous best friend's memorial service? No, that's not it. We've spoken about your non-booksta friends. Your husband and son. Our lives. Our shared hatred for any genre of book not classified as psychological or dark thrillers, and true crime. Rachel's name never came up." She reached for her coffee, not taking her eyes off mine. "Why isn't Doctor Ross here with you?"

If I didn't know better, I would've thought Morgan was a detective. One of the many reasons we connected right from the start – we both saw through the bullshit. We were similar in many ways, which was either hilarious or frightening; depending on how you looked at it.

"Jake hates it when people call him *Doctor* outside of his practice. He thinks I'm here on vacation with you." My husband didn't know about Rachel, or that I'd grown up in Marcel. When we met, I didn't want my past to influence any chance I had of a future with him. Mostly, I wasn't the person I had been when I left this place fifteen years earlier. *Correction: I didn't leave, I ran.*

Morgan finished her coffee. Her face changed into the one I'd seen in Marco Polo videos; her thinking face. "Lysa, what did you tell your husband? Why am I here, other than to meet you in person? We could've done that in the Bahamas or anywhere more fun."

"The least I can do is tell you *why* we are here." *Part of the reason.* "Jake doesn't know I grew up in Marcel. Or that I had a stepmother named Rachel."

Or that she murdered my brother.

Two

Morgan

Allysa always mentioned our similarities and to an extent we were similar. But I wasn't as perfect or admirable as she thought. Unlike her, I'd spent years becoming comfortable with who I was and burying my past.

"Wait a minute. We're going to your stepmother's memorial service, when you haven't even told your husband about her? Allysa, what's going on?"

I glimpsed something in Allysa's eyes. The *something* was as familiar to me as my skin. "Don't you dare lie to me. We're best friends. I flew in from Edinburgh to be here for you. Tell me the truth, and I mean all of it, or I'm blocking you on Instagram and getting on the first flight out of here." I grinned; Allysa and I often joked about blocking each other on social media.

Allysa shifted in her seat, tugging at her dress' sleeves. I'd never seen her wear a dress before.

"I asked you because you're good at reading people," she said, glancing past my shoulder.

"Right now, I can see that you're full of it. I might be good at reading facial expressions and body language, but I can't read dead people. And I sure as hell won't attend whatever it's called when people try to speak to the dead. I'm not a ghost reader."

Allysa pursed her lips and laughed. "I love you."

"I love you more." We played the 'I love you game' too often. I threw my hands in the air; fingers spread. "I'm *here* for crying out loud, which I won't do as neither of us are criers.

Dammit, Allysa, just tell me what's going on. Did you murder her? Yes, I'll get rid of the evidence for you, even though you're more than capable of doing it yourself. Wait, you wouldn't leave a crime scene or any evidence which can be traced back to you. If you did, it would be staged and the evidence will point to whoever you want."

"No, I didn't kill her."

I gestured with my hands for her to continue. Allysa didn't. "Who am I supposed to be reading for you? I can't go in blind. Give me *something*."

Allysa pulled her black hair away from her neck. It had finally grown to the length she wanted. I had talked her out of cutting it short again more than once. "Can't you just trust me?"

I shook my head and forced a sigh. "You know my secret." *The least damning one.* "We don't keep secrets from each other."

Allysa stopped the waiter as he walked past our booth and ordered us more caffeine.

Three

Allysa

"Jake knows I'm meeting you. He said it will be good for me after the past few months. Thank you for being here. Why are you living in Edinburgh now? Weren't you living in Majorca a few months ago?" Edinburgh was the third city Morgan had lived in since we met on Instagram not a year before.

Who could have ever guessed I would meet my best friend, my soul-friend in many ways, through the bookstagram community? I sure didn't. It offered me insight into what drew people to online dating. I had proposed Morgan try it, as she'd been single since we met. She refused, saying the men on those sites were either married, weirdoes or serial killers. *Agreed.*

Morgan stared at her coffee. "I live in the world. Any place can be home for however long I want it to be."

I grabbed my phone, found the photo I was looking for, and held it towards her. "Are you sure a certain Australian actor, who is currently in Scotland, has nothing to do with it?"

Morgan grabbed my phone and stared at the photo of her walking hand in hand with a man who was a fifteen on a scale of one to ten. "This isn't supposed to be public. We've kept it quiet for months. I can't be seen with him like this."

She placed my phone on the table and pushed it towards me as she grabbed her own from her black leather handbag, and stormed out of the restaurant. It stung a little that Morgan didn't trust me to keep her relationship a secret. Neither of them were married. The secrecy was therefore unnecessary, in my opinion.

I sent Jake a text, telling him to have a good day at the

office and to send my love to Daniel. Daniel would always be the best thing to ever happen to me. The resemblance between him and Sebastian was uncanny. If only my brother could've met his nephew.

Morgan returned to the table before I could dwell on the past.

"It's out. Yes. We're dating; have been for a while." Morgan slid into the booth with the grace of a female prison guard and dropped her phone in her handbag. She yanked it out again, waving it next to her head. *Even her phone is black.* "Do you think we should take an *usie*?"

My hand shot to my forehead. "A what?"

"An *usie*, like a selfie. We can post it and make everyone jealous." She looked at me as if I'd said the dumbest word ever.

"You mean a photo of the two of us?"

Morgan nodded; her palms facing the ceiling.

"Not yet. I don't know if either of them is one of our thousands of followers. I can't risk them seeing I'm here."

A lot had changed throughout the city since I left. That day, I'd vowed to uncover the truth and bring Rachel to justice. No matter the cost. I shouldn't have waited fifteen years; not that confronting her had ever made a difference. After all these years, the police remained adamant that my brother had left out of his own free will. They claimed to have investigated Rachel's alibi for that night, but if they had discovered the truth, they would've arrested her. Not for murder, but for all of her various other crimes.

I should've told them and not expected them to do their jobs. Of course, Rachel had them all in her pocket.

"May I ask you something?" Morgan sat in the passenger seat, fidgeting with the rental car's radio.

I swatted her hand away from the damn radio and switched it off. "I drive in silence."

"Liar. You listen to audiobooks and consider it reading,"

Morgan said to the passenger side window. The ocean was on her side; the city on mine.

"Are we having this discussion again?"

"Let's not, because I'm right. Your monthly updates should differentiate between books read and those you listen to." Morgan poked my shoulder. "You're real."

I slapped her hand away while keeping my eyes on the road. If this was her way of distracting me, it worked. "As real as I was last night when we hugged."

"Ah, yes. Our first time."

"How was your first time with the Aussie?"

Morgan sighed and cleared her throat. "What happens down south stays down south."

"Scotland isn't south, silly." I shook my head and laughed, even though Morgan didn't share in my amusement. "It's like we've been friends our entire lives."

"Because we both hate drama, and we're not very fond of people." Morgan snorted a laugh. "Fictional people and those who are part of the bookstagram community are our people. Some of them. The others we tolerate."

I asked whether she was worried that people would discover the truth about her, even more so now that her face was all over the internet.

"It's not like I'm in witness protection or anything. And to be fair, you hadn't known that we'd met years ago. Not until I told you the truth about meeting me at a CJ Green book signing. You fangirled so hard over your favourite author." Morgan laughed and tapped her fingers on her knees, as if typing on a keyboard.

"Mommy, how long until we get there?" she asked in her version of a whiny toddler voice.

Some days I wondered what Morgan had been like as a child, and whether she had ever been one. Other days, I wondered if she had ever truly grown up. For as much as I knew about Morgan Wright, she remained a mystery.

Which was fair. I didn't tell her everything either.

Four

Twenty years earlier

"Death is never pretty. People think dying in their sleep is a good way to go. Perhaps for them, but not for whoever finds them, or wakes up next to their no-longer-breathing-meat. You, *will not* be a pretty corpse. Serves you right."

She thrashed against the restraints. It didn't help her, but it made this all that much more fun for me. "What are you going to do to me?"

I couldn't suppress my laughter; not even if I were the one tied to the chair. "Do you think I'll tell you the truth?" Her badly coloured hair slipped through my fingers as I yanked the whore's head back, exposing her throat. To me, they were all whores, but unlike the others, this one opened her legs for money. *Disgusting.*

The blade traced the length of her external jugular vein. From her collar bone right up to her earlobe. Biology had always been my favourite subject. "When will you get it through your thick skull that he'll never want you?"

She swallowed hard. The cold steel remained pressed against her skin. "Who?"

I released her hair and stared at her reflection in the mirror. "See, this is the problem. You don't even know what you've done wrong. By the time I'm done, you will."

Our eyes met; recognition flashed in hers. "I remember you. Why are you—"

"Shut up! If I have to hear one more word in that whiny voice of yours ..." The blowtorch's blue flame hissed to life next to her cheek. "Be a good girl and stick out your tongue."

She shook her head. Her lips pursed tight. Tears rolled down her cheeks, dripping onto her pink shirt.

"Don't worry. The cat won't get your tongue, the police will. Now, say ah."

Five

Morgan

Allysa withheld a lot of information from me. For the time being, I bit my tongue. People often tell us more than they want when we fool them into thinking we believe their version of a story. If Rachel had been the evil stepmother Allysa made her out to be, I realised there were even more things she kept from me.

Half-truths scream full-lies.

"Rachel was a bitch to you and your brother, but it doesn't explain why he left without saying goodbye to you. From what you mentioned earlier, it's clear the two of you were very close growing up." I studied her face, hands, shoulders, legs; waiting for her body language to tell me the truth. Or at least steer me in the right direction.

Allysa kept up the charade. "That's my point. He wouldn't have."

"Have you considered the possibility he might've had a reason to flee Marcel?"

"My brother didn't *flee*." Her nostrils flared. "Rachel killed him."

I asked the obvious, "What reason could she have had for murdering her own stepson?"

Allysa's eyes closed for a split second longer than necessary to blink. "I suspect she was in love with him."

People murder each other for much less. I gave her the benefit of the doubt. "Tell me about your stepsisters. The more I know going in, the better."

"I prefer you go in blind. You need to draw your own

conclusions and be objective." Allysa's eyes never left the road ahead. Determination seeped through her pores.

For the first time in years, I had a best friend. I felt more than just a little rusty at the entire friendship thing. To have an almost exclusively virtual friend was one thing, but sitting next to her in a car – with the weight of what she had placed on my shoulders – proved nerve-wracking. I didn't want to fail her and lose our friendship. Allysa never belittled me. She never made me question my worth. Allysa was my biggest supporter and fan.

Despite being out of practise in the friendship department, I still excelled in detecting red herrings. If her evil stepsisters were lying, I would know. *It takes one to know one.* Allysa never referred to them as *evil*, neither did she call them her sisters.

"This explains your obsession with cold cases."

Allysa glared at me, just as I wanted. "I'm not obsessed. Someone needs to keep shining a light on the victims the police and the media have forgotten. The families are often too distraught and exhausted after years of not hearing a single word. I'm. Not. Obsessed."

"*Passionate* then."

She glanced at me with one eyebrow raised. "The fact I run an Instagram account dedicated to cold cases, means nothing other than that I believe parents and siblings deserve answers."

Projection much? I wondered how far to keep pushing her. For as close as we were and the details about our lives we shared, there were just as many things we would never divulge. If you weren't there when it happened then you'll never grasp it in its entirety.

As with all traumatic events, there is the person you were before, and the person you will become after. A specific day holds more power than you ever thought possible. Until you stand outside the trauma unit and the doctor gives you the life altering news. 'He didn't make it. I'm so sorry.' Sorry? What a pathetic word. It doesn't describe the soul-destroying years ahead of you. Losing your identity. Moments when the pain becomes so unbearable you can't remain on your feet. The nights when you get flashbacks of that defining moment, or the last time he touched you, said your name, and texted to say he loves you. Every time this happens, you lose him again. And more of the person you were before you heard the word 'sorry' dies.

"Morgan, where did you go? You zoned out." Allysa's hand rested on my arm.

Despite the air-con being on full blast, I couldn't breathe. I opened the window and inhaled salt and humidity. Not unlike the air of my youth. For the past fifteen years I had tried my utmost to avoid inhaling similar air to that which had once filled my young lungs. If, months earlier, I didn't promise Allysa to quit smoking, I would've lit one up.

She squeezed my arm. "Talk to me. What's going on? One minute you're giving me crap about the cold case account, the next you're staring at nothing and became unresponsive."

I placed my hand on hers, and patted it the same way my mother had mine on her more lucid days. "I do this when I need to prepare myself mentally for something. You know how much I hate crowds." I lied.

"There won't be many people at Rachel's memorial service. Ten, at most."

I shook my head and forced out a loud breath.

"Seeing as you believe I have ulterior motives for running the cold case account, why do they intrigue *you*?" Allysa steered the rental car off the main road and parked in front of a Victorian-style house.

"My best friend in high school disappeared the day we graduated." *Half-truth.*

She turned to face me. "I'm so sorry."

I swallowed the bile back down. One word held far too many memories. Being in Marcel, this close to *home*, might push me over the cliff I had been standing on for fifteen years.

Six

Allysa

The years had been good to them. *Of course, they were.* Life was easy for women like them. Beautiful, charming, intelligent, educated and both successful in their respective fields. I despised them.

"Lysa, put your sunglasses on. They won't explode if you keep glaring at them like that. I assume they are your evil stepsisters?" Morgan held her back rigid. A hint of a smile grazed her lips.

"Jen and Sara. Not my step-anything. We lived under the same roof for a few years. The end." I fought to slow my heart's rapid beating. My stomach churned the same way it had the day in court; the last time I'd seen my dad.

Morgan hooked her arm through mine and tilted her head, studying the few people who came to pay their last respects to a woman who didn't deserve it. Rachel deserved to be in hell for more reasons than just murdering Sebastian.

"I have a gun with a silencer in my handbag. Create a distraction – take off your clothes. You've got the ass and boobs for it. Now drop that hideous dress, Mrs Ross. I'll pop the bitches. Low calibre bullets. Minimal blood spatter. I'll be out of here before their bodies hit the floor." Morgan patted the black leather bag hanging by her side. "Damn, now that song is going to be stuck in my head for the rest of the day."

For a moment, I hoped she was serious. "Not until I have answers."

Light flashed in her blue eyes. "Yes," Morgan said, loud enough for people to turn and stare. "It's a tragedy that a wonderful woman like Rachel died. She was too young." Morgan's voice caught, and she reached inside her purse, removing a tissue and dabbed at the corners of her eyes.

I nodded, playing my part. "I always hoped to one day reconcile with her. But time waits for no one."

Fourteen people in the living room, including Morgan, myself and Rachel's daughters. The perfect ones. Jen and Sara. The ten strangers nodded solemnly and returned to their conversations. Two more people cared about the dead bitch than I'd expected.

Sara and Jen headed in our direction. No sign of their perfect husbands or exquisite children.

Morgan stepped in front of me and extended a hand towards Jen and then Sara. "I'm sorry for your loss."

Sara glared at Morgan as if she were decomposing in Rachel's living room. "And you are?"

"Morgan Wright. Allysa's plus-one on this sad day." Morgan returned to stand beside me.

Jen stepped forward, wrapping her arms around my neck. "I missed you, Alicia."

"I missed you too, Jennifer." If not for our friendship, our parents would never have met. Sebastian would still be alive. And my dad wouldn't be on government-enforced retirement.

Morgan turned towards me as she tilted her head. "*Alicia?*"

Jen and I both laughed. "No, silly. It's our nicknames for each other. We were friends long before my dad married Rachel."

"It's through us they met." Jen shook her head, but smiled. "While you're here, are you going to see—"

Sara crossed her arms over her chest and glanced between Jen and me. "Seeing as Allysa is now married, or is it engaged, as only you're wearing a ring, to a woman, I have to ask – did the two of you ever?"

Still the same bitch.

Jen slapped her sister's shoulder. "Allysa is married to Jake Ross. Morgan's in a relationship with that extremely attractive

Australian actor whose name I can't remember."

"I didn't expect you to be the type to waste time reading the tabloids." Acid dripped from Morgan's words.

"Saw it on Instagram. I follow Allysa's bookstagram account and then started following you because of your comments on her posts. I'm also following your hottie now." Jen grinned, not realising that she sounded like a stalker.

More often than not, I wished we could have private accounts to protect us from the weirdos and former best friends.

Morgan drew a deep breath. "Which of these old gentlemen are your husbands?"

"The silver fox in the dark suit is mine." Jen pointed in a direction I didn't care to look.

"Sara?" Morgan's protective side took a giant step forward. I waited almost a year to see it in action.

"My husband couldn't make it. He has too many surgeries scheduled this week."

Morgan popped her lips. "How inconsiderate of your mother to kick the bucket when he is busy. I'm sure if he wanted to, he could've had another surgeon stand in for him. I'm in the middle of an extremely important project, but dropped everything when Allysa mentioned she needed me."

My bestie didn't let up, instead she leaned forward and whispered. "Start checking his shirt collars for lipstick marks. And if you smell another woman on him, I assure you I've never come that close to any of my doctors."

Sara's face turned red; the colour almost matched her hair. "My husband isn't cheating. He is a respected neurosurgeon and a very important member of our staff."

Unleashing Morgan completely blind might not have been the best idea. "Sara is a paediatrician."

Morgan nodded. "Yet you could get away for the memorial service. But it's *your* mother who passed away. Again, my most sincere condolences. From what Allysa has told me, it's clear your mother was quite ... remarkable."

Sara turned on her heel and strutted away on very expensive shoes. Even as a child, she had hated confrontation, and loved money.

"Jen, do you think Mister Sara's husband is cheating?" Morgan clearly picked up on something so I decided to let it play out. "Or is her lover waiting in her hotel room? Do they have an open marriage or both just turning a blind eye for the sake of their children?"

Jen's eyes wouldn't meet ours. "Sara's life is private. And, for what it's worth, I'm the last person she'll ever confide in. Excuse me."

From across the room, Sara stared daggers at us while making small talk with two older women I didn't recognise.

"Sara was Rachel's favourite and ensured Jen always knew it." Morgan tapped black painted nails on her biceps. "No wedding ring on Sara's finger, but a visible indentation. A weak spot to exploit. When we leave, I'll run background checks on both of the doctors."

I caught myself before laughing out loud. "Morgan Wright, you're not a detective. But you're a master at reading people. Yes, Jen was treated like the runt of the litter. It got a little better for her once they moved in with us. Rachel had someone new to direct her vile verbal arrows towards. Me."

"Has Jen always spoken about men as hotties and silver foxes?"

"No. Back in school she wasn't very popular. Despite looking like a lingerie model, Jen was kind of a nerd."

Morgan faked shock and covered her mouth with her right hand. "*You* were friends with a nerd? How does the school's wild child and the family's black sheep befriend a geek?"

"You answered yourself. I didn't have friends, because they couldn't run fast enough and always ended up getting caught. Jen was a star athlete; she outran me. Two outcasts make the best of friends."

Morgan batted her eyelashes. "Like us?"

I placed an arm around Morgan's shoulder and pulled her

close. For the first time, she appeared vulnerable. As if I would decide to spend recess with Jen rather than with her. "You're the best friend I've ever had, Morgan Wright."

"Best friend? Why haven't you mentioned anything about your father?" Morgan walked away before I could tell her another lie.

Seven

Morgan

Throughout the service, Allysa kept mumbling under her breath whenever the minister said anything good about Rachel. She may have brought me along to be her tiny muscle with my people reading skills and ways to intimidate others using only words, but I also studied her. And learned a great deal. *Oh, Lysa, I hope this isn't the end of our friendship.*

Once the service concluded, the food eaten, and the guests departed (back to their homes, not dead) I poured myself another cup of coffee and took in the expensive furnishings. More questions for Allysa – what had Rachel done for a living, and why didn't she talk about her father?

A commotion from somewhere in the house drew my attention. Allysa's raised voice forced my feet to move faster than they had in a long time. Unlike her, I wasn't a fan of running. Some considered me a gym-rat, not knowing that I'd mastered the art of capoeira, after years of relentless training. When I had decided to be more physically active, it had seemed the most logical to learn a martial art which looks like dancing.

"I said no!" Sara screamed with her fists pressed at her sides. The draft coming from the front door stirred her red hair, making her appear even angrier.

I bit my tongue. *This is the reason we're here.*

Allysa stepped forward, moving closer to the staircase Sara barricaded using her petite frame. "Just let me search the house and go through her things. If you're so adamant that Rachel didn't murder Sebastian, then you don't need to worry about what I might find."

"Sebastian was of legal age and decided to leave. Why, after all these years, can you still not get it through your thick skull?" Sara remained in position.

Countless memories flashed through my mind. Rage opened its eyes. My body moved before my brain could order it to remain in place. I pushed Allysa aside and reached for Sara, yanking her from the bottom step. My fingers wrapped around her neck. I didn't squeeze. Not yet.

I pulled her face closer until we were eye to eye. "You know what your mother did. Either you step aside and allow Allysa to find the closure she deserves, or I'm going to make your life hell." A sinister thought came to mind; I kept my mouth shut.

Sara's eyes widened, but I didn't ease my grip. "Who the hell *are* you?"

I rubbed the tip of my nose against hers. "Wouldn't you like to know? Unfortunately, I can't divulge my job title or employer. Only the government knows I exist and what I spent years being trained for."

"Sara, just do as they ask. I'm tired of Mom's bullshit. She's dead and we need to clean up for her. Again. Story of my life. I'm glad Mom's dead." Jen moved closer to my side and laid a hand on my arm. "Please release my sister. I'll make us all some coffee; I don't trust Sara not to put something in it. And then she will tell you *everything.*"

Tears welled in Sara's eyes. She tried to shake her head, but my hold on her throat made it impossible.

"Every damn thing," Jen ordered. "Now, go sit in the living room while I make coffee. It's time to throw Mom's skeletons out of the closets. Out of this house. And out of our lives."

I released Sara and motioned for her to walk ahead of us. Allysa grabbed my arm to keep me from following Sara. "What the hell was that?"

"Me, being your friend. You deserve answers. If I need to bruise her sagging neck to get them, so what?"

Allysa shook her head hard. "Jen's husband is a prosecutor. If Sara mentions this to him, you might face assault charges."

I laughed. "Wait, what? They allow that grandpa in a courtroom? Aren't they afraid he might keel over during a trial?"

"He is fifty-nine, not ninety-nine."

I tried to remember his face and wondered about Jen's age. If she was thirty-eight, like Allysa and me, then not-a-grandpa was twenty-one years her senior. "When did they meet?"

Allysa started walking towards the living room. "She was of legal age. You forget I can read your mind."

Good thing you can't.

We waited for Jen to pour the coffee and hand us each a mug. Once she took a seat, away from her sister, I spoke. "You don't share paternal DNA."

Sara and Jen glanced at each other, but neither confirmed my observation. I'd never seen siblings look so much unalike.

"Ladies, we're not here to spew more insincerities about your mother's passing. Let's get on with it, or I will restrain both of you while Allysa searches the house and property at leisure."

Jen stared at the mug in her hands. "It's time, Sara. I'm tired of lying for Mom. She's no longer here, and it happened twenty years ago."

Sara downed her coffee and cursed as it burned her throat. "My mom didn't murder your brother. Neither did she hire someone to do it for her. Sebastian Pimento doesn't exist. He hasn't since the night he left this house of his own volition. Sort of."

Allysa shifted forward in her seat. "Then why didn't he say goodbye to me or my dad?"

"It was part of the conditions of his departure," Sara said, staring at the coffee table.

"You make it sound so formal. Just tell us what the hell happened. And if Allysa's brother is still alive, as you claim, where is he?" Their little avoidance game was getting old – fast. *Much like Jen's husband.*

"Mom didn't approve of our relationship, despite us not

sharing the same DNA. Sebastian and I didn't care, we were in love."

Allysa gagged and stood to pace the length of the living room; a fist pressed to her mouth. "I can understand that he might've found you attractive, but he despised you, Sara."

"We were young. You think with different parts of your body then and don't consider what a future together will be like. Mom focused on nothing other than my and Jen's futures. Mom had it all planned out, and she ensured she provided us with the means to reach her goals. I became a doctor because Mom wanted me to marry a doctor and what better way to meet one? Jen studied law, because how else would she meet a lawyer to marry? Mom didn't speak to Jen for an entire year after she heard Jen's a criminal defence attorney."

Allysa laughed from where she stood by the big window. Moss-coloured drapes framed the view from the house. "That's rich coming from Rachel, considering how she made the money to send both of you to the University of Marcel. Let's not forget the cute convertibles she bought you, or the designer clothes. No trace of the *slum* she raised you in was to linger. She reinvented you. It would've been less of a hassle to send you across the country to a different university, but no, Rachel had to keep her little girls under her eyes and yank those chains if needed."

I raised my left hand. "I have so many questions. Lysa, you can fill me in later. Right now, someone tell me what Rachel did to make money and what happened to Allysa's brother? Why was he banished from the trashcan?" I glanced at Allysa. "Sorry, but I'm getting a trash-to-tiaras vibe from the two of them."

"Crystal meth," Jen said. "That's how Mom put us through university and ensured we have the lives we do now."

"Strange, because you don't appear thrilled with your lives." I shrugged, loving the family drama unfolding in front of me. It was much more fun when it was someone else's drama. "Okay, so Mommy was a drug manufacturer. Non-blood-related brother and sister were getting it on. I'm yet to see a reason for the young prince being banished from the land. Will he one day return and stake his claim in Sara once again?"

Allysa spun around. "Ew, dammit, Morgan. You're talking about my brother and that piece of designer-label-wearing-shit. Sorry, Sara, but there has never been any love lost between us." She took a deep breath and wrapped her arms around herself. "I've spent the last twenty years of my life searching for Sebastian Pimento. Nothing. He disappeared off the face of the earth."

Jen stood and handed something small to Allysa. "Sebastian no longer exists on paper, but Terry Holt does. Mom sent him to Wild Bay to go work for one of her contacts there. I found this copy of the driver's license Mom had made for him, and kept it in the hopes of one day being able to give it to you."

Bile fought its way past my heart beating in my throat. I took a deep breath, forcing myself to appear unaffected. I wanted to scream. *My Terry!*

Allysa couldn't learn that the only man I ever loved was her brother. I had tolerated my late husband, luckily, I didn't have to for long.

"This is Sebastian? He's in Wild Bay? Morgan, we need to leave. It's only a three-hour drive. We can be there by early evening." Allysa turned to Jen and Sara. "What's the name of Rachel's contact? I'll start there."

Against my better judgement I asked Sara, "What happened to the baby?"

Sara opened her mouth, but no words came out. Jen stared at me. "How did you know?"

I forced a shrug and tried for my most baffled facial expression. "Lucky guess. Well, not lucky, let's rather call it *educated*. Two teenagers were getting it on while living under the same roof, yet one gets sent away – not forgetting the name change – but Sara was allowed to stay and become a doctor. An unwanted pregnancy might warrant such drastic actions. Allysa, how did your father feel about his wife's decision?"

Allysa continued to stare out the window. "I'm not sure if he knew. I sure as hell didn't. How did I not realise you were pregnant? Sebastian disappeared, and I can't remember seeing much of you or anyone else after that."

I walked to Allysa, placing my hands on her shoulders. "It's a normal trauma response to block out certain events when your mind's sole focus was on the loss of your brother. Taking into consideration that you had thought he was murdered, that's a lot to process for a teenager."

Jen stood with the obvious intention of walking over to comfort Allysa. One look from me froze her to the spot. I shook my head. "No, you sit your ass down. You kept the truth from your so-called best friend. You have no right to play bestie now. It's too late."

"You never met my mom." Jen slumped down in the chair. "Back then, Allysa and I spent as little time as possible at home. When we had to be there, we stayed up in our room."

I could've wasted time saying how grateful I was to never have met Rachel. Truth be told, I could've postponed the inevitable with a whole range of trivial things. But I knew Allysa. She wouldn't rest until she had answers. *Time to get the show on the road.*

"Sara, what happened to the baby?"

Tears rolled down her cheeks. Sara rested her forehead on her palms. "I gave him up for adoption."

Jen placed a hand on her sister's shoulder. "I still don't think it was Sebastian's baby. Not with what Mom forced us to do."

"I hate her," Sara whispered loud enough for us to hear. "I'm glad she's dead and can't control our lives any longer. Finally, I can search for my son."

"Sara, I'm sorry, but Jen has a point." Allysa lifted a hand to silence Sara. "Jen told me about the *private lessons* Rachel forced you to have with some of her best paying customers. How can you be sure the baby is Sebastian's?"

"Because Rachel gave us condoms for our *lessons*. Sebastian and I never used protection. We were in love."

I wanted to jump over the coffee table and snap Sara's self-righteous neck. For lying to Allysa. For deceiving Terry. Sebastian. It didn't matter.

I knew the truth.

Eight

Eighteen years earlier

The smell of scorched meat hung heavy in the stale air. This was her fault. If only she had listened to me, she wouldn't be tied to the chair. Every time she turned to look at a piece of herself lying on the table next to her, she cried. This one hadn't talked as much as some of the others. I never gave her the chance.

Who are you? Why am I here? I remember you. The police will look for me. My father has a lot of money, if you let me go, blah blah blah.

She made up for her inability to speak with ugly crying.

"I warned you." I tapped the blade against her temple and studied the tear drops rolling down her cheek, the snot streaming over her bruised lips. "Inside this thick skull of yours, you thought you stood a chance with him, never realising how good you *had* it."

There wasn't enough time to enjoy what I still needed to do. Always somewhere to be, work to do, or people to meet up with. Not even as a child did I have time to play.

I grabbed the syringe and explained to her what to expect. "Don't worry, I'll leave your other eye. For now. You're going to need it a little while longer."

Her attempt at screaming was comical and horrific. Even to me.

Once her mouth couldn't open anymore, thanks to the duct tape, I continued showing her the errors of her ways. Sure, people would report her missing, but the police wouldn't come knocking on my door. They haven't any of the other times a young woman went missing, or when their bodies were found where I had left them. Disposing of the corpses took a lot of planning; this area was rife with curious animals. Sometimes I resorted to hiding in nearby trees to scare the scavengers away. Every piece of them had to be found. I didn't care for any of it. Except the most important part.

I approached her from behind; she focused on my every move in the mirror positioned in front of her. An old scarf my father had loved wearing in winter kept her head in place.

The needle punctured her eye; the pupil contracting with the sudden burst of pain. Slowly I pulled the plunger back, extracting the vitreous humour. Her once beautiful hazel-coloured eye was now deformed and shrivelled. Sometimes, when I had more time, I also removed the aqueous humour, leaving their eyeball completely drained of fluid.

"This is going to hurt. You should've got it through your thick skull that he'll never want you." I grabbed the spoon.

Nine

Allysa

Years of my life wasted, trying to prove that Rachel had murdered Sebastian. Terry Holt. The name kept repeating in my mind. A broken loop. A reminder that my brother was alive. *I hope.*

My stomach remained in a knot as I raced back to the hotel. Whether or not Morgan wanted to, she was coming with me to Wild Bay.

"How did you know about the baby?" I asked.

Morgan readjusted her sunglasses and tucked her blonde hair behind her ears. "I didn't. Nothing more than a guess. It's a reasonable conclusion, considering the facts. Before we left, what did Jen say to you?"

I chewed my tongue, reaching for the water bottle in the cup-holder. Even after the last drop slipped down my throat, I still didn't have the words to tell Morgan the truth. A lie I had told her when we first became friends came back to bite me in the ass. It wouldn't open a can of worms; Morgan learning about Rachel the meth-maker had done that already.

Did I want to tell her what Jen had said? No. The alternative seemed the better option – lie. Again.

In time it would start raining poo, but there wouldn't be time to grab an umbrella, as my dad had liked to say. I told Morgan the truth.

"Wait, what? Your father is in prison for drug trafficking, without the possibility of parole?" Morgan tapped a finger to her mouth. "You need to go speak to him and hear his side of the story. None of this makes any sense. Until an hour ago, I thought your father was dead. We'll put a pin in that one and circle back to it later. If I was reading a psychological thriller, I would suspect the evil stepmother had something to do with it. Seeing she had loved making money from drugs."

A grin spread across my face. "And if you were the author?"

"Morgan Wright isn't an author, merely an avid reader."

I failed to contain my laughter and focused hard to keep the rental in the right lane. "No, Morgan Wright is not. However, CJ Green is a *bestselling* thriller author. What does CJ think?"

Morgan touched my shoulder and rolled her eyes as soon as I turned my head towards her. "Send CJ an email. I'm sure she'll respond within twenty-four-hours. If that fails, send her a DM on Instagram."

One of the many reasons I loved her – Morgan always knew how to lighten the mood. I often wondered whether she ever experienced a bad day or even suffered from PMS.

Morgan Wright: a ray of sunshine dressed in black.

"Do you want me to go to Wild Bay with you? I don't want to be in the way of you finding your brother. It might be best if you ask Jake to join you. This is a family matter."

"You are family. Not by blood, but by choice. Morgan, please come with me." If it came down to it, I would confess that Jake knew nothing about my life in Marcel. Nothing with any truth in it.

Morgan reached into her handbag and pulled out a pair of over-sized reading glasses, despite having perfect vision. "CJ will speak to you now."

"I love you." I laughed.

"That's an odd thing to say to your favourite author. A comment like that will get you flagged as a potential stalker. Or worse – blocked."

"Not CJ, silly. I meant *you*. Morgan."

"You wanted CJ's opinion, so here she is. If you say you love her, or anything too familiar, she goes back in the bag."

Morgan made a valid point. I'd read every single one of CJ Green's novels and I was yet to come across another author who could write as many plot twists without making the story unbelievable. Her research was factual, to the point of being scary. If it wasn't for a post I had once seen on Instagram about thriller authors being some of the nicest people you could ever meet, I would've feared her. Perhaps I did.

Then again, many people feared me ... for different reasons.

As the hotel came into view, I asked CJ for her opinion. Morgan answered without looking up from her phone. "I booked us rooms at a newly refurbished guesthouse right on the beach. I've found that establishments under new management go above and beyond for their guests."

"Did you learn this from following your Aussie around the globe?" I still didn't understand why she kept their relationship a secret. I wondered how they had met. "How did the two of you meet?"

"He is the main character in a movie adaption of one of CJ's books."

Before the next question left my mouth, Morgan jumped out of the rental car and rushed towards the hotel's entrance. When I asked her about it later, she claimed to have needed the bathroom and that she knew I was anxious to get to Wild Bay.

I didn't give it much thought.

Sebastian is alive.

Ten

Morgan

Nothing good ever comes from going back. Whether it be to an ex, the town you grew up in, or prison. With every passing minute the bile rose higher in my throat. If Lady Luck existed, then the entire population of Wild Bay would've died since the last time I had set foot in that horrid, backwards, inbred little town.

Vacationers saw it as paradise. The locals called it hell.

Allysa and I had grabbed our belongings from our rooms at the hotel and left Marcel. I offered to drive, giving her time to process the reality of hearing her brother was alive.

"CJ hasn't given me her opinion," Allysa said from the passenger seat.

I didn't want to lie to her when the possibility existed of the truth coming out. Not all of it, but enough to destroy our friendship. Best friends weren't easy to come by. At least not ones I could be ninety percent of myself with.

Evasion seemed my best option. "I'm sorry I didn't tell you about selling the rights to Predator. It's surreal that a part of my imagination will come to life on screen. And I signed a non-disclosure agreement with the studio. They want to go public once production wraps up."

Even sitting beside me and wearing a safety belt, Allysa managed to wrap her arms around my chest and squeezed, releasing her hold when I coughed. "I knew one of your books was going to be made into a movie or a series. I understand why they chose Predator, but I think it will be even better as a series."

As long as I evaded the truth, I tossed another factual bomb at her. "How do you feel about Sabine's books being made into a television series?"

Allysa screamed so loud my ears buzzed long after she stopped. "Are you freakin kidding me right now?"

Evasion is a gift. "No. I'm waiting for the contract. Depending on the response to the pilot episode and the success of the first series, the production company will decide about buying the rights to rest of the books in Sabine's series."

"Do you have any idea who you want to be cast as Sabine?" Allysa beamed and turned to face me as much as the safety belt allowed. She looked ready for a run, wearing her trademark tank top and shorts. Me? Always ready for a funeral or to rob a bank.

"That's out of my control." Unlike many other things, including the new man in my life. I had been adamant I wanted Wyatt in the lead role. If not, I wouldn't have sold the rights. *Life works out when you force it.*

Wyatt ended up in my life and bed. Whether he made it into my heart remained to be seen. I hadn't been in love since I was twenty-three years old. Friendship and being in a committed relationship were both foreign concepts to me.

"Why do you not want people to know that you're CJ Green?" Allysa asked.

I smiled, grateful that I didn't have to lie. "To keep my personal life and my author life separate. Yes, I know, readers love connecting with authors, but I'm extremely private. CJ creates a smoke screen. I post what readers expect from an author. You won't see any CJ posts from my time in Scotland. Not until the official media release. Morgan Wright joins in follow trains, posts book reviews, and shares photos of random things which get the most likes and engagement. Guess now that the entire world knows about my relationship with Wyatt, I'll need to post something to appease the masses."

I hate social media.

Whoever took and posted the photo of us walking down

Princes Street deserved whatever I decided to do to them.

"How does Wyatt feel about it? He lives in the public eye." Allysa handed me a travel cup of coffee.

A three-hour drive couldn't be undertaken without caffeine, I had told her before we left Marcel. I forced the lukewarm fluid down my throat.

Minutes ticked by; the distance to my past getting smaller. My only hope was that no one recognised me. People's faces don't change much, unless you don't leave it to time and natural ageing. I hadn't; my late husband never gave me much of a choice in the matter. Despite knowing that I might walk past unnoticed by most of Wild Bay's residents, there was one I couldn't. No matter what work had been done to alter my appearance, he'd recognise me in any crowd.

The sight of the main street forced me to take a deep breath and exhale slowly. Ghosts dwelled these streets; welcoming me *home*. Back to hell. Back to everything I had spent the past fifteen years trying to forget. Some things one shouldn't forget. Instead savouring it and replaying it in your mind until you've had your daily dose.

For Allysa's sake, I kept glancing at the rental's GPS system and pretended not to know the location of the guesthouse. Years ago, the house had belonged to Mr and Mrs Green, until they'd decided to leave Wild Bay.

"As soon as we've checked in, we need to head to the bar where Sebastian worked," Allysa said, staring out of the window at the ocean.

I'm not setting a foot inside Perk.

Eleven

Allysa

Part of me felt relieved when Morgan said she couldn't come with me to Perk. She claimed she had to catch up on emails. Typical of her to be a control freak even after selling the rights to Predator. I guess it was what made her so successful in the first place – her attention to detail and drive to succeed.

I didn't want her to witness the inevitable melt down once I laid eyes on my brother. I doubted he still worked at Perk. Sebastian would've found a way to break free from Rachel's hold.

Why had he left without telling me? We were close growing up. Perhaps we weren't. I never realised Sara was pregnant because I'd been too engrossed in my own life. As Jen had said, we were all trying to survive living with Rachel.

My body shook as I stood outside Perk's doors. Inside, people were laughing. The salty ocean breeze enveloped me and the smell of dead fish invaded my nostrils. Warm air brushed against my skin.

Strange how your senses heighten when adrenaline spikes in your veins.

I willed my feet to move, hating Rachel for robbing me of two decades with my brother. Reaching for the brass door handle, I decided that once I located Sebastian, I would visit my dad. *Seb can come with me.*

After downing a second beer, I requested to speak to the owner. The bartender asked whether he did something wrong.

"No, not at all. It's regarding a personal matter." I offered him my most charming smile.

The bartender walked towards a door to the right of the bar and I caught a glimpse of a tattoo behind his left earlobe. In my line of work, I saw that cartoon skull often. The first time had been on one of Rachel's friends. Their presence in Wild Bay meant I needed a gun. And to get Morgan as far away as possible. Anyone associated with me could be caught in the crossfire.

An informant had warned me they'd come for me. I expected nothing less, not after what I'd done.

"How can you have something personal to discuss with me if we've never met?"

I turned towards the voice and stared up at Donna Perk. Somewhere in her late fifties, her stance and the irritation flashing in her eyes reminded me of Rachel.

I held out my hand. "My name is Allysa Ross. I believe my brother used to work here. Sebas … Terry Holt. Rachel, my stepmother, your friend, sent him here twenty years ago. Not sure if you heard, but she passed away last week."

"I don't know a Rachel." Donna turned her back on me.

I grabbed her arm and stood, trying to intimidate a woman twice my size. "Cut the act. She supplied the drugs, and you made enough money to buy half of this town. Where. Is. My. Brother?" The information Jen had given me proved useful as the colour drained from the old bat's face.

Donna pulled her too-tight jeans up on her large frame and instructed me to join her in her office. She asked me to sit; I didn't.

"Tell me where I can find my brother, or your life is about to turn into a living hell." I considered telling her I knew her new boss was looking for me, but didn't want to make this fight easy for them.

If someone did to my son what I did to his…

Donna leaned back in her oversized fake leather chair and studied me. The smell in the confined space was as stale as in the main bar area.

"I won't ask you again."

She lit a cigarette and blew smoke into the air between us. "Terry is dead."

I opened my mouth, trying not to inhale the cloud of slow-killing death. "What's his new name?"

Donna cocked her head to the side, taking another drag. "No, not like that. You better sit for this."

My insides coiled. I wanted to let out a blood-curdling scream, but hated that phrase. Instead, my breathing increased as I pushed my fingers through my hair and stared her down. "Tell me."

Twelve

Seventeen years earlier

It baffled me how so many stupid women either lived or found their way in to our small town. *Wild Bay – magnet for the dumb.*

"Silly girl. If you listened to me and kept your hands to yourself, you could've spent today at the beach. Yet, here you are."

One eye watched as I stepped around her and reached for the next lesson. I bent down, resting my fingers on her skinny knees. Blood trickled from her empty left eye socket. Some things belong in pairs.

An absolute shame that I had to teach them one at a time.

Perhaps one day I might have two friends to play with.

True friendship is supposed to be a special thing; a bond stronger than blood. It could be interesting to test their knowledge of each other. My only friend knew everything about me and turned it into weapons aimed at me.

A gurgling sound erupted from her throat. It grated on my nerves.

It shouldn't have surprised me that teaching them took so long, after all, most children attended school for twelve years. *An utter waste of time.* Nothing I learned there had prepared me for life. My knowledge came from experience.

In the distance a rooster announced the new day. Was this the mute and half-blind bitch's last? How many things were on my to-do list? I ran through them all and realised today didn't hold enough hours for the final lesson.

This silly girl caught on really quick as to who I was. What the media called me. No one knew me. Not the real me. At a young age I'd learned who I was didn't matter. Not when those close to you had bigger problems. *Great way to grow up, being pitied, ridiculed and feared by idiots.*

The holiday season was drawing to an end. I needed the rest and assumed so did the police.

A cool breeze brushed the hair from my neck. I didn't let it fool me; this would be another hot day. Even hotter for the dumb slut once I shut the doors.

I was a brilliant teacher. From the start I told them what to expect. *No surprises in my classroom.*

Not feeling in the mood for a headache, I grabbed the respiratory mask, eye goggles and gloves. Unnecessary, but the last thing I needed was to be off my game at work. I could've explained it away, but didn't want to take the risk.

"I have places to be and you're going to learn another valuable lesson. What did I tell you?" The sound of my laughter filled the structure. "That's right, your tongue is over there." I pointed at the chunk of muscle.

"Did you study science in school? If not, I'll explain how generous I am, considering what you did."

With her hands fastened to the back legs of the wooden chair this wouldn't take long to set up. I'd learned the hard way with the first student. *Practise makes torture perfect.*

"You thought I'm dumb because of where I work. Jokes on you, silly slut. I could've gone to any university I wanted. Who knows, I still might."

I pulled the plastic buckets closer and positioned them under her hands. Rope kept her arms in place. Pouring the white crystals into the containers, it reminded me of big salt granules. Salt would've been pointless for this lesson.

"The first time I considered using hydrochloric acid, just to get my point across. But I don't want your *eye*, nose and mucous membranes to burn. The ventilation in here isn't good enough."

The silence became suffocating, or it may have been the restricted oxygen supply due to the mask.

I hoped she savoured every sound. Next lesson? Her ears.

With a hose positioned in each bucket, I opened the tap. She made that horrible gurgling noise again. If I had more medical knowledge, her vocal cords would lay next to her tongue and shrivelled eye.

"I need to head out for a few hours, but don't worry about getting bored. The sodium hydroxide eating away at your skin and meat will keep you busy."

My laughter drowned out the annoying sound coming from student number ten.

Outside the doors, life and love waited.

Thirteen

Morgan

The moment Allysa entered my room at the guesthouse, she sank to her knees, sobbing into her hands. The scream lodged in her throat as she stared up at me. Pain distorted her beautiful face.

I knew that scream. It had been stuck in my chest for decades. Grief.

I was powerless to do anything but wait for the shadow, which had followed me for years, to rip my friend to pieces. *It's what the shadow does best.*

I wrapped my arms around Allysa and held her, knowing nothing I said would help. *Words can't comfort shit.*

Once her breathing returned to normal and she stopped rocking, I brushed the hair from her face and pressed my lips to her forehead. Grief had pushed my soul through the shredder with no one around to hold me. It wasn't necessary to close my eyes to see the events of that day replay in front of me. Some memories can't be buried.

Allysa needed me more than ever.

"Do you want me to contact Jake?" I asked.

She shook her head.

"Are you sure Donna told you the truth?"

Allysa nodded.

I stood and pulled her up with me. "Okay, here's what we're going to do. You're going to take fifteen minutes to yourself, while I go buy us some burgers. You haven't eaten anything today, and this is going to be a long night."

Despite Allysa being taller than me, I held her as best I

could. "It's a full moon tonight, and we're going to find the weredonkey."

Allysa's chest expanded. "What the hell is a weredonkey?"

"There's a drove of wild donkeys around these parts," I improvised. "While you were out, I read up on Wild Bay."

"A drove?"

I stepped back, but held onto Allysa's hands. "A herd. A pace. Whatever. It's said that one of them was bitten by a werewolf and turned into a weredonkey. It doesn't bite or eat people, just kicks the shit out of them."

Allysa lifted her face to the ceiling. "What would I do without you?"

"Read. Run your cold case account. Workout. I don't know. Suffer. All the boring things you did before we became friends."

She glared at me. I held up my hands. "Okay, you would've been wife and mother of the year and still a bad*ass* thriller reading chick. And it isn't fair that you're this beautiful. Not cool, Lysa."

"I expected to find Sebastian, not hear that he is dead. *Murdered.* By a serial killer." The words hung in the air.

I took a moment to arrange my thoughts. "Did the police catch the killer?"

Allysa shook her head. She sat down hard on the bed and fisted the duvet. "No. But I will. Tomorrow morning, you and I are going down to the police station and we'll talk to the lead detective. Tonight, I'll see what I can find online about my brother's murder. Dammit, I forgot to bring my laptop."

"Use mine. I'll go and see if I can find us decent food in this hill-billy town. Allysa, please take a few minutes for the reality to sink in. I know it's easier to stay busy than face the darkness. It's your new way of life. Nothing will ever be the same. Trust me."

Allysa grabbed my hand as I turned towards the desk for my handbag. "Who did you lose?"

Who didn't I? "My husband." Easier to mention the one

person whose death brought me the least amount of pain. No turmoil, just money. The very reason I had married him.

"You never told me you were married." Allysa stared up at me and pushed her fingers through her hair.

To shrug or not to shrug? I did what I did best. I lied. Again. "Because it almost killed me." It wasn't a complete lie. In time, he would've killed me. "I was very young and most days it feels like someone else lived through it. We can talk about it later. Right now, *you* need *me*."

I left Allysa in my room and walked down the familiar street. Nothing about this hellhole had changed. It seemed ridiculous that I expected the ocean to look different.

The one thing that had changed? Me.

As the sun faded behind me, I wondered how to be the person who Allysa thought I was. And keep the truth from her. No matter the cost.

My late husband had left me with enough money to never have to work again. The only benefit of marrying an older and childless man. I made more than enough from my books, not to mention the movie deal, to be my own woman. Money opened a lot of doors for me. Including hiring a private investigator in Denver, Colorado. Allysa's home city.

Allysa Ross didn't just read and review books, and run a cold case account on Instagram.

Fourteen

Allysa

Morgan had threatened to feed me the burger like mother birds feed their chicks. If not, I wouldn't have eaten a single bite the previous night. No one, except Jake, ever took care of me the way she did. We managed to sleep a few hours, but by the time I woke up, Morgan already sat behind her laptop, continuing the search.

Twenty years since I'd lost my brother; years believing Rachel had murdered him. She didn't end his life, but she had destroyed it. I'd mourned Sebastian every day, but the crushing blow of Donna's words left me drained.

How could I process the new shitstorm of emotions when I had experienced so many of them throughout the past two decades?

The sun warmed my face as I stared out over the ocean, clutching the mug to my chest. A caffeine hangover was the least of my worries.

I pulled my phone from the back pocket of my jeans and calculated the time difference. Jake and Daniel were still asleep. I sent Jake a text telling him Morgan and I decided to stay a few more days, claiming we were having too much fun.

A week before, hunting a murderer would've been fun, but this was personal.

Something doesn't add up.

"You're still wondering whether the police made a mistake?" Morgan said from behind me.

"Don't you?" I kept my eyes on the golden line on the horizon.

Morgan came to stand next to me. She stretched her arms above her head and bent forward, groaning louder with every move. "We're too old for these late nights. I'm going to need caffeine in one of those bags a nurse sticks into your arm in hospital."

I turned to her; a mischievous smile on her face. She knew how much I hated when people failed to get basic medical information right.

Morgan rolled her eyes before I opened my mouth. "Yes, Mrs Ross, intravenous fluid regulation. IV line. Bag filled with caffeine. You're the former paramedic. I'm the burnt-out author. Oh, that reminds me, what do you think about us getting matching tattoos? We're basically the same person; might as well get matching ink. Or we should do another buddy read. This time fiction, not true crime, all things considered."

"I'm going to need something stronger than coffee in order to deal with you today. I swear you're worse than my son. It's like you drain the life right out of me some days."

Morgan bumped her hip against my thigh. "I love you more. Why don't you take a shower? You look like something that will scare the weredonkey. When you're a little more presentable, we'll drink three cups of coffee, get a good buzz going, and head to the police station."

"Are you sure you want to come with me?" I didn't expect her to remain in Wild Bay with me. This went beyond normal friendship responsibilities.

Morgan downed her coffee and waited for the seagulls to stop screaming. Her words, not mine. "Damn, those things are loud. I won't leave you to face all of this on your own. Why you refuse to tell Jake is beyond me, but I respect your decision. It's not like Jen is here. Why did you lose contact?"

"Sebastian disappeared and my dad went to prison. I knew Rachel was responsible. It's difficult to be friends with someone who obeyed her mother to a fault, despite knowing what she's capable of."

Morgan remained quiet; her mind working in overdrive.

I saw her get this way when writing a book. Or as she called it, 'typing up the incident report'.

I didn't know how to tell Jake that most of the woman he loved had never existed. I spent my entire adult life cladding myself in lies, much like an armadillo's scutes. If the possibility existed to ensure he never found out how flawed I was, how trailer-trash my childhood had been, I would grab it with both hands. For him, I'd lie for the rest of my life. Not to hurt him, but because I loved him, our son, and our life together. *Dreams do come true.*

Jake came from a wonderful family, unlike me. Things hadn't always been like that. Before my mom died in a hit-and-run, life had been good – perfect compared to the aftermath. I vowed a long time ago to be the glue that kept my family together. The same way my mother had.

I needed to make amends with my dad. Before I faced him, I had to find the person responsible for Sebastian's death. How do you beg for someone's forgiveness, and tell them their son had met a brutal end, in the short time allowed by the warden?

"Promise me here and now that, whatever happens, it won't have an impact on our friendship." Morgan's eyes filled with tears.

I placed an arm around her shoulders and hugged her to me. "Promise. Why would it?"

"Grief changes you. People avoid you because your pain doesn't fit in their perfect lives. You avoid them because their perfect lives remind you of the clusterfuck your life has always been. Some of us are destined for lives filled with pain." Morgan shook her head. "Millions of people are worse off than we are. I have no right to feel sorry for myself."

"Neither of us have had *ideal* lives, yet think about how far we've come? From the first DM I sent you, I had a feeling we would be friends. I never expected you to become my best friend, not with us living on different continents. You understand me in ways very few people do. Not even Jake."

Morgan nodded. "You're my safe space and there's nothing

I won't do for you. If you want me to see this investigation through, I'm here for you. It bugs me that in all these years, the police haven't arrested a suspect for the murders."

Her use of the word *investigation* didn't sit well with me.

Did she know? Or did her storyteller brain embellish?

Fifteen

Morgan

Gold digger. Sugar baby. Leech. I'd heard every word imaginable when Ray Wright and I had dated. He hadn't cared that I was young enough to be his daughter, and all I saw was a ticket out of the hell my life had been. Of course, it hadn't been all bad. But the walls closed in on me in a small town where everyone knew everyone's business.

The woman staring back at me in the mirror kept me sane. Soon after meeting Ray, I wrote my first novel. Therapy is for the weak, and I had needed a better way to process my grief and childhood. Writing dark thrillers was my choice of therapy and self-care. I wrote late into the night or any minute Ray had allowed. He had wanted a trophy wife, and I had sparkled, despite the unpolished piece of rusty, weather-beaten discarded steel I was.

I am.

At the time, Ray Wright had been one of the most eligible bachelors in London. His house in Kensington Gardens made up for his violent temper tantrums. The thousands of pounds he had spent on me made up for the sadistic streak he hid from the rest of the world. None of Ray's previous girlfriends stuck around; clearly, they hadn't been as desperate as I was at the time.

A knock on my bedroom door yanked the memories of that night on Ray's yacht from my mind and thrust me back into the present. F-bombs exploded in my mind; a war zone saw less carnage.

Allysa eased the door open and stared at my now brown

eyes. Her head tilted to the right, then the left. "Why the hell is CJ here?"

"Don't judge me, but when I do research for a book, I go full CJ. Coloured contacts, fake reading glasses, the entire persona. Sebastian's murder isn't just another book I'm writing, but if I'm going to help you, I need CJ's analytical brain. Her way of understanding evil."

Allysa nodded and pursed her lips. "Do you think it's because we studied psychology that we find the criminal mind so fascinating?"

No. "Yes. However, your childhood was shaped by criminals in the sense that a hit-and-run driver killed your mother. Rachel manufactured meth. And your father is in prison. On top of that, your brother disappeared and for years you believed the very woman your father married had murdered him."

"What about your childhood?" Allysa asked.

My formative years weren't her business. Friend or not. "We don't have time to discuss the intricacies of my first years on this earth. Rachel knew Sebastian had been murdered because Donna told you she informed her. I wonder whether Sara and Jen also knew and lied to you yesterday?"

Allysa shrugged, pulling at the hem of her azure blue tank top. "It doesn't matter. The most important thing is to find out as much as possible from the detective who handled the investigation. Then we do the police's work for them."

My hand lifted to my mouth. "You're not thinking what I suspect you're thinking?"

The person standing in the room with me wasn't the Allysa Ross I had gotten to know. But the Allysa my private investigator had compiled a file on.

Wyatt didn't sound thrilled when we spoke and I told him my plans had changed. Instead of being naked and curled up in bed with one the of the most gorgeous men in the world, I headed towards the police station. Wyatt gave me butterflies;

the second man to ever do so.

The idea of walking through the station's door set off a stampede of starving rats dashing towards a corpse inside my stomach. I swallowed back the bile and hoped more than ever *he* wasn't on duty.

Allysa waited impatiently for me to end the call with Wyatt. "Lover boy okay with you not being back for a few days?"

I nodded. "I'll send him some nudes later to make up for it."

A couple of people on the street turned to look at us as Allysa's laughter filled the morning air. "*You* send nudes? We're not as young or perky as we used to be."

"True, but I've had some help in the things-going-south-department. You don't land a man like Wyatt Samuels, at our age, if you can't keep up with him. Damn, he's ripped and still trains like he's doing triathlons. Stamina for days." The memories flooded through me and sent shivers down my spine. Until I remembered the reason we stood outside the police station.

Perhaps I was in love with Wyatt, because only one other man had made me feel ... anything. The love of my life. Half of my soul. The one man who would never hold me again. Never again tell me he loved me, or that he believed in me. Not a day went by that I didn't wish things could've worked out for us. If only he hadn't been so narrow-minded.

Allysa led the way into the station and walked up to the front desk. I lingered behind her, keeping my focus on the worn floor tiles.

"Good morning, may I please speak to Detective Boyle regarding the murder of Scb ... Terry Holt?" Allysa asked the officer sitting behind the desk. "My name is Allysa Ross. I'm Terry's sister. An old newspaper article, my friend found online, mentioned Detective Boyle as the lead investigator."

The officer picked up the phone and five minutes later, Detective Boyle headed down the stairs.

He looked at me, then at Allysa. Boyle returned his attention to me. A hint of a smile tugged at the corners of his mouth. *He knows.*

Will Boyle extended his hand towards Allysa and then asked us to follow him to his office without shaking my hand.

Once we reached his office, Detective Boyle motioned for us to take a seat. The intensity in his gaze felt like a punch to the solar plexus. It was a mistake coming, but I also needed answers. The worn file laying on his desk mocked me.

"The change is rather remarkable, Mandy," he said.

I didn't react when Allysa spoke. "Her name is Morgan Wright, not Mandy."

Detective Boyle smirked. "I knew you'd change your name. So, you married Mr Wright. I always had this gut feeling he was Mr Wrong, in more ways than one."

You have no idea. "I've always preferred Morgan. I'm not my mother."

"Welcome home, *Morgan*. Fifteen years is a long time," Will said.

Sixteen

Sixteen years earlier

Perfect auburn hair. Exquisite emerald eyes. Well, eye. A natural athletic build most women, and men, would kill for. Ironic – she was going to die.

I studied what little remained of her hands. Maybe I should've become a doctor. The human anatomy always fascinated me. So did chemistry. But a medical degree didn't come cheap. Unlike most of my students, I didn't have a rich daddy or a trust fund.

"You're a remarkable student. I've enjoyed our time together very much. It was dumb of me to remove your tongue before asking how you keep your hands so soft. Kept. My apologies for being inconsiderate of your feelings."

I wrapped my fingers around her gorgeous hair, yanking her head back. One eye stared up at me. This one wasn't as weak as the others. That stubbornness had led her to my classroom.

"The first time we spoke, I gave you the benefit of the doubt. Men threw themselves at your feet. Pretty little thing like you must be used to the attention. Why didn't you listen to me? You've been able to hear since before birth; eighteen weeks into your mother's pregnancy, to be exact."

An ability many people take for granted. There were days when I wondered what was the point in wasting energy on these women who would never learn from their mistake. One which proved fatal – for them.

Women have thicker skulls than men. It's a scientific fact.

I didn't know whether my students' skulls were thicker than that of the average female, or if they were just arrogant and thought themselves better than me. I never offered them a chance to explain themselves.

There was no going back once they were dragged into my classroom. Such privileged lives they lived, and to think I only ever asked them for one simple thing.

My left hand held her head in place, while my right reached for the dropper. She flinched as I yanked her hair to the side. "My voice is the last thing you'll ever hear."

I counted out loud with each drop. "One. Two. Three. Four." The liquid slipped from the glass tube and disappeared down her ear canal.

A high-pitched keening sound filled the humid air. *One ear done, one to go.*

Sulfuric acid is dangerous in the wrong hands. Lucky for her, I knew my way around acids.

Pointless to say anything; I left her to think. It was all student number thirteen could do. *She better use her brain while she still has it.*

Seventeen

Allysa

Morgan? Mandy? Whatever the hell her real name – she needed to explain herself. I couldn't exactly have it out with her in front of the detective. Instead of confronting Morgan, I pushed my hands under my thighs, desperate to control the rage-induced trembling.

"Mrs Ross, I believe you came to see me regarding a cold case?" Boyle stared at Morgan, not even glancing in my direction.

"I need access to your case file on the murder of Terry Holt." No matter what Morgan's deal was with the detective, Sebastian deserved my focus.

Later, I could decide what to do with my so-called best friend.

After cleaning his glasses and repositioning them on his nose, Boyle met my stare. "Civilians can't access case files. I didn't invite you into my office without doing a background check. Terry Holt was an only child. Care to explain why you're wasting my time asking questions about a murder which happened fifteen years ago?"

Morgan sighed and leaned forward, resting her elbows on Boyle's desk. "Will, I didn't come to this shithole town to reminisce or see the sights. You're going to play nice. Make us a copy of that file." She pointed at the folder to his left. "And on your way back, bring us some coffee. Milk. No sugar. Allysa and I will be here for a while."

His laughter sounded like a cadaver dog picking up the scent of decomp. "Now why would I do that, *Mandy*?"

Morgan stretched her arms above her head. "One word: proof."

Boyle swallowed hard, grabbed the file, and stormed out of the office. He slammed the door with such force that the window rattled.

I turned to Morgan, who reached into her handbag and offered me gum instead of an explanation. She shrugged when I declined and folded her arms over her chest. As much as I wanted to hate her for lying to me, never mentioning she once lived in Wild Bay, this was the exact reason I had asked her to come to Rachel's memorial service.

What Morgan lacked in physical size, she made up for in verbal intimidation. How could one word turn Detective Will Boyle into her lap dog?

"You and I need to have a serious conversation," I said.

Morgan nodded. "Later. Right now, we need to be a united front. Will isn't easily intimidated, and I promise you, he won't give us *everything*. No matter what, we're not leaving without answers. We hold the smoking gun."

"You're holding it. I'm just here as your sidekick. I hate sidekicks." I wanted to be angry with Morgan, but she was right. Uncovering the truth about Sebastian's murder trumped any animosity I felt towards her. For the time being.

Boyle returned and handed us each a mug of light brown coloured liquid. He kept the file clutched against his ribs and stared at Morgan. The anger radiating from him made me worry he might reach for his gun and shoot her, if not both of us. "You can look at it, but it doesn't leave my office."

Morgan yanked both files from Boyle's grip. "Such a waste of trees to make us a copy if you won't let us take it. Where is the rest?" She threw the papers back at him and slumped down in her chair.

"This is the entire file."

Morgan stood and walked around the desk. She pushed Boyle down in his chair, making herself comfortable on his lap. Morgan lifted his left hand to her face. "Good for you,

Willy. Did you have to blackmail her into marrying you?"

"*You* want to talk to *me* about blackmail?" he scoffed.

Morgan pressed her nose to his cheek and inhaled. "Still the same aftershave. No matter where I am in the world, if I catch a whiff of this putrid stench, it makes me nauseous. I told you to play nice, but you're holding out on us. Be a good little detective and go make us copies of the other case files."

Boyle stood, easing Morgan from his lap. His hands lingered a fraction too long on her waist. "You asked for Holt's file. This is it." He lifted the brunette wig from Morgan's head and tossed it onto the desk. "That's more like it. Sorry sweetie, but flirting won't work with me. I'm a married man."

Morgan laughed, throwing her head back and slapping Boyle on the shoulders. "Flirting? Oh, Willy. Just like old times. I'm shocked you ever made it as a detective. Fifteen years later and you're still stuck in the same job. In the same shit town. Enlighten me, what's the most exciting case you've worked on in the past decade and a half?"

She didn't give him time to answer. "Busting teenagers for drug use or drinking in the cemetery or on the beach? Arresting rowdy tourists? It isn't nearly as fun as hunting a serial killer, is it?" Morgan shook her head. "The one case which could've been your ticket out of this dump and you didn't catch him. Poor Willy. You know what? *You* failed the victims and their families. Look Allysa in the eyes and tell her you did everything possible to apprehend the man responsible for her brother's murder."

Boyle crossed his arms over his chest. The sly grin reached his eyes. "In that case, I guess I need to tell you we exhausted every resource to solve *your* boyfriend's murder. Or did you forget about him as easily as you forgot about your mother? I expected you to be here for her funeral. Guess jetting around the world with a man older than your father was more important."

I reached for the mug, focusing hard to calm the tremble in my hand. *Who the hell is this woman?*

Morgan stared up at Boyle and tightened his tie. Without letting go, she pouted, a single eyebrow raised. "Video footage. Proof. Now get us all of the case files. Or you're going to prison. Not that you need to worry about bumping into anyone you sent there. Small town detective. Small town crime. A serial killer laughing at your incompetence. Jokes on him, though. Allysa and I will do your job for you. Run to the coffee shop down the street and buy us decent coffee."

Boyle yanked his tie from Morgan's grip. "Serial killer? Why do you think Holt was one of The Skull Keeper's victims?"

"Donna Perk has quite a mouth on her," I said, watching the colour drain from Boyle's face.

Eighteen

Morgan

After we returned to my room at the guesthouse, I waited for Allysa to punch me. To my surprise, she didn't. In her shoes I would've strangled me. "I got us all the case files, didn't I? This is the reason you came here – answers."

I wondered if it was my friend, or Terry's sister, who threw the glass against the wall. Maybe there was no coming back from this for us.

"Allysa, come on. You lied to me about the reason you wanted to meet in Marcel. Not once did you tell me about your childhood or share details about your family. Now you're upset with me for not telling you about growing up in this shithole? You don't know what my life was like before I met Terry." Tears flooded my eyes. I had loved him. *I always will.*

With my back to her, I continued. "While I lived here, there were at least three other men named Terry Holt. I couldn't have known the one I had dated was your brother when Jen mentioned the name." I lied.

"Did you love him?" Of all the questions, I didn't expect this one.

I turned to face Allysa; her face contorted by rage and grief. "Yes. I wanted to spend the rest of my life with him. Sara claims they were in love, but it's nothing compared to what we shared." The weight of a thousand bricks fell from my shoulders. For once I didn't need to lie.

"Then why are you here and my brother is dead? *Murdered.*"

I needed time to decide how much to tell her, so I walked to the mini fridge and grabbed us each a bottle of water. "Terry never told me *why* he had to stay in Wild Bay. I wanted to leave this place as soon as I could think for myself. For most of our relationship, I begged him to leave with me. He refused. Now I understand it was because of Rachel."

"You lied to me." Allysa took the bottle of water I held out to her without looking at me.

"Dear pot, kindly refrain from calling the kettle black." I smiled when she did. "We both have our reasons for not being truthful about our childhoods, but the most important thing is to find the person responsible for murdering the man we both loved."

Allysa pushed her fingers through her dark hair and tied it into a messy bun. "The other victims and their families also deserve answers and closure. Not that closure exists when losing a loved one in a brutal or sudden manner."

"Closure and acceptance aren't the same." I sank down next to her on the bed and placed my arm around her. "If we aren't friends at the end of this, I'll understand. Can we please put all of our emotions aside and focus on what we need to do? I didn't blackmail an officer of the law for nothing."

Allysa rested her head against mine. "What is it you have on Detective Boyle? I swear if you called him 'Willy' one more time, I would've burst out laughing."

"Will and I go way back. He was a few years ahead of me in school. I won't bore you with the details. *What* I have on him is important. It's enough that he also gave us the other seventeen case files. I ensured he included the autopsy reports and crime scene photos. Lysa, I'll read through Terry's file. I don't want you to have your brother's last moments ingrained in your memory. Remember him the way he was the last time you saw him."

People rarely speak about it, but the weight the ones who identify a loved one carry is unfathomable. That moment, the sight, smell, sounds, all of it forever carved into your soul. I knew that better than anyone. I'd seen enough death to last most people a lifetime. As did the woman next to me.

Allysa rested her elbows on her knees, tossing the bottle between her hands. "It doesn't matter whether I see Sebastian's file. If I see the crime scene photos of the other victims, my imagination will fill in the blanks for me."

I shut my eyes and swallowed hard. Before we had left his office, Will pulled me aside and warned me Terry's murder differed from that of the other victims. If it meant I had to chew and swallow every last page in Terry's file in order to protect Allysa from the truth, I would.

To shift her focus onto something, or someone else, was my only option. "Lysa, if you never realised Sara was pregnant, how did Rachel find out?"

"Did Sebastian tell you about the pregnancy? Is that why you asked Sara?"

I nodded, knowing I blew my cover story of not knowing my Terry was the same one Jen had told her about. To push the one responsible for sending Terry to this town – and indirectly to his death – in front of the Allysa-bus seemed fair. She had, after all, lied to Allysa more than once. Every one of my lies was to protect Allysa from the truth. Whereas Jen had done it because she'd always been a two-faced bitch. *Good thing she didn't recognise me.*

"Jen told Rachel about the pregnancy. Your former bestie spent a lot of time in Wild Bay over the summer holidays. Did she ever tell you that?" I hugged Allysa to me. "Jen has a lot of explaining to do."

Neither of us moved a muscle, despite the pounding on the wooden bedroom door.

Nineteen

Allysa

He barged through the door, not even giving me time to open it wide enough. Rude. Detective Boyle paced the length of the room, stopping to stare at the copies he had made for us, which laid on the desk in Morgan's room. "What exactly are the two of you up to?"

I couldn't bring myself to read the files. A part of me didn't want to see how savagely my brother had died. Another part wanted to do the same to the person responsible. I knew which part of my psyche would win.

Morgan pushed to her feet. "You better be here to give us your list of suspects. If not, get out."

I bit my tongue; excited to watch round two of this ongoing fight. My money was on Morgan.

"I can lose my job for giving you that." Boyle pointed at the case files.

Laughter filled the room and mixed with the salty ocean breeze drifting in through the open sliding door. "Will, I'm not here for shits and giggles. Neither is Allysa. Do you really think we don't have more important things to do than *your* job?"

Morgan held up a hand before Boyle could speak. "Suspect list. Now."

Detective Boyle pushed his fingers through his thinning hair. "I understand the magnitude of losing someone you love, especially when it's a violent death. You have my sympathies, but Mandy, you can't storm into my office and blackmail me into giving you information about a case like this."

I stepped closer to Morgan's side. "Her name is Morgan."

"Morgan Wright. CJ Green. Mandy. Whatever you want to go by. You might have changed your appearance, but deep down, you're still the same girl you've always been. Poor little Mandy. Your parents didn't make things easy for you, but you perfected being the joke of the town."

Despite not being happy with her myself, *no one* spoke to my friend like that. "Back off, Detective. You've had fifteen years to solve the murders of eighteen people, but you're no closer to finding the killer than you were back then. Let's all take a moment and consider that, by working together, we'll be able to bring my brother's murderer to justice. And do the same for the other victims and their families."

"What happened after we left your office?" Morgan asked. "For the record, we didn't storm into your office. You invited us. Get your facts straight."

Boyle shook his head and stared at his shoes. "Donna Perk arrived a few minutes after you left."

Morgan and I shrugged at the same time and waited for him to continue.

"Her son was a person of interest during the investigation. We spoke to Corey Perk more than once during that five-year period. Donna is worried about what it will do to his fragile mental state, having all of this brought up again." He lifted his eyes to mine. "Whatever you said to her, she's not happy. Trust me, Donna Perk isn't the type of woman you want to mess with."

Neither am I. "A small-town drug dealer is the least of my worries. If her son is innocent, she has nothing to worry about." I refused to let Donna or her bosses intimidate me.

Morgan crossed her arms over her chest. "Why is Corey no longer a person of interest? Did his mommy pay you to look the other way?"

Boyle straightened his back. "No. There's irrefutable evidence that Corey wasn't involved in Terry's murder. You don't get an alibi more solid than his."

"I will be the judge of that," Morgan said before I could.

As unsure as I was about the state of our friendship, no one had ever stood up for me the way she did. Except my dad. Before Rachel had wrapped him around her pinkie. Perhaps it was time to forgive him. He may have some answers about what really happened. Back when Rachel ran our house with an iron-fist when he wasn't there. At least she never sold me to her clients the way she had her daughters.

Sudden movement to my left.

Morgan lunged forward. The tip of a knife pressed against Boyle's chin. "Suspect list within the next twenty minutes, or I'm going to destroy this town and its two-faced people. Starting with you, *Detective*." She tapped the blade against his skin. "Some crimes don't have a statute of limitations."

Boyle didn't move a muscle, not even to take a breath. "I've never committed a crime."

Morgan moved the blade to his cheek. "While you're on your way to the station to fetch us the list of suspects, think about the *Mandy* you knew. Do you remember me as a trusting teenager?" she asked, with a smug look on her face.

Putting space between them, Morgan returned the knife to her side, where she had kept it hidden. *Who is she?*

Boyle stepped back, bumping his legs into the desk. "You're bluffing."

"Maybe. Maybe not. Guess you should head to the station. Twenty minutes and you better be standing here with *everything* you haven't given us already. Will, trust me, Allysa is not the type of person you want digging into your life. As for me? I'm not helpless, pitiful little Mandy anymore. The people round here might remember my parents, but there's an entire world outside the town limits."

Morgan turned to the sliding door and stared towards the ocean. "Twenty minutes. Or you'll see what growing up here turned me into. It isn't pretty."

Boyle walked to the door and glanced over his shoulder at the woman I didn't know anymore. "Weren't you the last person to see Holly alive? Strange thing that you're staying here, in the Green's former house, and using her surname for your pen name."

Morgan's fingers curled into her palms, but she kept her back to Boyle. "Don't you dare mention her name. If anyone is to blame for her disappearance, it's you."

After Boyle left, I asked the first of many questions. "Morgan, who is Holly?"

Twenty

Sixteen years earlier

Sometimes I wondered whether I should've changed my lesson plans around. For the fun of it. For mine, of course, not theirs. More than once, I considered taking one of their friends. Being tortured is one thing, but to witness what I did to someone you claimed to love ...

These women threw the word 'sister' around as if it meant they were more than temporary acquaintances. No friendship lasts forever. Unless you're stuck in a small town and have no choice. How many of the people I knew would remain in contact after one or both of them left Wild Bay? Here, even families turned their backs on each other.

One thing which isn't temporary is true love. Lust is as short-lived as it takes to orgasm. But real love, eros as Plato defined it, is only obtained once you appreciate the beauty within a person. It transcends the physical and connects the souls. My soul was bound forever.

Student number fourteen would never experience it. A miniscule part of me felt sorry for my students. What was the point of learning a lesson if you wouldn't be able to apply it?

In reality, I couldn't teach them and send them on their merry ways.

Mute. Half blind. Deaf. Faceless.

No way they could step back into society, let alone have the opportunity to touch another person again. Not with their mutilated hands.

With one eye, my student studied my movements. She squirmed at the sight of the syringe.

It's rather comical watching someone try to swallow pills and water without a large part of their tongue. I didn't perform major glossectomy surgery on them. I had, however, done enough research to know how to perform it.

The difference between being a butcher and a teacher? Knowledge.

"Calm down, silly. It's just morphine for the pain. I'm not a monster." The words left my mouth before I realised she couldn't hear them.

With the skinning knife in hand, I stepped closer to the chair. The morphine and restraints keeping her neck in place made the next lesson easier. Every teacher needs the right teaching aids.

I stared up at the exposed wooden beams. The pulley system waited patiently to lift her from the chair once I dismissed her from the classroom.

I got to work. This job didn't pay the bills or contribute towards my other responsibilities.

I pressed the tip of the blade to the spot where her left ear and hair met. Blood trailed down her face as the knife glided along her hairline.

Beauty truly is only skin deep.

Twenty-one

Morgan

Will clearly forgot what I was capable of when pushed to the limits. The point where there were no other options left. Except self-preservation and survival.

I'd survived more than most people. The lucky ones – born with smiles on their faces and die with those same idiotic grins. Those who never shed a single tear other than for their own egotistical reasons. I'd never been a fan of people; despite the impression I gave on social media. *No one is who they pretend to be.*

Allysa Ross. My best friend. The perfect mother and wife. An advocate for the victims long forgotten except by their loved ones. That was the image she projected into the world. The information my private investigator had gathered proved even she wasn't who she claimed to be.

I bit my tongue. If things turned out as I hoped, it wouldn't be necessary to tell her that I knew.

"What the hell is the deal with you and Boyle? Did he *hurt* you? Morgan, you better start talking. Now." Allysa crossed her arms over her chest and tried to stare me down.

My shoulders lifted as I exhaled louder than necessary. "No, he didn't, not in the way you think. I was of legal age when I did what was needed to ensure he looked the other way."

She covered her face with her hands. "For once, give me a straight answer. And tell me the truth. I'm so tired of this silly little dance we've been doing around the subject of our childhoods."

Rich coming from you. "When my father passed away, I did some things to ensure my mother and I didn't end up homeless.

No, it wasn't legal. You know how little teenagers get paid for waitressing and other menial jobs. I didn't have any other options. Will knows about it because he was one of my best customers, before he joined the police. After he became a police officer, I needed to do certain things to remain out of juvie. I'm not proud of what I did, but there wasn't anyone else to take care of my mother." The closest I came to telling the truth in days.

"Were you a prostitute?"

"No. I worked for Donna. Guess that means Rachel owned me back then."

Allysa grabbed her sunglasses and stepped out onto the balcony. I didn't know whether to follow her and explain the rest or leave her to mull over the fact that I had sold drugs to high school students and tourists. People visited Wild Bay for more than just the scenery. That's how I had met the monster whose surname I took. *Among other things.*

"Are you joining me or not?" Allysa asked.

After fishing my sunglasses out of my handbag, I joined her. The air clung to every part of my skin. Even as a child, I had hated the humidity.

"Did you ever meet Rachel?" Allysa didn't look at me.

"No. Jen spent most holidays here on her own. I have to speak to Corey."

She turned to me. "Why do you want to waste your time with Donna Perk's son, seeing as Boyle said Corey had a solid alibi?"

This remarkable woman's ignorance baffled me. Perhaps grief and the reality of her brother's death impaired her logic. "Will isn't above taking bribes. Although I doubt he'll allow Donna to suck his dick. I say Corey remains a suspect."

I checked the time on my phone. Will had three minutes left to hand over the list of suspects. "We need to post and engage on Instagram, otherwise we're going to lose followers."

Allysa pulled her phone from the back pocket of her daisy dukes and took a photo of the ocean.

As soon as she posted it, I liked and shared it to my stories. "We should take one together. An *usie*. It will show Jake we are having fun. Imagine how jealous all our bookstagram friends will be when they see us together." I cocked my head to the side and waited for her to argue with me. "I don't have to add our location."

"How is it possible to see two different people when I look at you?" The pot called the kettle black, yet again.

"Lysa, face it, neither of us had childhoods that people want to talk about. Is it any surprise that we both omitted certain details? No. So what if your stepmother manufactured drugs and your father is in prison? Does growing up in this horrible place change anything about me? No. Our pasts shaped us into who we are today – survivors. The only thing that matters is that your brother and my first love was murdered. It's up to us to find who is responsible."

I stepped closer to her and grinned. "I think we both agree that we have no intention of involving the police once we track down the killer."

Allysa smiled and hugged me tight.

Twenty-two

Allysa

How had Sebastian's name ended up on a list of suspects in a serial killer investigation? Terry Holt's name, to be exact. I asked Detective Boyle.

Boyle loosened his tie and rolled up his sleeves. "Terry didn't grow up here, and a few months after he arrived, the first victim's body was found. When I questioned Holt, he wasn't forthcoming about what had brought him to Wild Bay."

I considered asking Morgan for her knife and do more than just threaten the detective. Sebastian wouldn't have hurt a fly. He had dreamt of becoming a doctor – to save lives, not take them. If it hadn't been for Rachel and slut-Sara, he may have gone on to do great things. Sebastian's grades had been good enough. He could've received a scholarship.

Anger pulsed through me, making my hands tremble. It was time to reach out to a local contact. I needed all the tools necessary to teach these fools a lesson. Sebastian deserved to have his death avenged. I may have failed him in life, but I wouldn't in death.

Everyone responsible would taste my wrath before I returned home to my husband and son.

Grabbing the case files, I waved them at Boyle's face. "Why did you black out crucial pieces of information? This reads like something issued by an intelligence agency."

Morgan lifted both arms into the air and stretched her back and neck. "Willy, have you been sampling some of Donna's product?"

"What the hell are you talking about? Of course not. I

know the shit she's been cutting it with. Every week we have a handful of people who OD on her bad products."

Morgan inspected her nails. "Doubt she's cutting it. Donna needed a new supplier after the previous one died. You just can't trust anyone these days."

"You know a lot for someone who hasn't been around the past fifteen years."

"Oh, Will, even as children, you underestimated me." Morgan turned to me. "Don't worry about the blacked out words. *Detective Boyle* forgets that I found two of the victims. Unlike him, I never forget. Every. Little. Detail. Forever ingrained in my mind."

Boyle nodded. "All things considered, I thought it best not to remind you of all the horrors you've witnessed."

"Remind me?" Laughter bellowed out of the woman by my side. "A mutilated body is kind of high on the list of things one can't erase from your nightmares. Tell me, do the faces of the dead haunt you at night?"

It struck me hard – the similarities between Morgan and the female characters she wrote. This was her fight with Boyle, and I didn't intend to get involved. For the first time, I saw the real Morgan.

"I don't have time for this, *Mandy*. I'll see you when I arrest both of you. You've always been a rule breaker, and your friend is on a personal mission. The two of you trying to play vigilantes will be a delightful change of pace to my normal work. Have fun, ladies. I will see you soon. Oh, Allysa, word of advice, stay away from Corey Perk. Donna will feed you to the sharks and watch them rip you to pieces. Her son is off limits."

The second Boyle closed the door behind him, I grabbed the case files and spread them out around the room.

Unable to stick the crime scene photos on the wall, I improvised and used the white floor tiles as a chessboard of death.

Morgan bent down and picked up file number eighteen before I got to it. "You don't want to remember your brother like this. Trust me. This killer is unlike any you've read about. And it's personal for you, Lysa."

"If you loved him, it's also personal for you." I continued to stare at the horror surrounding me. No need for the blacked out words in the autopsy reports; the crime scene photos told me everything I didn't want to know.

The suffering the victims had endured was ... unimaginable.

Morgan had scanned through the files during the short drive from the police station to the guesthouse. She remained motionless, clutching Sebastian's file to her chest. "Terry wasn't tortured like the female victims were. What the killer did to him ... he wasn't alive."

My head spun as a million thoughts collided at once. My brother was brutally murdered, yet I felt relief that Sebastian hadn't endured the horror the killer had subjected the female victims to. What did this say about me?

I ran to the bathroom just in time, dropping to my knees and clutching the toilet. Coffee exited my body. The entire day neither Morgan nor I once considered food.

Dusk descended on the town, dragging me into the reality of the darkness that still lingered unseen. Even though the killings had stopped, evil remained free.

How did the killer manage to leave no forensic evidence? He isn't a ghost.

Morgan occupied my spot on the floor, staring at the destruction of human beings around her. She shook her head. "All these beautiful young women ... the things he did to them ... but he didn't rape them. I checked the autopsy reports. We need to speak to the medical examiner."

I found a mint on the bedside table and popped it into my mouth after returning from the bathroom. "And tell Doctor Linetti what? That we are concerned citizens?"

Morgan smiled, but it didn't reach her eyes. "I am CJ Green, and I'm doing research for my next psychological thriller. It would surprise you what people tell me when I use that line."

Doubt it. "I need some time to myself. I'm going for a walk on the beach to clear my head and get my thoughts in line."

Morgan returned her focus to the files. "Get something to eat while you're out."

"Or you'll feed me like a mama bird?"

Despite the retreating sun, moisture filled my lungs. I'd always hated the humidity growing up in Marcel. Morgan and I had been born in the same country. Something else we had in common, other than a surprisingly long list of things. And my brother. Sebastian to me. Terry to her.

I reached for my phone when my feet touched the sand and checked that no one was within earshot. No need for a burner phone, not with my contacts. The good ones. Unlike the person whose number I dialled.

"You promised no more favours."

"Hello to you too. Have you set a date for the wedding yet?" The sand was warm underneath my butt.

"That's none of your business."

I rolled my eyes, despite it not being a video call. She didn't know my face and never would. "Your fiancé made it my business. Are you ready to visit him in prison? Your bestie is quite talkative when given enough tequila. She mentioned you're getting cold feet. I hope the proof I sent to you is the reason you're coming to your senses."

"He didn't hurt that child. Ed loves children. That's why he became a teacher."

Some people. "Augusta, you better listen to me, because I'm only going to say this one more time. Ed is a paedophile. You'll be lucky if you get to visit him in prison. Right now, I'm leaning towards saving his victims from the turmoil of going through a trial. Do you understand what I'm saying?"

"If you want me to leave him, I will. I've heard what happens to them in prison. Please don't let Ed end up in there."

I didn't have time for this. "You can leave him, but it won't change his fate. However, whether you live is an entirely different matter. You're as despicable as he is. Because *you* decide to look the other way. I can't. I won't. And I will come for you myself. Trust me, sweetie, you don't want that. I'm rather fond of skinning—"

"Okay. I'll leave Ed and do whatever you want." Augusta sobbed in my ear.

I hated her even more. "Good girl. I'll send you a list and the delivery address. Talk to you soon and don't worry, you'll land on your feet. One day you'll thank me for saving your future children from the paedophile you love."

The sound of snot moving backwards in Augusta's nasal passages made me sick. "Wait, you're not asking me to kill someone this time?"

Twenty-three

Morgan

Grief is a strange thing. You can be busy with everyday life and the next moment, it hits you. No, it doesn't just hit you; it destroys you all over again.

I sank to the floor and cried. How could the man I had loved, still loved, be rendered to nothing but paper?

Terry had been much more than my first love. At a time when I'd known nothing but being the town joke, he had brought light into my darkness. Terry had given me hope for a future beyond this horrible town. In the end, it came down to me to get myself out. Without him.

Over the years, I often thought about him and our love. In the moments where his smiling face, the sound of his laughter, the way his body moulded to mine became too much, I reminded myself that I had made the call. It ended with me watching taillights disappearing into the dark.

I cried without making a sound; the pain was too intense. In the rare moments I allowed the memories to consume me, grief stole my voice. Terry and I had been more than lovers and best friends. With each other, we were vulnerable; our true selves. Our souls were bound together. We'd been able to sense each other's emotions even when we weren't in the same room.

We never told anyone about the eternal vows we had made to each other. No one had witnessed it; no white dress for me or a tuxedo for him.

Next to the lagoon, we had promised forever to each other. The words I spoke that day had meant everything. Not one I uttered to Ray Wright had come from my heart.

My heart and soul forever belonged to Terry.

I still didn't understand why he had refused to leave this hellhole with me. If he had feared Rachel finding him, we could've paid for new identities. For him, I would've run for the rest of my life.

Death stared up at me from the mutilated bodies of seventeen women. Death pressed against my chest as I clutched Terry's file.

A file.

That's what we all become in the end; pieces of paper to show we had existed.

I didn't want to see the photos of his butchered body. A body I knew better than my own. His beautiful face was unrecognisable without his skull to give it shape.

Terry hadn't told me everything as I'd thought. Then again, I never told him everything either. I hadn't wanted to disappoint him.

Self-preservation and survival.

I forced myself up from the floor, willing my feet towards the bathroom, where I washed my face. If I didn't fight back against the heartache and avalanche of emotions, I would end up in a mental health facility. Years ago, I'd come too close to ending up in one. Age and experience are outstanding teachers. The difference between me and most people? I paid attention.

When life knocks you down, you get back up.
When life destroys your soul, you learn to live without it.
If the darkness is heading towards you, threatening to this time consume you for good, you embrace it and allow it to change you.
That's what survivors do.
One day at a time.

I didn't care about tomorrow. I hadn't since the last time I'd come to Wild Bay.

My stomach interrupted the staring competition between me and the woman in the mirror. *I'm not my mother.*

***

It took ten minutes to walk from the guesthouse to Perk. I needed food and to dig a little on my own. Allysa replied to my text message, saying she didn't want to join me. She wanted more time to herself.

"Is Corey still working here?" I asked the waitress as she wrote down my order. She reminded me of a younger version of myself.

"Donna's son?"

"Yes, Corey and I went to school together. I hoped to see him while I'm in town."

Younger me shook her head. "I've never met him. Not once in the three years I've worked here."

I reached for the menu and handed it to the waitress. "Please tell Donna a customer wants to speak to her."

"Did I do something wrong? I can't get fired and Donna has been in a terrible mood for days. Whatever happened last night, it sent her over the edge." Younger me divulged more than I would've to a customer.

I reached for the waitress' arm and gave it a gentle squeeze. "No, silly. Donna knows me because Corey and I were friends. We lost touch over the years. You know how it is once you leave this place."

She shut her eyes and took a deep breath. "Not all of us are lucky enough to get out."

"Then you do whatever it takes and find a way out of here. If you don't, this place will kill you." Younger me didn't realise her tip would be more than enough to get her out.

Ray Wright's money had gotten me out. Despite what it had cost me. It was only fair that it helped someone else.

Holly and I had often come to Perk for the ribs. Tonight, I ordered the same in her memory. The good ones and the bad.

Holly and I had two sides; one of them we reserved for each other. Holly had loved to call me 'sister', the way other best friends did back then. Every time she had called me that I felt nothing but gratitude for being an only child. I'd heard about sibling rivalry, but with us, it turned into a war.

Everything had changed when Holly learned about the one thing I had that she didn't.

The sight of a familiar face yanked me out of the past. *Jen.* I waved her over. The sincerest smile plastered on my face. As fake as her new hair colour.

"Hello, Morgan." She made herself comfortable and raised a hand in the air.

"You don't remember me at all, do you, *Jenny?*"

Her eyes widened as she lowered her arm. "Only one person has ever called me Jenny."

I reached across the table and pushed her now blonde hair behind her ear. If she wanted to look like me, she needed to get it right. "I always wear black. You should try harder, *Jenny.*"

Jen rolled her eyes. The same way she had back then. "I have no idea what you're talking about. Where is Allysa?"

"She has gone home. Family emergency." I stared at wanna-be-me and did my best to look sad. "Too bad you kept your mouth shut for twenty years. Not surprising at all, considering how utterly self-absorbed you were at ages eighteen to twenty-three. Five years is a long time. What surprises me the most is that the serial killer didn't want you. It's possible he knew your skull is as putrid as the rest of you. That's the most logical reason he never wasted time on you."

The waitress placed the ribs in front of me and I told her that Jen wouldn't be staying.

"Who are you?" Jen clasped her hands on top of the table to stop them from shaking.

I lifted the steak knife, pointing it at her ashen face. "Did Mommy know you came here over the holidays to slum it with Corey? Maybe that's why the killer let you live. You weren't single like his other victims."

With my free hand, I reached for the fork and lowered the knife. "Jenny, go home. This is no place for a weakling like you. Terry told you the same thing every time you set foot through those doors. Now, you best be on your merry way, because I'm hungry and aching to bury this knife in your eye."

Jen pushed her chair back, still trying to place me. *Idiot.* The sight of her hurrying out of Perk increased my appetite. In more ways than one.

It baffled me that a woman as intelligent as Jen didn't realise, I lured her to Wild Bay. The photo of Allysa and me, with the iconic lighthouse in the background, was all it took. The lighthouse would always hold a special place in Jen's heart. It's where she had met Corey.

Instead of The Skull Keeper.

I cut into the rack of ribs with a grin on my face. Allysa responded to my text message with a smiley emoji. In the past she always responded with a skull emoji. I doubted she'd ever use it again.

Twenty-four

Fifteen years earlier

The final lesson was always bittersweet. It signalled the end for this specific student. As a graduation present, I left her remains where they would be found.

Often, I already knew my next student's face. Unless the tourist season drew to a close. When these spoiled, self-entitled women left Wild Bay, my life returned to normal. There were fewer things to juggle and less lies to tell. For a few months I breathed.

Until they started driving into town again.

Sometimes I wondered what life would be like outside of this place. Would I be a different person? *Or is teaching women part of who I am?* A part I couldn't leave behind. There was only one way to be certain – I needed to get out. For good.

She didn't make a sound when I dragged the mirror closer. The others had tried but managed nothing more than the irritating sound which drove me insane. Perhaps I enjoyed hearing it, seeing as I decided against sticking duct tape over their mouths. Humans are multi-faceted creatures. Even ones like me.

One eye focused on the exposed meat staring back at her. *Nothing more than a once pretty face*. We're all the same; only the outer layer differs.

I swatted the flies away. They didn't have to wait too long to lay their eggs. Death meant new life for the flies, beetles, spiders and other creatures who feasted on my students. Meals were served until the medical examiner removed the bodies from the ecosystem. Nature moved along, on to the next meal.

Similar to how I shifted my attention to the next student.

The cycle of life is natural and quite beautiful.

I controlled the stages of death.

Mother nature took care of the stages of decomposition.

Two more teaching aids waited to be put to use. This part I enjoyed the most; from a scientific point of view, more than it ended their despicable lives. Good thing I knew that the average male skull is 6.5 millimetres thick, whereas the average female skull is 7.1 millimetres.

I picked up the drill and positioned the tip of the concrete bit against the occipital bone, to the right of her spine. I squeezed the speed trigger and counted. Twenty seconds.

After extracting the drill, I reached for the syringe containing concentrated hydrochloric acid and emptied it into her skull.

Dissolved grey matter and blood rushed out of the hole. It formed the most intricate pool at my feet.

Memento mori. My death art.

Twenty-five

Allysa

It's not that I didn't want to join Morgan for dinner at Perk. I needed time alone. The way I spent most of my days. People aren't very pleasant creatures, except for the few I allowed into my life. Dogs would always be my preferred company. With a dog, you always know where you stand. Besides, the Morgan I knew ordered me whatever she was having and would leave it in my room.

The Morgan I thought I know.

The breeze blowing in from the south cooled the dampness on my neck. I wanted to shut my eyes and forget the horrors I had seen. A dozen scenarios played through my mind. The question would remain unanswered until the killer laid at my feet.

Many serial killers decided to stop killing. Gary Ridgway, Dennis Rader, and Joseph DeAngelo were the first names I thought of. I'd always enjoyed reading true crime books as much as psychological thrillers. *You can't hunt what you don't understand.* Why did this murderer stop?

"You have some nerve," a familiar voice said.

I kept my eyes on the darkening water. "My brother was murdered. What kind of sister will I be if I don't turn every stone?"

Sand exploded against my back. "Do you have any idea what your digging will do to my son? The actual killer is either dead or long gone."

"Then Corey's mental and physical wellbeing is of no concern. Boyle claims he has a solid alibi for the time of

Sebastian's murder. I don't understand why everyone is so worried about Corey. Unless he has something else to hide. Maybe he terrorises babysitters in his spare time."

I felt her hovering over me, but refused to look at her. A solid object pressed against my skull. Experience told me it was the barrel of a revolver. "Donna, you're not the first person to put a gun to my head. Your boss' son tried and look where it got him. Are you sure you want to piss me off?"

"Rachel shouldn't have agreed to your father's terms. The woman was a dumb, self-serving bitch."

No point in telling her not to speak ill of the dead when Rachel deserved to be called much worse. "I just want to ask Corey a few questions, that's all. Donna, I'm trying to find the killer. Don't you and the rest of the town's residents want answers? Go tell the families of the victims that you stopped me from exploring every avenue in order to bring them closure and their daughters' killer to justice. Have you ever spoken to a mother who doesn't know where her child's body is because the killer refuses to disclose the location to the police? Imagine knowing who slaughtered your son or daughter and you don't have a body, or any remains, to bury. Sit and listen to a father whose nine-year-old went out for a bicycle ride but never came home."

I pushed to my feet and turned to face her. Donna didn't expect me to lift the barrel and position it against my forehead. "Thing is, you won't be talking to them hours after their child goes missing. No, you'll sit there and hold their trembling hands *years* after everyone else forgot their baby ever existed. Some of the young women who were murdered in your town, their parents have been waiting twenty years for an answer which might allow them to sleep at night."

Donna lowered the revolver and pushed it into the back of her jeans. "That's their children. Mine is off limits. He has been through enough."

I lifted my pointer finger into the air and asked her to give me a minute while I made a call. "Donna Perk has been selling bad products. Police say they have a handful of ODs a week. It won't be long before someone moves in on her territory. Are you interested?"

I listened to the man on the other end of the line. Despicable as they came, but effective for far more reasons. "Remember about the five favours you owe me? I want to cash one in. Yes, Donna Perk. Thanks. Not going to say I owe you, seeing as you still owe me plenty for Atlanta."

I handed the phone to Donna and smiled as fear transformed her face. In the fading light, she looked even older.

She shoved my phone in my hand and turned to walk away.

"Not so fast, old lady. You're a dead woman walking. Take some time to appreciate the sight of the ocean. The smells and the caress of the wind on your skin. It's a matter of hours before your execution. Ensure that you enjoy whatever you eat tonight. Don't even consider running. It's the difference between a single bullet and being tortured to death."

As I watched Donna hurry to her Harley Davidson, the message alert tone on my phone sounded. *Morgan.*

I sprinted in the direction of the guesthouse, slowing my pace to an evening stroll as soon as she came into view. It helped that no matter the weather, I ran every day.

Morgan wasn't joking when she'd mentioned Jen's ridiculous change in appearance. Few women can pull off being blonde without looking trashy.

I hid behind an SUV and waited.

Jen used Instagram to stalk not only me, but Morgan as well. Another reason I hated social media. Some people were there for the right reasons, but they became less by the day. One more drama-filled post and I would delete my bookstagram account. The cold case account proved far too valuable to shut down.

Jen walked without a care in the world; her focus on her phone. Certain individuals just scream potential victim.

I grabbed her from behind, covering her mouth with my hand and pushed her against the side of a delivery van.

"Go home," I whispered against Jen's ear.

She mumbled against my palm. I released her and took a big step back. "You scared me to death."

"Too bad you're still breathing. Go. Home. Now."

Jen stepped forward, but stopped when I crossed my arms over my chest. "I need to be here for you while you process your grief. I'm sorry I didn't tell you the truth earlier. We can move past this and be best friends again. Sisters."

My nails dug into the skin covering my triceps. "For twenty years, you lied to me about Sebastian's whereabouts. And now you want to be here for me while I process my grief?"

I walked away from my once upon a time friend. "In this town, nothing good happens to women like you."

The memory of Jen's bruised and battered body filled my mind as I put distance between us. She knew what I had done for her.

Sometimes when sleep evaded me, I wondered whether that moment had turned me into who I became or if vengeance had always been inside me. No one hurts the people I love. Back then, I had loved Jen.

It's a shame what time does to people.

Twenty-six

Morgan

My breath caught in my throat. Goose bumps rippled across my skin. A million tiny feet scurried across my neck. "Kill it! Please."

Allysa stood next to me on top of the unmade bed and grabbed my hand. "You're on your own with this one, my friend."

I turned to the woman who, in my eyes, was fearless. "Wait, you're afraid of spiders, too?"

"Not afraid. Petrified." Allysa rubbed her arms and neck with her free hand. "What the hell is that thing?"

"A king baboon spider. When I was a child, we saw them around town and on the farms. The story goes some idiot smuggled them here from East Africa to breed and sell. He didn't think ahead, he just kept them in his house and eventually they found their way back to nature."

Allysa stomped her feet and shivered. "Do they eat baboons? I swear that thing is big enough to take down a baboon. Where is your knife?"

I pointed towards the desk on the other side of the room. "Allysa, if you love me, you'll kill that spider."

She shook her head so hard I moved with her. "No. There are limits to every friendship. This is it for me. You always claim to love me more – you kill it."

"With what? Do you see any assault rifles, grenades, or a small atomic bomb within reach?"

I had climbed out of bed to make coffee and opened the sliding door. The instant I'd turned back to the coffee machine, the devil's spawn ran into the room. Instinct had forced me to run, jump on the bed, grab my phone and call for help. So much for the badass image Allysa put out into the world. In her defence, the thing was the size of a dinner plate. Nevertheless, a true friend would kill to save her friend from something that hideous.

"Morgan, you've attended autopsies, sat across the table from serial killers, gone with the police on a ride-along in gang territory, all for research for your books. But a spider is your nemesis?"

I kept scanning the bed and floor, wondering where the monster was hiding. "You haven't seen when they stand up ready to strike at you. Or heard the horrible sound they make by rubbing their legs together. Screw this. I'm on the first flight out."

A knock on the door made us both jump, higher than when the spider had run towards Allysa when she had entered the room.

"Morgan," Detective Boyle said.

"He has a gun." I pulled my hand from Allysa's. "It's open, but there's one of *them* in here, Will. Get your gun ready and shoot it. Allysa and I are on the bed. Don't hit either of us by mistake. I promise to not call you Willy again."

Boyle laughed so loud it sounded as if he stood next to us. "I can't believe you're still afraid of the silly things?"

Now wasn't the time for flashbacks of all the times Will had chased me around after catching one of the spiders when we were young. He had always carried a clear plastic bag around with him for this very reason.

"One word – chicken." I smiled, despite the creature from hell hiding under the bed. Most probably.

Will eased the door open, scanning the room. He stepped across the threshold, careful to not make any sudden movements. The gun remained holstered at his side. *So much for that idea.*

Allysa and I held our breaths. Without saying it, I knew we

both hated needing a man to rescue us. We were stronger than that, or so we thought. *Damn, spider.*

"Where did you last see it?" Will asked, taking another slow step further into the room.

"I think it's under the bed," I said.

Allysa pointed towards the bathroom. "In there."

Will shook his head and repositioned his glasses. "Typical eyewitnesses. For all I know, Morgan's little friend ran out the sliding door."

He grabbed my knife from the desk and began his search for the rust-coloured monster of my nightmares. I threw my arms around Allysa and we clung to each other.

My eyes remained closed until Will said, "Suspect is down."

"Did you kill it?" Allysa asked.

I opened my eyes and released my death grip on Allysa. Will wiped the knife with the white robe, which belonged to the guesthouse. He lifted the knife by the blade and held it towards me. I shook my head hard. "You can keep it."

Allysa crossed her arms over her chest and I realised we were still wearing pyjamas. Hers a SpongeBob theme. Mine in my favourite colour, but leaving little to the imagination.

"Will, do you mind giving us an hour to shower and get dressed?"

He nodded. "Sure, the body isn't going anywhere. Neither are the two of you."

Twenty-seven

Allysa

Why Boyle wanted to speak to us made little sense. Not that much ever did before my second cup of coffee kicked in. The adrenaline rush from seeing that monstrosity of an eight-legged beast wore off as I rinsed the conditioner from my hair. I sent Jake a text message and promised to call him later. *Ten a.m.*

I hadn't intended to sleep late. There was too much to do. The previous night Morgan had told me Jen didn't recognise her. This came as a surprise considering how many vacations Jen had spent in Wild Bay. Morgan might've had some surgery done, but not nearly enough to wipe her face and voice from someone's memory.

The scent of ribs still lingered in the room, but I didn't dare open a window or the sliding door.

Morgan held out a mug towards me as I stepped into her room. I couldn't help it – I scanned the floor, walls, ceiling and every other surface. If not for the man laughing at me, I may have checked underneath the bed too.

"Ladies, you need to come with me. We're taking a drive to the police station." Boyle tilted his mug back and swallowed.

"There's no need to write a report about killing a spider. It's an obvious case of self-defence. We will say the spider ran into the knife, making it suicide by cop." Morgan pushed her hair behind her ears.

"I don't have time for jokes."

I moved to stand beside Morgan. "We're not going anywhere until you tell us what this is about. Yesterday you said the next time we see you will be when you arrest us. If that's the case, you're wasting your time, Detective. And ours."

Boyle held up his hands. "You won't be setting foot inside the police station, not yet anyway. The morgue is next door. That's where we are going."

"Fantastic. We were hoping to speak with Doctor Linetti today." Morgan lifted the mug to her mouth, but didn't take a sip.

"I need Allysa to identify a body." Boyle kept his eyes fixed on me. "I doubt you want her sister, Sara, driving all the way down here. Let's spare her the trauma, seeing as she recently lost her mother."

"Jen?" Morgan asked.

Boyle nodded. "How are the two of you with seeing a mutilated body on an empty stomach?"

Morgan reached for my hand. I didn't resist. My mind went into overdrive. "Detective Boyle, is that your word choice when notifying families or loved ones of a death? I assume you're trying to rattle us. It won't work. Morgan and I have nothing to hide. Yes, we will go with you and I will identify Jen's body."

Despite how much I hated Sara, no one deserves to see their loved one dead. I remembered what it had done to my father to identify my mother's remains.

"You said her body is mutilated? Did she die in a car crash? I don't want Allysa to identify the body, if that's the case. For personal reasons. If you want to know, you can do some detective work." Morgan squeezed my hand.

Boyle shook his head. "We found a driver's license at the scene. Jen Burke. An abandoned vehicle caught the attention of a passing motorist. The vehicle came back as registered to Mrs Burke's husband."

Boyle motioned towards the door. "It appears your presence has awoken the beast from its slumber. The Skull Keeper is back."

***

Morgan drove us to the morgue. Boyle didn't object, stating I needed time to prepare myself before viewing the body. Sometimes all the time in the world isn't enough.

Morgan tried to make jokes as we followed Boyle down the passage. The morgue looked straight out of a TV series. White tiles covered the floors and walls. Fluorescent tubes positioned overhead. And the smell? Not one I'd encountered before.

It made sense that Morgan felt comfortable surrounded by the dead, as she often attended autopsies for research purposes. I wasn't a stranger to corpses, even those of my own making, but being inside a morgue gave me the creeps.

Boyle made the introductions and asked Doctor Linetti to hurry; there was another crime scene. Morgan and I glanced at each other, but neither spoke.

Doctor Linetti reached for the body bag's zipper. "My apologies. I didn't have time to take her out. Will, you could've warned me. This isn't fair to Mrs Ross."

Boyle shrugged, not offering an apology or adding that we'd seen the case files. "Allysa, are you ready?"

"Does she have any tattoos or birthmarks? I don't have to show you her face?" Doctor Linetti offered me a sad smile. I liked her. Boyle lacked her sense of compassion.

Jen had a scar on her left hip; she refused to tell me how she got it. Identifying her by the scar made sense, but I wanted to see everything. I needed closure on my hatred of my childhood friend. Even I had a limit to the anger and resentment I could carry around. "No. I have to see her face."

Morgan placed her hand on my back. "Jen recently coloured her hair blonde and had it cut. It looks like mine. Is that enough for you?"

Boyle and Doctor Linetti glanced at each other and shook their heads.

"Show me." I wish they never did.

Twenty-eight

Fifteen years earlier

With every passing day, the end came closer. My entire being screamed in silent frustration. This couldn't be how it ended for us.

I found myself at a crossroads. In the figurative and literal sense of the word.

If I kept driving down the left road, it meant one less student. Not that I was worried the police were catching on. I heard more inside information than most police officers who turned out to be the killer. No one ever noticed who was listening while they talked shop over a couple of beers.

'He always looked so harmless' the neighbours say after a violent predator's arrest. The media feeds these brief sentences to the masses, creating a world in which we mistrust everyone. The man who makes our coffee, the neighbours' thirty-year-old son who still lives with them, the pastor, every teacher, even the cashier at the convenience store could be a human trafficker, serial rapist, or paedophile.

Fear unites people in unimaginable ways.

Yet, for five years, the residents of Wild Bay hadn't cared about living with a serial killer in their town. A few of my victims were locals, and in the public's opinion, the women were destined to die young. They cared even less for the self-entitled, trust fund, bitches who drove into town in cars which cost more than the average two-bedroom starter house in these parts.

The worst of it? None of those women had earned it. No, their daddies bought it for them. How would they ever learn respect and responsibility when they received everything as they exited the womb?

The burden rested on my shoulders. I had to step up and teach them about the ways of the real world. Even though theirs was much bigger than our small town; we knew the meaning of hard work. We all understood that money didn't fall from the sky. Here, we worked for what we wanted, and fought for survival. *Is love stronger than the need to survive?*

An invisible wall closed in on me. Not the police. It was the reality of what my life would be like in five, ten, thirty years, if I didn't get out. Wild Bay would wrap its icy-black hands around my throat and squeeze the carbon dioxide out of me. This place didn't deserve to kill me.

I took lives.

A serial murderer.

A survivor.

Instead of going left, I steered the car down the path on the right. It led straight to the lighthouse. It was where I said he'd be waiting. Women are easy. The daughters of wealth, at least. Mention a candlelight dinner under the stars and you've got them – not hook, line and sinker – tied up in my classroom.

Twenty-nine

Morgan

Allysa and I didn't have time to speak to Doctor Linetti. After Allysa identified the piece of skin as Jen's face, Will ushered us out of the autopsy room and straight to the rental car. I glanced at her as I put the car in reverse. We followed Will to the morgue; we were following him to the crime scene.

With the medical examiner's van blocking his view, I pursued. Tiny skeletons danced in my stomach. *Butterflies can't survive inside a thriller author.*

"Where are we going?" Allysa retied her hair into a sleek ponytail.

I wanted to ask why she wasn't wearing daisy dukes, but it might've been due to me teasing her the night before, saying it made her look Texan. "Will insisted on putting you through that horrific ordeal, the least we can do is find out what the hell is going on. I doubt he asked Doctor Linetti along for a B&E. And we're not breaking the law by following them."

"He suspects we murdered Jen." Allysa stared out of the side window.

I laughed. "Yes, because it'll take both of us to kill her. Either of us could do it in our sleep. Without leaving a single piece of forensic evidence. For five years, The Skull Keeper ran circles around Will and the rest of the Wild Bay Police Department. I remember they even brought profilers and more experienced homicide detectives in from Marcel. Nothing. The killer just kept on doing his thing."

"You shouldn't let Detective Boyle hear you say we can get away with murder. I bet you a cup of coffee and a peanut butter and chocolate cupcake he's going to question us both about Jen's murder before the end of the day."

I gagged. "You know I hate chocolate. No deal, you're right. Lucky for me, I kept my pose with her last night, despite wanting to stab her with a steak knife. The police should question Donna."

Allysa turned to me. "Why her?"

"She hates Jen. Well, hated. Or can you hate the dead? I'm confused when it comes to these things."

"Why did she hate Jen?"

I shook my head. A montage of memories flashed through my mind. All of them ended with Jen storming out of Perk and Donna drinking herself into a stupor. "Jen broke Corey's heart."

Allysa dragged her hands down her face. "Jen changed a lot after Sebastian disappeared. She became reckless and stood up to Rachel even more. Jen wanted a man to love her. No one knows who her biological father is. Rachel refused to tell her. I don't think Rachel had a clue as to who impregnated her. She slept around a lot before she met and married my dad. Whenever they had a fight, she threw it in his face."

The ME's van came to a stop and I realised where we were – the road to the lighthouse. Tourists never ventured out here. The lighthouse and the tiny peninsula on which it stood were the only part of Wild Bay reserved for the locals.

None of the residents dared to come here during tourist season and the mayor had installed a sign saying that trespassers would be shot. Ironic, as the mayor at the time had ended up with a bullet in his head. The police hadn't been able to pin it on Donna, but we all knew she was behind it. Donna Perk didn't take orders from anyone, and that mayor hadn't liked to climb into other people's pockets.

In the end, the residents of Wild Bay elected a new mayor. Donna continued running her main business out of Perk. And the sign remained in place.

"I can't follow them any further than this. There's one road leading to and from the lighthouse and not far behind this tree line it opens up." I kept the car travelling at a law-abiding speed and knew where to make a U-turn.

Allysa turned around in her seat and stared at the sign attached to the gate. "Who shoots people who wants to see a lighthouse?"

Teenagers high on drugs and alcohol can be rather destructive when they want to be. None more so than those who breezed in and out of town. Where else would they go to have sex when their parents were at home waiting for them? The police had extra patrols on the beach in order to ensure none of the out-of-town-idiots drowned during a night-time swim. It happened more often than people cared to remember.

I gave Allysa a shortened version of the reason for the sign.

While we waited for Will to question us about Jen's murder, which he no doubt planned to, I suggested we get lunch. Afterwards, we needed to reread the case files.

I understood why The Skull Keeper remained free. You can't arrest someone without enough evidence.

The dead answer questions as to the manner and cause of death. But I'd never heard of any corpse saying the killer's name.

No trace evidence or DNA on the bodies or where the victims were found.

You're clever, but is it enough?

Thirty

Allysa

Morgan insisted we stop for lunch and, to my surprise, I enjoyed the alfredo lasagne rolls, even more than the delicious ribs she had watched me eat the night before.

After my second beer and countless minutes staring at the crashing waves, I turned to Morgan, who typed away on her phone.

"Do you want another beer before we head back to my room?" Morgan asked.

"That's the worst pickup line ever."

Morgan lifted a finger to the side of her face, then continued typing, and downed her glass of water before looking at me. "Who has motive to kill Jen, other than the two of us and Donna Perk?"

Luckily, there weren't any other patrons within earshot. "You need to stop saying things like that. I know getting arrested will be great publicity for your next book release and add to your badass author persona, but I prefer to stay under the radar. I've got a family to think about."

After what felt like hours, Morgan lifted her eyes to mine. "Touché. I don't have anyone who cares about me. Let's focus on tracking down your brother's murderer, and then you can go home to your family."

"What's wrong?" Morgan wasn't above being a bitch at times. None of us are. *Something happened.*

"Life. This place. I hate being here, but I won't leave you on your own. It might not seem like it, but I want Terry, sorry Sebastian's murderer, brought to justice. The thing is, Lysa, I lived here when the murders happened. I remember what the newspapers reported. The things some of the junior officers discussed, not realising everyone paid attention to their every word. Strangest thing – the murders never deterred anyone from coming here for the holidays. There was no decline in tourism. In fact, it boomed."

I gulped down the last of the beer, contemplating what Morgan said. "Maybe it's the same as people who don't move from an area when a serial killer is lurking in their midst. They can't fathom that evil will come for them. Too many people live in tiny bubbles, thinking nothing bad can happen to them or their loved ones."

Morgan reached for my hand. "Not you and me. The reality of life smacked us in the face when most children learned to ride their bicycles."

"What happened here? Why did you tell Boyle you're not your mother?" I squeezed her hand.

Morgan stared out over the ocean, not releasing my hand. "Ah, my mother. Amanda York. The town crazy. Mental health and personality disorders were a taboo subject back then. Years later, I learned the word *schizophrenia* and what it means. Until the moment someone put a label on my mother's behaviour, I just thought she was different. My father took care of her until she became my responsibility."

"Did your dad up and leave you?"

Morgan shook her head, then nodded. "You could say that. Lysa, I can talk for days about all the things my mother did when not taking her medicine, but I don't want to discuss my father. Please."

I drew my bottom lip between my teeth, thinking about how little I had shared with her until I didn't have a choice. Morgan may have learned about my childhood, but as for the image of me being an average stay-at-home mom? *Could people be any more wrong?*

Morgan signalled the waiter and asked for the dessert menu. My curiosity peaked; Morgan hated anything sweet.

When the waiter returned, Morgan asked, "What happened at the lighthouse?"

"Nothing." The waiter needed to work on his poker face.

Morgan touched his arm and smiled up at him. "I grew up here, probably left around the time you were born."

The waiter asked us again to call him Kevin. "Depends how old you were when you left. Ten?"

"Oh, sweetie. My friend's the MILF, I'm just an ILF. And way too experienced for you." Morgan didn't give the red-cheeked Kevin a moment to process. "What happened at the lighthouse? Who died?"

Kevin pursed his lips and shook his head before glancing over his shoulder.

Morgan let out an exaggerated sigh. "Have you ever heard about the York family?"

He nodded.

"I'm Morgan York."

"Good thing I didn't believe you. My parents have only mentioned a Mandy York."

Undeterred, Morgan leaned back in her chair and crossed her arms underneath her boobs. "People used to refer to me as Amanda York's daughter. Then one day they shortened it to Mandy. Oh, I heard all the other words along with it. Poor child growing up with a lunatic. When will Mandy snap and become as crazy as her mother? I can continue, but that will be a waste of our time and you still have youth on your side. I'm not that lucky."

The waiter glanced at me; I refused to help him. "Well, barely legal Kevin, are you going to answer, or is there some other humiliating memory you want her to recall?" I asked.

"Donna Perk. Word is she was *murdered*."

Morgan tapped her forefinger on her nose. "Now, who is stupid enough to kill Donna?"

Kevin shrugged. "I heard she ran the drugs and police in this town."

"Listen up young man, this almost-old-lady is going to

drop some bombs on you. The truth kind, not the F kind. Never trust anyone. Not even when they tell you a story they could've overheard in this little town where gossip gets traded like currency. With Donna Perk, the less you know, or assume, the better. For all you know, one of us killed her and we're wondering who needs to be silenced. Never think a woman isn't capable of committing a violent crime just because she doesn't have a Y-chromosome. And if you say 'Yes, ma'am', I will gut you with this straw."

I pinched the bridge of my nose with my thumb and forefinger, staring at the table. My stomach shook, but I pursed my lips and tried not to get a headache from the building pressure.

"Now, fetch our bill. Considering the life lessons I unloaded on you, I doubt you need much of a financial tip. There are things money can't buy, like wisdom."

Kevin swallowed hard and placed his hands behind his back. He nodded and moved to turn away from the table.

"Dude, calm down. Don't get all emotional and stuff. Maybe I will change my mind by the time you return to our table." Morgan forced a sweet smile.

"What the hell is wrong with you?"

She shrugged. "Who has the balls to go after Donna Perk?"

As we walked out of the restaurant, I overheard a conversation. Before Morgan closed the car door, I asked, "What did that lady mean when she said she wonders if this is enough to bring Corey into town?"

Morgan slipped on her sunglasses and placed both hands on the steering wheel. "Jen did much more than break Corey's heart. She destroyed his world. No one has more motive for wanting her dead than him and Donna. If Donna's dead, that leaves Corey. Guess it's time we pay him a visit."

Thirty-one

Morgan

Corey Perk. The best-looking boy in school grew up to be an even more handsome man. The last time I saw him was the day I'd left Wild Bay. I couldn't leave without saying goodbye to him, even if he hadn't been conscious. We had lived close to each other and because of the limited number of children, we became friends. In Corey's defence, even in a big city, I would've been friends with him. He wasn't anything like his mother.

Things changed for all of us when Terry moved to town. Corey no longer held the title of Most Eligible Bachelor. And, by then, everyone knew his mommy was a drug dealer.

Everything went to shit the moment Jen had made her first appearance at Perk. The Corey I had known became a different person, and not for the better. What he saw in Jen remained a mystery to me.

I explained the intricacies of spending half of my life in a small town to Allysa. The gate opened; she stormed in and began to dig. It's what she did best.

"How did you and Sebastian meet?"

The memory of that night was so vivid I didn't need to close my eyes to remember. I stared at the winding road ahead. The passing farmland seared into my subconscious. Along with every day I'd spent here. "I waitressed at Perk. Donna hired Sebastian as a bartender."

"How did you two get involved?"

To be on a witness stand would irritate the living daylights out of me. I preferred to ask the questions. "The physical attraction was immediate, from my side at least. He admitted he had trouble working that first night as he struggled to keep his eyes off me. Looking back, I think what cemented it for us was the fact that neither of us wanted to talk about our lives before we met. We dated for five years, and with Jen's appearance, or rather almost constant presence, he ended up telling me what had brought him here."

I didn't give Allysa time to ask another question. "Jen threatened to tell me about Sara, the baby, and his father being in prison for drug trafficking. Sebastian knew I didn't care about any of it, but with Jen, it always became a battle of wits. He beat her to it, not telling her. When she came to me, I laughed and told her to leave him alone. I threatened her with The Skull Keeper, saying everyone in town knew who he was and that he got rid of our problems without payment."

Allysa turned to me. "What?"

"I lied. No one knew. Jen backed off for the rest of the season, but came back for Corey's heart and soul. I warned him that she did it to make Sebastian jealous. It's weird not calling him Terry. To me, he'll always be my Terry. The man I loved."

I wondered what Allysa would've been like as a sister-in-law.

"Morgan, I'm sorry for asking you to come with me, for even asking you to Rachel's memorial service. This can't be easy for you." Allysa placed a hand on my shoulder.

"It isn't, but I want answers as much as you do. Sebastian was my first love; the best friend I ever had. After I met him, I realised how destructive some of my other friendships were. My heart will always belong to him."

"Then why did you leave?" Allysa didn't remove her hand.

I shook my head and forced the tears back. "I wanted to be someone other than *Mandy*. I don't know if things would've turned out different for Sebastian if I'd stayed here. We might've broken up. Or he may have left me now that Rachel is dead; with three children to raise on my own and a mortgage to pay. Wild Bay was his prison."

Allysa hugged me as best she could. "At least he found love here. Thank you for loving my brother and keeping Jen away from him."

"I didn't kill Jen. And I should've done a better job of protecting Corey from her."

Allysa stared out the window. "If Donna worked for Rachel, why didn't she tell her about their relationship? Rachel would've had a heart attack."

Laughter bubbled out of my could've been sister-in-law. The irony of her words wasn't lost on me. I told Allysa I couldn't say, but if I were to venture a guess, Donna didn't want the trouble of informing her boss that Jen was slumming it with Corey. In reality, he had been the one diving in the dumpster. Corey had deserved better than that woman. I didn't care if Jen rested in peace.

"That's weird," I said, bringing the car to a stop on the dirt road. Allysa opened her window before I had the chance to tell her not to. Dust bellowed into the car. *City girls.*

Yellow tape informed us what had happened here. I stared at the house; no sign of Corey. A yellow aeroplane stood inside a hangar. *At least Corey fulfilled one of his dreams and became a crop duster.*

"This is where they found Jen's body," I said.

Allysa turned to me with raised eyebrows.

"The Skull Keeper left his victims throughout this entire area. The body of the first victim was found in this exact spot."

"Corey found her?"

Something inside the house drew my attention. It wasn't a door opening or the movement of a curtain. I shook my head; the wind brushing my hair across my face. "I did."

Thirty-two

Twenty years earlier

In the distance, the sun made her appearance. She didn't do much more than rim the horizon in warmth. I rubbed my arms, grateful for the layer of protection the overalls offered against the cool morning wind. One last thing to do before I left; I didn't want to rush this. The previous night I'd slept well; better than expected, considering I'd made the leap from teacher to murderer. Not much of a leap, as there wasn't a different outcome planned for my first student.

People always say you never forget your first, but staring down at what remained of her, I felt nothing. Slaughtering chickens and livestock left a scar on my psyche, even though their deaths were always quick and painless. They didn't deserve to suffer. Those who torture animals deserved to spend time in my classroom.

If the police paid attention, the sequence of my lessons wasn't hard to understand. The medical examiner would explain it to them.

I doubted those unversed in the art of death could appreciate the detail. The devil wasn't in the details. It was in the scene itself. Perfection. All of it. I hoped those who saw her corpse grasped the tremendous amount of work I'd put into this woman's last days.

Light coming from the house drew my attention. No doubt the owner's son would be considered a person of interest.

I smiled. Soon, the names of every man in town would be on that list. Maybe even that of a few tourists. But returning the spotlight to the residents of this shitty place wouldn't be difficult. I had it all planned out – murder a few local women out of season; tourist season, to be more specific. Outside forces didn't govern my hunting season.

I erased and covered my tracks before heading home. There were a few things to take care of.

Student number two didn't have much time left. I hoped she enjoyed the day by going to the beach or having her nails done. Soon she would learn what happens to those who ignore me. I warned the bitch as often as I had the one lying in the field.

"Have at it," I said to nature's creatures. "You better hurry. She'll be found soon."

Thirty-three

Allysa

Morgan pressed a palm to her chest, staring at the front door. "What's wrong?" I asked.

Without giving an answer, she climbed out of the car and walked up to the house.

Perhaps seeing the crime scene tape brought back memories of her discovering the first victim. I kept my mouth shut, studying her. The slow steps she took. The way she kept rubbing her arms. Morgan was far too confident to have worried about seeing an old friend.

A terrible stench assaulted my nose. Growing up in a city and choosing to live in an even bigger one hadn't prepared me for being in the country. I didn't have any frame of reference to place it. "What the hell is that smell?"

"Pig manure. There's a lagoon on the farm to your left." Morgan continued staring at the weathered door.

"A lagoon?"

Morgan tilted her head to the right and left. "A lagoon is a large open-air pit where pig waste is left to be broken down by anaerobic bacteria. It's then used to spray crops. Great fertiliser."

Without warning, Morgan ran to the front door, hitting it with the side of her fist. "Corey! It's Morgan!" She kept pounding on the door. No one answered.

I reached for the handle and let us in. Morgan called out again; no response. The smell inside the house, on the other hand, I knew. Someone had recently discharged a firearm.

We made our way through the entryway and turned left

into the family room. A figure sat in a wheelchair.

"Corey!" Morgan screamed, falling to the floor. She covered her eyes and released a sound I often heard coming from distraught families. Morgan rocked back and forth, clutching her knees to her chest.

I grabbed my phone and contacted Detective Boyle as I stepped away from the nonhuman sounds Morgan made.

Boyle said it would take them fifteen minutes to get out to the farm. Enough time to investigate the scene for myself.

A shotgun lay on the carpet, the barrel pointing towards Morgan.

Blood, hair, skull fragments and grey matter coated the walls and ceiling. I stared at the carpet and furniture. *What goes up, must come down.* Skull fragments were everywhere. I'd never seen anything like it.

The note stuck to the wall opposite the body made my blood boil.

Corey's death could've been avoided. Basic human decency goes a long way. Boyle needed to explain himself. If he wasn't responsible, I intended to go after whoever had made the call.

It was always a strange sight, seeing a suicide victim who took the time to dress up. I doubted the Sunday best Corey wore was his first choice when he'd dressed himself for the day.

No matter what I tried, Morgan didn't respond to me. I said her name; she covered her ears. When I touched her shoulders, Morgan swatted my hands away without opening her eyes. The deafening scream was replaced by a keening sound I knew. Grief.

Why for Corey? A man she hadn't seen in years and who, by all accounts, hadn't been on the best terms with when she'd left Wild Bay two decades earlier.

"Morgan?" Boyle's voice filled the house. He didn't look at me before picking her up and carrying her outside.

I followed them, but remained at a distance. Boyle pressed

my best friend's head to his chest and stroked her hair. Morgan mumbled with her eyes shut. I moved closer without stepping into the invisible bubble around them. This behaviour was a stark contrast to the previous animosity between them.

Doctor Linetti stared at them. Tears spilt down her cheeks. She quickly brushed them away and headed towards me. "Where is the body?"

"In the living room. He left a note."

Her emotions remained hidden despite my quizzical stare. "That poor young man didn't deserve this. Not after everything he'dd survived. Three bodies and the day isn't even over yet. It's like *he* is back."

On autopilot, she dressed in a white disposable coverall, covered her shoes and pulled latex gloves over her hands. The other investigators did the same. For the third time in less than twenty-four hours, they were about to face death.

From the research I'd conducted on Wild Bay, there weren't any murders mentioned in the online newspaper articles. The Skull Keeper had introduced destruction to this tranquil place.

Morgan's sudden movement pulled me away from the clinical scene in front of me. "No paramedics. No hospital. No. Same." She lifted her head from his chest and placed a hand on Boyle's cheek. "It's the same, Will."

"Okay. At least have Doctor Linetti take a look at you. Morgan, it's time for you to leave Wild Bay."

Blonde hair swayed from side to side. Morgan pushed to her feet and reached for my hand. "No. Allysa needs me."

I placed an arm around her and pulled her close. "Detective Boyle is right." *Shoot me now. Too early?* "Have Doctor Linetti assess you and then we can leave. You're more important than finding Sebastian's murderer."

Boyle cleared his throat. "Morgan can leave town. But as for you, Allysa, I have a few questions for you. Since you arrived in town, there have been two murders."

The hair on the back of my neck stood up. "Make that three. You, or someone else in your joke of a police department, are responsible for Corey Perk taking his own life." I pointed at the front door. "Go look for yourself, *Detective*. Corey left a note. Who calls the only relative to come and identify a body? Even more so when that person is in a wheelchair. Surely one of Donna's employees could've done it."

Boyle met my stare. "How we conduct investigations is none of your business. You're a civilian and the sister of a murder victim. Not very objective, are you?"

"The Skull Keeper didn't murder Terry. Neither did he kill Jen." Morgan took a deep breath. "The victims were tortured before death. Terry, rather Sebastian, and Jen weren't. The victims' bodies were naked; Sebastian and Jen were clothed. Their skulls not being found isn't enough. Anyone in your department could've read the reports. Copycat? Maybe. How do I know *you* didn't murder the man I loved? Let's face it, *Willy*, you had enough motive to want to hurt me. What better way than taking away the one person who meant everything to me?"

Morgan's back.

I glared at Boyle. "We're leaving. If you want our statements, come to the guesthouse."

Thirty-four

Morgan

Did I feel bad about faking my emotional response at seeing Corey's body? No. His wasn't the first suicide by shotgun I had seen. After the first one, especially if it's someone you love, it kind of numbs you to the sight of a headless person.

Will's reaction was exactly what I wanted. Playing coy with me never worked for anyone.

I smiled when Allysa handed me a mug filled with coffee. *How do people function without caffeine?*

On the way back to the guesthouse, Allysa remained silent. In due time, she would bombard me with questions. It was only fair that she learned a bit about the twenty-three years I had spent in Wild Bay. The weight of all the skeletons rested on my shoulders. I kept secrets. Unlike Holly.

Will knew better than to admit to anything which might add his name to the list of suspects in The Skull Keeper investigation. And Holly's disappearance. I pushed his name to the top of Allysa's suspect list.

"When you're ready to talk about it, I'm here." Allysa motioned for me to follow her out onto the balcony.

The moisture in the air wasn't as bad today; the wind helped. "My father committed suicide."

Allysa didn't look at me. Another reason I liked her – she knew when to probe and when to discuss books.

"Will must've read the file. The circumstances of my father's death weren't made public. Good thing it happened before my uncle had resigned from the police. Not long after, he and my aunt left Wild Bay." I hated them. "At the time, I thought they didn't want to help take care of my mother."

Allysa lifted the mug to her mouth. "How old were you?"

"Fourteen." I'd grown up quickly after my father committed suicide.

Dear old daddy had forgotten about the exclusion clause in his life insurance policy. Two months short of the two-year period expiring. He had thought he could buy his way out of debt, not realising it would thrust me into the very hands of the men he owed money to.

Fourteen is considered too young to drive, buy alcohol, or consent to sex. The perfect age to have forced me into selling drugs to pay off my father's debt. They had threatened to contact a social worker and have me placed in foster care. They had said a crazy woman couldn't take care of a child. They weren't wrong. But I knew what happened to children under the government's supposed care. The decision hadn't been hard – I'd rather sell drugs than be raped.

They supplied whatever the clients wanted, from party drugs to scheduled medicines. In no time I'd sold to teenagers, housewives, and businessmen. The affluent and the junkies. During those years, I'd learned a lot about people and myself. Not to mention the other criminal titbits I had picked up.

Allysa placed the mug next to the chair, stretching her legs out and rested her feet on the balustrade. "What's the deal with you and Boyle? Don't lie to me."

"We were involved, but it didn't work out." Holly being the reason I had lost the protection of a police officer. She had hated that I was dating someone older. My supposed best friend had despised a lot of things about me, and told me often that craziness and failure were in my DNA. If she had ever said one good thing to me, I couldn't recall it. We'd been friends because there hadn't been many girls our age. I've always preferred having male friends. Less drama.

Time to change the subject. "Lysa, you need to go see your father. Why haven't you?"

Allysa pushed to her feet. "He transported Rachel's drugs.

He brought that bitch into our lives, and where did it get any of us? Sebastian ended up here. My dad is in prison. I didn't have anyone."

She turned to me; her eyes hidden behind her sunglasses. "My dad never even got a parking ticket. How, or why, he went from being the best dad to trafficking drugs, I'll never understand."

"You can ask him. I'm surprised you wrote him off."

"I didn't. He asked me to stay away. Not a hard thing to do when all the love you have for someone turns into hate. I still can't comprehend why he—"

A knock on the door interrupted her. I made my way through the room, enjoying the coolness of the tiles underneath my feet. My eyes scanned the floor and I remained on high alert for sudden movement. At any moment, another eight-legged devil's spawn might come looking for revenge.

Will stepped into the room before I opened the door wide enough. "Ladies, it's time you tell me exactly what it is you're doing in my town."

Thirty-five

Allysa

Since identifying Jen's body, the taste of bile lingered in the back of my throat. Not because she'd been violently murdered. Anyone who saw the loose skin which used to be someone's face without feeling sick would have to be a psychopath. It might even upset the most hardened criminals. Serial killers are a different species.

Knowing that my brother had suffered the same fate made it worse. More real. Sickening. Innocent people didn't deserve to die like that, even if I no longer cared for Jen. I reminded myself that Sebastian's mutilation had happened post-mortem. *Small mercy.*

"Jen stalked you and Morgan," Boyle said once we were alone in my room. He pulled out the desk chair and moved it closer to the chair next to the bed.

I sat down when he told me to. "You're going to need to give me more than that."

"Unlike The Skull Keeper's other victims, Jen's phone was found with her body. She'd made multiple screenshots of your and Morgan's Instagram posts. We even discovered she'd sent you a friend request on Facebook. It's still pending." Boyle took out his phone and held it in his hands. Most of the detectives I knew no longer made notes in a pocket-sized notebook.

"I haven't been on Facebook in months." Facebook friends aren't real friends. Ninety-nine percent of people befriend you in order to pry on your life. Who cares what happened to a person you haven't spoken to since the last day of school? I sure didn't.

"Where were you last night?" Boyle asked the obvious.

"Here, in this room, with Morgan. She brought me ribs from Perk and I passed out early. Yesterday was a long day."

Boyle's fingers tapped away at the phone's screen without him breaking eye contact. "Passed out or fell asleep?"

"Detective Boyle, not that it's any of your business, but I don't sleep well. I haven't in years. So, after an emotionally taxing day like yesterday, it's common for my body to shut down and force me to rest. Do you want to discuss this with my GP? I can give you his number." The knowledge that Donna Perk wouldn't see the sunrise proved to be a far better sleeping aid than any pill a doctor had ever subscribed.

"Where did Morgan go after she left your room?"

I pursed my lips. "What motive could either of us have for wanting Jen dead? Don't you think *if* we wanted her dead, Morgan and I could've come up with a more creative idea than to kill her the same way Sebastian had died?"

"We have eyewitnesses stating they saw Jen and Morgan having a conversation at Perk."

I gestured for him to continue. "And? A conversation between two people who bumped shoulders at Perk years ago isn't enough for you to consider Morgan a suspect."

"How well do you know Donna Perk?" He repositioned his glasses on his nose.

"I met her once. I'm sure you can round up some eyewitnesses at Perk to confirm this. Seeing as that's where Sebastian had worked, it's the most reasonable place that I started looking for my brother. Donna informed me of his death."

"Did you get into an argument with her?"

I threw my hands in the air. "You're wasting your time, Detective. I didn't murder Jen, and I met Donna Perk once. Who contacted Corey and asked him to drive to the morgue to identify his mother's body?" Holding a hand up, I continued. "Have you read his letter? I have. Someone played a very sick and twisted game with Corey by leaving his ex-girlfriend's body on his property. As if that isn't bad enough, you informed him of his mom's murder, not by sending an officer to his house. No, you told him over the phone. How did Corey lose his legs?"

"Were you aware that Jen stalked you?"

My entire body trembled with rage. Far too often, I'd experienced first-hand how the families of victims were treated by law enforcement. Once upon a time, I had considered joining the police. That dream had crashed and burned when I saw how blasé the police were about Sebastian's disappearance. All things considered, I should've sent them a gift basket as their nonactions sent me down the path to who I became.

"No, I did not. It's impossible to be certain who stalks you when your account isn't private. I'm a bookstagrammer. It's standard practise to have a public account."

Boyle stood and walked to the mini-fridge, removing a bottle of water. He drank half of it and placed the bottle on the desk. "And your cold case account?"

"It's not a stretch that I would devote my time to be a voice for those forgotten by the police and public."

Boyle sat on the edge of the desk and adjusted his tie. "I'm going to prove Terry Holt was The Skull Keeper. Someone turned the tables on him and murdered him the same way he butchered seventeen young women."

Thirty-six

Fifteen years earlier

It didn't take a clinical psychologist to realise *Jenny* had serious daddy, mommy, and sister issues. If she got a few drinks in, her tongue became rather loose. I grinned. Soon, her tongue would be free from her disgusting mouth forever. The perfect end to my teaching days – Jen's skull with the others. The coup de grâce to my time spent in this horrible place and the despicable people who called Wild Bay home.

A part of me didn't want to take Jen's skull. Now, as for teaching her my various lessons, I considered adding a few special ones just for her.

Jen felt unseen by her family, but I saw her. The way she flirted with every man in Perk, sometimes even women. Unlike my other students, Jen didn't come from legally gained money. Weird how people act all high and mighty when they are the spawn of scum.

Everything she owned was bought with drug money and the deaths of those who'd OD'd on her mommy's products. I asked her once where her daddy was; she drank even more than usual that night.

A quick text message to her phone and she headed out the door. Corey was working the bar alone tonight. One day he might realise I did him a favour by removing the vermin from his life. A handsome young man like him wouldn't be single for long. As soon as he forgot about the bitch who had controlled him for five years.

Unlike Miss-Out-Of-Town, I knew a shortcut to the lighthouse. After parking my car out of sight, I walked to the spot where I waited for her to arrive. My students tended to be punctual. Physical perfection made for the perfect lure. *Idiots.*

While waiting for headlights to become visible through the trees, I considered adding another lesson; one especially for Jen. It was only fair, as she received more warnings than any of the others. Hack off her feet? Stick a firecracker up one of her orifices? Burn her legs? The possibilities were endless. My time wasn't.

Jen never made it to the lighthouse, or to my classroom. She lived another day to spew her toxicity on everyone she met.

If I ever saw her again, the hypocrite would suffer. Once I selected a student, she wasn't free to leave town unless inside a coffin.

Good thing I knew where Jen lived in Marcel. *One day I will hunt you down.*

Thirty-seven

Morgan

"Take a seat. This is going to take a while." Will's left thumb rubbed against his wedding ring. His eyes moved over every part of me, lingering on spots he had, years ago, thought belonged to him.

The man in front of me didn't resemble the one he'd been when we were involved. Never was the five-year age gap more apparent. Men around here spent too much time in the sun and aged faster than anywhere else I'd travelled to. Perhaps this hellhole drained the life out of them. If I had stayed any longer, it would've snuffed the life out of me. A serial killer had been the least of my worries.

"Were you aware that Jen stalked both you and Allysa on social media?" Will made himself comfortable on the bed.

I took a seat at the desk, putting as much distance between us as possible. "*Detective*, I am a best-selling author. Having fans or weirdos popping into my DMs isn't anything new. However, I don't recall Jen reaching out to me. I did my own digging after she mentioned she started following me. She used an avatar instead of a photo of herself as her profile photo."

Will's head tilted to the right. "DMs? Avatar?"

Careful not to smudge my mascara, I covered my face with my hands. "You're not on social media, are you? I thought with the town's low crime rate, you would keep yourself occupied during shifts. DMs are direct messages. An avatar is a graphic representation of someone. So instead of having a photo of herself, Jen had a picture of an animated character with a book. Again, not unusual."

This wasn't the time to mention that Jen had another account – one she had used to post bad reviews of, not only my books, but numerous other authors. I doubted she'd even read any of the books she trashed.

It's easy to be a troll when hiding behind a screen and not using a real name or a photo of yourself. It's part of what authors endure. The good reviews always outweigh the bad. People could say what they wanted about my writing, but nothing mattered as long as I enjoyed the stories I wrote.

"It's no secret that you hated Jen. You got along well enough with everyone else when you were a waitress at Perk. Why the animosity towards her?"

"Will, please name one person, other than Corey, who didn't hate Jen? She always thought herself better than everyone else. Corey was a consolation prize for her as she made no attempt to hide who she really wanted – Terry."

"Is that why Corey and Terry never got along?" Will removed his tie and placed it on the bed.

"Until Terry moved here, Corey held the title of the most handsome man in Wild Bay. I think he always knew that Jen dated him to make Terry jealous. People expect these things to not affect men. But Corey had little else going for him, considering everyone in town knew what Donna did. None of the local women wanted to get involved with a man whose mother had a volatile temper and was involved in organised crime."

Will walked to the coffee machine, not saying a word until he held a mug out towards me. I never drank this much caffeine unless on a deadline.

"Donna hated Jen more than the rest of us combined. Since learning more about Jen's past, I suspect Corey saw a bit of himself in her having grown up fatherless and having a drug dealer for a mother. Maybe Donna didn't want Corey involved with the daughter of her supplier." I shrugged; careful not to spill the coffee.

"Morgan, why are you not married? You're Instagram

posts shout of someone who is utterly alone. It's always selfies, photos of books, or something random. Even your author account comes across as dark and cold."

Every thriller author has a dark side. How else will we write what we do?

"*Detective Boyle*, where is your partner? The detectives I've interviewed never questions eyewitnesses or potential suspects alone." I lied. In smaller towns and cities, detectives and patrol officers often work alone unless on a special assignment or training a rookie. "Am I a suspect?"

"Where were you last night?"

Playing the faceless shadow in your nightmares. "I ate dinner at Perk, where I ran into Jen. We chatted for a while. I'm sure you've already established this, otherwise you wouldn't be asking. After dinner, I came back here and gave Allysa the food I had ordered for her. The two of us chatted for about an hour and then I turned in for the night. What did Corey write in his suicide note?"

Will shook his head. "I can't share that information with you."

"How did Corey lose his legs? Please. What happened to my friend?" I'd witnessed enough interrogations to know how to turn the tables. Everything my detective friends had taught me came in handy, not only for my books.

It must've been my sad smile, because for the first time since Allysa and I walked into Will's office, I caught a glimpse of the man who had offered me protection. Not the condom kind.

"Fifteen years ago, the last time Jen had visited Wild Bay, her fiancé came looking for her at Perk. He had asked Corey if he knew Jen and where he might find her. Imagine this big shot lawyer from Marcel, whose face had been on the news countless times, is your girlfriend's *fiancé*. To say it crushed Corey is an understatement. That night he drank himself into oblivion, got high for the first time, and headed out to the lighthouse."

"Corey never used drugs. He hated them."

Will nodded. "I know, but that night, everything changed for him. The short version: Corey crashed his car, the wreckage was unlike anything I had seen in a long time. The doctors needed to amputate both his legs at the knee."

My shocked expression was forced; none of that was news to me. But it didn't hurt to appeal to Will's gentle side. On cue, tears rolled down my cheeks.

I lifted my eyes to his. "It isn't fair. Corey deserved better than the shitty hand life dealt him. No father. A dictator for a mother. And I had tried to warn him about Jen. We all did."

Will handed me a tissue, giving me the chance to ask, "How did Donna die?"

"It appears she committed suicide at the lighthouse."

I swallowed, dabbing the tissue to my eyes and cheeks, and went in for the proverbial kill. "Were you aware that, before Terry's murder, he had resigned from Perk? He'd planned to leave town. Donna didn't want to hear it as Rachel, her supplier, had saddled Donna with the responsibility of keeping Terry here. Back in the day, I heard Rachel's name whenever *they* threatened me. Will, it seems the people my father had owed money to were better connected than either of us thought."

He refused to meet my stare. "I'm sorry I failed to protect you."

"We both failed to keep my mother safe. There's no point in dwelling on the past. If I were you, my focus would be on establishing the time of death for Jen and Donna. Perhaps fifteen years ago, Donna murdered Terry to prevent him from leaving town, and murdered Jen last night to keep her away from Corey. With all the bad products she's been selling, it's only a matter of time before someone else moves in on her territory. Trust me, drug dealers don't hand over their turf without a fight. More often than not, they'll go for your loved ones first. Like they did with my mother. Nothing Donna did or didn't do would've kept Corey safe, except ending her own miserable life."

Will pushed to his feet and paced the length of the room. I stared at a random spot on the wall, ignoring his movement. "I have two questions for you and then I'll tell you what I think happened fifteen years ago when your boyfriend – sorry ex-boyfriend – lost his head."

My nails dug into the material covering the chair's armrests. I controlled my breathing. The invisible spot on the wall morphed into scenes of vivid brutality. Will's blood pooled at my feet.

Most authors see the scenes as they write it. I wasn't any different. My imagination was more real to me than the lines on my palms.

The figure in my peripheral vision stopped moving. "How well do you know Allysa Ross?"

"She's my best friend. I know Allysa better than anyone." Thanks to the private investigator in Colorado.

"Were you aware of the fact that she met with Donna late yesterday afternoon on the beach?"

"Allysa mentioned running into her." *Friends cover for each other.* "What is it to you?"

Will picked up his tie and stroked the length of the material. "An off-duty officer noticed Donna heading to the beach and kept an eye on her. From where he stood, their meeting didn't appear friendly. He didn't venture too close, but it appears Donna held a gun to Allysa's head."

I laughed and rose from the chair. "Oh, Will. Is that all you have? Allysa has a way of rubbing people up the wrong way because she doesn't take intimidation well. Donna is – was – used to people doing whatever she wanted. Including the police. Imagine her shock when the sister of a man she had murdered years ago, waltzed into her bar. Allysa isn't the type of person you want digging around. Speak to any of the numerous victims' families she has helped to find closure, or the bodies of their children. Allysa Ross is like a well-trained German Shepherd. She will give her life to protect the people she loves. But if you get on her bad side, Allysa will take you down and rip you to pieces."

Time for him to leave; I lifted my arm towards the door.

"One more question. Why did you marry Ray Wright? You were happier than you've ever been in your entire life while you and Terry dated. Why did you leave him for a man old enough to be your father?"

"That's two questions, and I decline to answer either. My life choices have nothing to do with you and in no way pertain to your investigations. Get out. You've been here long enough."

Will reached for the door handle. "I'm going to prove Terry Holt, or rather Sebastian Pimento, was The Skull Keeper. Someone in this town took the law into their own hands. That same person murdered Jen, leaving her body for Corey to find when he checked on the fence this morning."

Thirty-eight

Allysa

Donna's death had gone as planned. She had begged for her life, and tried to negotiate not ending up with a bullet shattering her skull. My contact wasn't an amateur. *Neither am I.*

The footage was shared on the dark web to a site created specifically for Donna's execution. It ceased to exist seconds after I watched the video. It ended with Donna's body disappearing into the dark as it fell towards the rocks below the lighthouse.

The same rocks where the police had, fifteen years earlier, found the mangled remains of a motorcycle registered to Terry Holt.

The question of why Morgan had lied to Boyle regarding my encounter with Donna needed to remain unanswered. Morgan hated having her privacy invaded. *Sorry, not sorry.* Other than dogs, Morgan Wright was the most loyal creature I knew.

I waited for her to knock on my bedroom door. We needed to compare notes after being questioned by Boyle. Her angle of pointing at Donna as the person responsible for Sebastian and Jen's murders didn't come as a surprise; the logic in it quite reasonable.

The door opened. Morgan grinned as she walked towards where I stood on the balcony. "Will is going to regret trying to pin seventeen murders on Terry. I'll gut him like a fish if he mentions it again."

Murdery-Morgan was my favourite. The blood lust visible in her eyes reminded me, yet again, how similar we were. One difference being, Morgan didn't know what it felt like to take a life other than on paper. She'd never witnessed the moment a soul exited the body, leaving nothing but a biodegradable corpse behind.

"It's easy to accuse the dead of crimes they never committed. Question is: why didn't Boyle do it years ago? Sebastian would've made the perfect scapegoat for the murders, considering it started soon after he arrived in Wild Bay."

Morgan removed a knife from underneath her black shirt and ran a finger along both sides of the blade. "I have my suspicions, but I prefer to check my facts."

"What did Boyle ask you?" I stepped closer to the railing and closed my eyes, taking a deep breath. The crashing waves were louder than the rumble of my stomach.

After inspecting her nails, Morgan answered, "Guess the same he asked you. Where I was last night. Did I know Jen stalked both of us on social media. Why you met with Donna at the beach yesterday afternoon. And to top it all, he wanted to know why I'm single and why my Instagram accounts are devoid of love and warmth."

Morgan threw her hands in the air. "I couldn't tell him I'm not fond of people, or that murder and destruction fill my mind more often than coffee goes down my throat. Of course, I threw it back at him and asked why he didn't bring another detective or officer along to question us. He never answered me."

"He still has a thing for you."

The sound coming out of Morgan was unlike anything I'd ever heard. "Will is trying hard to remain on my good side. I hold the power to destroy his entire life. Fun fact – whatever he felt for me hadn't meant jack-shit once Holly made her move on him. Can't say I blame him for falling for her. She didn't give up until she got what she wanted. *Our* friendship is real. What Holly and I had was destructive. I didn't shed a single tear when she went missing; a part of me breathed for the first time in years."

"Morgan, what did Holly do to you?"

"Too many things. All I'll say is she and Will started seeing each other behind my back. Idiots thought I wouldn't find out when I had more eyes and ears in this town than the police." Morgan took a deep breath. Calm spilled over her as her shoulders settled back to their normal position and her smile turned genuine.

I read her body language every time she sent me a video, as she did mine. Our bond that strong. "I'm right there with you. Boyle won't pin the murders on my brother."

"Jen stalked us." Morgan turned to me. "I want to see which posts and content she took screenshots of. Is it possible Jen murdered Rachel in an attempt to get you to Marcel?"

"No, she isn't capable of murder. Sara, being a medical doctor, knows how to make it look like a myocardial infarction."

Morgan shook her head and returned her focus to the ocean. "You don't know the Jen we were subjected to whenever she came to town."

I retrieved my phone from where it lay on the bed, ignoring the missed call from Jake. It didn't matter to me that Sara had lost her sister so soon after losing her wretched mother.

"What do you want, Allysa?" Sara asked.

Weird that she knew I was on the other end of the line. This number didn't exist to anyone apart from my closest friends and Jake and Daniel. "How did you know it's me?"

"Who else is cold enough to call my mother's number?"

Biting down on my lip to hide my smile, I failed as the corners of my mouth still lifted. "I don't have your number, and you've always been the problem solver. I assumed you'll have Rachel's phone and handle all matters pertaining to her illegally obtained estate. Or did she keep the cash in a safety-deposit box instead of investing?"

"Get to the point."

"I want to offer my condolences. You losing Jen in such a horrific way so soon after Rachel passed away … I know what it's like to lose your mother and a sibling."

Sara didn't speak, but I heard her breathing. "You've also

lost your father, even though there is time for the two of you to rebuild your relationship. Go see him, Allysa. Life is too short. My mother took my father's identity to her grave. At least you can make amends with yours. It's time he told you the truth about what led to his arrest, and his subsequent confession."

"Why are you saying this now?" Sara had always been vocal about her hatred towards my dad. Unlike Jen, she'd never accepted him as a father figure.

"My mother can't control us from the grave."

You're welcome.

Sara and I ended the conversation on better terms than expected. Morgan waited for me to process, knowing when to give me space. "Tomorrow morning, I'm going to see my dad."

Thirty-nine

Morgan

Moonlight danced on the dark water. The sound of crashing waves heightened my fight and flight response. Freeze is for the weak. To run depends on the situation. As for fight? It was how I survived my childhood.

Allysa decided to leave early the next morning to visit her father in prison. I didn't plan to go to my mother's grave. Amanda York, crazy of Wild Bay, rested alongside her husband. The man who had destroyed my innocence by burdening me with taking care of my mother. Not forgetting the debt he owed, which I had repaid. With interest.

You could learn a lot from criminals if you listened and never asked questions. Nine years of my young life had been spent selling drugs and observing. It was a miracle I passed high school and had time to read. Perhaps not, if you considered the majority of my sales came from tourists during the holiday seasons.

I'd worked hard my entire life, starting on the farm when I'd been old enough to do whatever my father needed help with. Being married to Ray Wright was the hardest I'd ever worked for anything. Even my brief marriage had gone according to my plan.

People who don't plan set themselves up for failure.

Clear Inbox – check. Phone sex with Wyatt – double check. Shower – check.

Seventeen case files positioned on the floor and my grilled chicken and salad taking centre stage, I snapped a photo and uploaded it to CJ Green's Instagram account. With long enough copy, informing fans and haters that the files were for research for a future novel. After including the right number of hashtags, I posted it. The photo was staged as most others on social media. I often wondered how many hours people spent capturing the perfect photo or making a faultless reel.

Including food in the photo showed I had the stomach for death; as expected of a thriller author. Especially one who wrote novels as dark as mine. If an ME allowed it, I would eat during an autopsy. Decomposition, and the brutalities humans inflict on others, never bothered me.

Allysa had declined when I proposed we go out for dinner, so we'd ordered in instead. We both ate alone. She needed to prepare for tomorrow. Not that she had said it. Did I understand her better than anyone because her brother's soul was part of mine? Was our bond this strong because I loved someone who shared her DNA? Without Allysa knowing it, I was her last link to Sebastian.

Terry Holt's case file remained on the desk, even though the files were unmarked and didn't give any indication of whose murders I conducted research on, I refused to include his in my post. The Skull Keeper hadn't murdered the man I loved.

Who identified Terry Holt's remains?

I jumped to my feet and grabbed the file, skimming through the information until I found the name – Donna Perk. It made sense. She had been his employer and Corey had still been recovering at home. Even though Terry and Corey hadn't got along, they were the closest thing the other had to a friend in Wild Bay. When Jen wasn't in town, they had surfed or went to the gym together.

I wiped my eyes, fighting with everything in me against the memories bubbling to the surface. Grief pushed its icy hands into my chest and ripped me open.

"Why didn't you come with me?" My voice broke.

The image of Corey's headless body in the wheelchair morphed into the image of The Skull Keeper's first victim. The one I had found. In truth, Judo had alerted me.

Horses weren't an uncommon sight on any of the farms surrounding town. I had often found my mother talking to our horses. Watching her with them was one of the few good memories I had of her. In those moments, she'd appeared calm. Normal.

Judo had been mine, purchased with my money. A gift to myself on my seventeenth birthday. The last gift my father had given me was the sight of him pulling the shotgun's trigger on my fourteenth birthday.

I rocked until the images stopped haunting me. For now, they let me be, but the ghosts always came back. Too many of them. I knew them each by name.

A note in the first victim's file caught my attention. Detective Boyle had made a note wondering whether this was, in fact, the killer's first victim.

No evidence on or around the remains. Nothing on the eye, tongue or the skinned face. Not even in the victim's hair. Skull not found. Extensive search of the area conducted.

The Skull Keeper was sadistic but never raped the victims. They were all dead before their heads were severed with what the ME suspected was an angle grinder. Unlike Terry and Jen.

Terry's death had differed in other ways; his tongue and eye weren't found lying next to his body. Neither had his body shown any signs of mutilation or torture.

Forty

Twenty-four hours earlier

Jen had escaped her fate fifteen years ago. Sure, I could've wasted time hunting her down. Once I left Wild Bay, I'd had bigger problems to deal with. She walked around town, acting like she owned it. A decade and a half later, she was still the same.

The first time I had seen her walking alone at night, one word came to mind – victim. How Jen managed to not get mugged baffled me. Perhaps she had. I didn't care enough to ask.

Jen kept her eyes fixed on her phone's screen. It cast a faint glow on her face. She walked and typed – as risky as texting and driving – unaware that danger closed in. Most of my students had been so engrossed in their own little worlds they never noticed me until it was too late.

Who glances around a dark street? Who keeps their phone tucked away and their car key ready in hand? Who scans other vehicles when walking through a deserted parking lot at night?

Survivors.

Who accepts an invitation to meet at an isolated place with a man who didn't say more than a few words to them?

Victims.

The very women who thought themselves better than me.

I grabbed Jen's head and jabbed the needle into her neck. Stealth and experience were on my side.

She glared at me. If morning wasn't approaching, I would've

taught her all the lessons. Duct tape protected my ears from her shrill voice. *Small mercies.*

The locals never ventured out this way at night. Not even teenagers dared to set foot in a place everyone believed to be haunted. Little did they realise how many lives had ended here. It had looked different back then. No time to reminisce; I'd waited years for this moment.

"*Jenny*, you won't be getting the full experience of being my student. Fifteen years later, and I honestly think putting a bullet through your thick skull is the best option to end you. I don't have time to waste on you. However, the second to last lesson is one of the quickest."

I laughed, reaching for the knife. Over the years, I'd learned so many new and exciting things, and wanted nothing more than to put them to use.

Perhaps coming out of retirement, so to speak, would be permanent.

The police would suspect Jen's death was the work of a copycat, forgetting even murderers could evolve. In this case, improvise.

Unlike most people, I wasn't afraid of getting older – I embraced the knowledge that came with it. If you bothered to pay attention to life's lessons and make the most of what was at hand.

Jen tried to move her head as the tip of the knife touched the skin next to her left eye. Botox did a great job of keeping the inevitable lines at bay.

Super glue anchored her head to the tree stump. Whoever had felled it had done so at the perfect height for me to work effectively. "Either you rip your scalp off, or you hold still. The choice is yours."

Tears streamed down her cheeks. The faint light cast by the flashlight allowed me to catch a glimpse as reality settled in. "Yes, *Jenny*. I am the one the police call The Skull Keeper. Twenty years ago, I warned you. Did you listen?"

I stepped behind her.

Rope kept Jen's arms to her sides and her body to the stump. I didn't bother to tie her feet.

Blood trickled down her jaw, leaving a trail on her neck. Such a shame I didn't have a mirror positioned in front of her. The silver strip covering her mouth muffled her screams. Nothing contained the sound of glee spilling out of me.

My joy was short-lived; she passed out. *Oh well*.

Jen came to before I severed her head.

Forty-one

Twenty-four hours earlier

The gaping hole inside me filled with suffocating dread as the prison came into view. Morgan had offered to come with me, and now I regretted telling her I needed to do this on my own. Before I left the guesthouse, she'd asked me a question to ponder during the drive. *What's the most boring job?* Two hours later, I'd narrowed my answer down to ten occupations.

Rows of pine trees and mountains surrounded Marcel Correctional Centre. No windows faced the outside world. The prisoners were allowed to see nothing but the sky above the recreation yard. I assumed they considered it a good day when a bird flew overhead, and didn't defecate on them. Although, some cultures consider it good luck. The sheer number of pigeons surrounding the building made me wonder how often it happened.

Standing next to the rental car while staring at the building and wondering about bird poop, my phone rang. "Hello, I miss you."

"Allie, when are you coming home? I'm worried about you." Jake and I lived in the same house, shared the same bed, but our worlds couldn't have been more different.

"It will only be a few more days. Are you bored without me there to drive you nuts? If you want, we can try phone sex later?" Sometimes I wished Morgan didn't tell me everything.

Jake laughed. "If you're serious, I'm game."

"I'm going to book a weekend away for the two of us. We need some time to ourselves." *As do most parents.* But I needed to come clean about my past in a neutral environment. The chance of Daniel overhearing was a risk I refused to take.

"Agreed. I'm going to a dental conference next Monday. Do you think you'll be home by Friday?"

Not once in all the years we'd been married had Jake attend a conference. "Are you cheating on me? I warned you before we got married what I'll do to you if you cheat on me. You've seen my forensic and thriller books. I'm going to take my sweet time and no one will ever find a single strand of your hair." I teased. Jake was the most trustworthy man I'd ever known.

The sound of my husband's laughter grounded me. "Slow down. No need to sharpen your scalpel collection. A weekend away will do us both good. A package was delivered to our house in Colorado yesterday. The sender listed their name, but didn't give a return address. For the first time ever, it's not an Amazon delivery."

All my book mail and purchases were delivered to our second home. "Who sent it?"

"Rachel Pimento. The house keeper will send it here for you tomorrow."

I pursed my lips. With my dad on the other side of the fence, multiple gates, and thick walls, I struggled to focus. My stomach sat in my throat. Rachel had never taken our surname.

"Allie, are you there?" Jake asked. "Do you know who sent it?"

"Yes, I ... will be back as soon as I can. Jake, I love you. Tell Daniel I'll call him after school."

"Allie, whatever you're up to in Wild Bay, promise you'll stay out of trouble?" I loved it when he called me Allie, but not that he knew I was in Wild Bay when I hadn't told him. *Something is wrong.*

"Are you able to take Daniel to lacrosse practise tonight?" No matter what case I worked, I tried my best to not let it influence our family life.

"Yes, I double checked that he has all of his gear. That child will forget to brush his teeth as old as he is. He takes after you in more ways than you care to admit."

One of my contacts could keep an eye on them until I returned to Texas. Jake, being a true Texan, believed in owning handguns for self-defence. He had inherited several handguns and rifles to add to his own collection when his dad passed away. Firearms and the house in Colorado.

"I'm sorry I can't be there with you. And for the record, *you* are the most forgetful one of the two of us. You can't even remember where we made love for the first time." Neither of us would ever forget our first trip as a couple.

"It was in Paris, such a cliché, if you think about it." Jake always joked about Paris, as that was where we conceived Daniel. "Allie, I need to go. You better be home by Friday or I won't go on a romantic trip with you."

"I'll be home as soon as possible."

Underneath the table, my legs jumped. Would my father recognise me? After arriving in The States, I'd become as American as possible. I'd grown up referring to him as my father. Now I waited to face the man who had sacrificed everything for me.

Our eyes met. He stopped in his tracks and sank to his knees. I ran to him, only to be stopped by a guard. To see him cry shattered the heaviness inside me.

The guard's smile was warm, as he led my dad to the table where I took a seat.

"Allysa?" My dad wiped his eyes with unshackled hands and shook his head.

I nodded. "Rachel's dead. It's time for the truth, Dad. After all these years, I deserve to hear from you why you did it."

In time, if she hadn't already, Morgan would realise my dad wasn't in prison for drug trafficking. In rare cases a first-time offender received such a lengthy sentence. Drugs weren't the police's biggest discovery when they had pulled my dad's truck over that day. Rachel had made sure of it, or rather, her minions had.

"I made a huge mistake marrying her. I wanted to give you and your brother the same things and opportunities Rachel did for her daughters. We were on the verge of being kicked out of the house. I was desperate."

None of it made sense, except him admitting marrying Rachel was a mistake. I reached for his hands across the table. "Dad, you provided fine for Sebastian and me. We didn't need all the things that the she-devil gave her daughters. Do you know where it got them? Sara is miserable and Jen is dead. Look where being involved with that woman got you?"

"Jen's dead?" He stared at me. The harshness of prison life etched into every line on his face.

I nodded. "Unrelated. Sort of. I didn't come here to talk about Rachel's spawn. Dad, why didn't you tell the police that Rachel ran the operation? The police didn't even find your DNA on the bodies. You didn't have to confess. You're innocent."

He hung his head. "I didn't know the gun was there until the police hand-cuffed me and read me my rights. No matter what I said, this is still where I would've ended up. Besides, Rachel threatened to have her most loyal customers teach you about sex. I refused."

"Did you know that's what she did to Sara and Jen?"

The colour drained from his face. Moisture filled his eyes. He shook his head, sending tears down his wrinkled cheeks. I watched the wet trail disappear into his grey beard.

"Why did you tell me to stay away?" Thirty minutes wouldn't be enough to ask all the questions I had, or tell him of Sebastian's death. I didn't have the words or the heart, but I owed my dad everything.

If not for him, I would be on the other side of the table.

"I didn't want you to see me like this. I wanted you and Sebastian to move on with your lives and get as far away from Rachel as possible. How did you get your name on my visitor's list? Last I heard, a prisoner needs to put a person's name on it."

I smiled. "I'm rather resourceful. Knowing the right people makes all the difference. That's also why I came to see you today. I have proof Rachel framed you. I'm getting you a new lawyer and we will start the paperwork to file for your appeal."

My dad shook his head and turned to the clock on the wall. He lowered his voice. "I'm not doing anything of the sort if it gets you in trouble."

The guard was standing too far away to hear me whisper, "Nothing points to me. I'm getting you out of this place. Soon."

My dad opened his mouth to protest, not knowing who I was now, but I spoke first. "We don't have much time left. You need to be the man I remember. The man you were before Rachel stuck her claws in you. You're a grandfather. Your grandson deserves to get to know you. Pimentos don't give up. You taught me that."

"Sara had the baby?"

I couldn't hide my surprise. "You knew?"

He nodded. "It's part of why I agreed to keep my mouth shut. Sara was desperate to escape Rachel, and she thought having a baby would derail Rachel's plans for her life."

My breath came out slow as my hands rose to cover my face. "Sara gave the baby up for adoption."

"No way Sebastian allowed his child to be taken away from him."

"Dad, I didn't want to tell you this." I pushed my fingers through my hair, unable to tell him Sebastian had been murdered.

He swallowed hard. "Tell me what?"

The words lodged in my throat; I reached across the table and squeezed his hand. "I no longer live in Marcel. After finishing school, I left the country."

During the rest of our time together, I told my dad as much as possible about my life.

Before I left, I reminded him that he had another grandson, Daniel, who I had named after him.

I left the prison with more questions than when I had walked in.

Something good had come out of Rachel's death. It didn't weigh on my conscious. My dad didn't deserve to be in prison, and neither did I.

Not when you rid the world of evil.

Forty-two

Morgan

Allysa kept up the lie. To call her out on it wasn't an option. Her past didn't have a bearing on our friendship. Did she need to admit her father had been found guilty of committing a double homicide? No.

Did I expect her to tell me she had been the one to pull the trigger when she hadn't been old enough to own a firearm? No.

Soon after realising Allysa could be the only genuine friend I'd ever had, I hired the private investigator. Holly had destroyed all notions of female friendships for me.

The last words she had said to me broke the rusty, weathered axel our friendship rode on. I'd also deserved more. Better. When Allysa and I had met and connected through DMs, I realised the possibility existed to have what I'd dreamt about since being a little girl – a sister.

If not for my father, my mother would've aborted me. She had reminded me of this whenever she swallowed her pills. Amanda York knew what lurked in her DNA even before the first time she had heard the voices. How strange the things normal mothers fear for their children. Mine had feared that I too was cursed with schizophrenia like her and my great-grandmother.

Oh, Mother.

Instead of asking about Allysa's visit with her father, I asked if she had given my question any thought.

Allysa sighed and retied her long black hair in a ponytail. "Any type of administrative job. I can't see myself, behind a desk every day, doing the same thing over and over." She shuddered.

The puffiness under her eyes tugged at my heart. She hated crying; few people saw her tears. I was the same.

"What is the job that would kill you?" she asked.

"Being an ice-cream truck driver."

Allysa laughed and sat down hard on the bed. The skin of her tanned legs against the white duvet was another reason I envied her. "What? You've got to be kidding me. Why?"

I shrugged, pushing my hair behind my ears. "Have you heard those freakin songs they play? Imagine listening to that the entire day. Oh, hell no. I'll definitely become all kinds of murdery. On the positive side, I would have a mobile freezer to transport bodies." *New book idea.*

"We've often discussed committing murder, but if it comes down to it, do you think you have the stomach to do something as horrendous as this?" Allysa pointed at the case files on the desk.

"Depends on my motive. If it is to rid the world of evil or those I consider deserving, then yes. Children or people in general? No."

The smile on Allysa's face told me I gave the right answer. It helped to be prepared for tests.

"Have you had lunch yet?" Allysa walked to the desk and pulled out a few take-away menus from the top drawer.

Nothing had passed my lips the entire day except coffee and water. I'd become engrossed in the case files; food never crossed my mind. The skull-less faces, tongues, shrivelled-up eyeballs and decapitated bodies didn't bother me at all. It was what *wasn't* in the police and autopsy reports which kept my focus.

"I checked the dates the victims disappeared. Either Corey or Terry was always behind the bar. If neither of them could work a shift, Donna manned it herself. Will lost some footing with that if he is still trying to pin the murders on Terry."

"It's weird when you call him *Terry.*"

I stared at the black nail polish on my toes. "To me he was Terry. I'll try harder to refer to him as Sebastian."

Allysa pulled me in for a hug. "That's it, we're getting Chinese food. You need your favourite comfort food, and I need a hug."

I didn't remove my arms from her waist. Very few people hugged me, and in moments like these I realised how much a simple gesture could mean to someone like me. People tend to take it for granted; I kept it locked away in my heart.

"Lysa, Sebastian and Jen's murders differ in some ways. Not enough that I think the same killer isn't responsible." Allysa asked me to elaborate. "Jen's head was held in place with super glue or something similar. She was alive when the killer removed her face."

Allysa squeezed me against her and stepped back. "How did you convince Boyle to give you information on an active investigation?"

"I didn't. When you looked at what the killer left of Jen's face, you saw someone you once loved. I compared it to what I'd read in the files, but I also found two of the victims. While you were away, I called the medical examiner who helps with my books. He agrees with me."

Confusion danced across Allysa's face. "How do you know about the glue on the back of her head? Dr Linetti didn't allow us to touch anything."

"While Will asked you to write your name down when you confirmed her identity, I risked it, as Dr Linetti had her back to me. There were bits of bark stuck to Jen's hair. Lysa, I think Jen was tied to a tree, and the killer held her head in place with glue."

Allysa didn't say a word, but the cogs in her brain turned at lightning speed.

"The Skull Keeper is back, but he doesn't have access to where he tortured and killed the other victims."

Allysa tapped a finger on her lips. "He either doesn't have access to the original property, or he no longer lives alone."

I studied the menu and decided on beef chow fun. Allysa chose the same and called the restaurant, asking them to deliver it to the guesthouse.

"Will lived on his own back then. Now he's married."

Allysa turned to me, tilting her head to the right. "Is he capable of this?" She pointed towards the files.

I shrugged. "It explains why the crime scene investigators found no physical evidence. We are taught to trust the police from a young age. If you were walking down the street at night and saw a police officer approaching, you'd feel safe, right?"

Allysa laughed. "No. How many serial killers turn out to be police officers?"

I smiled at her. "You and I know that. But how much do university age women know about the real world?"

Forty-three

Allysa

Parents often pay as much for the sins of their children as children pay for the sins of their parents. Everyone knows someone whose child became a drug addict and ended up stealing from them. Parents abuse their children in the most horrific ways. The sword cuts both ways.

My dad had paid the ultimate price for my sins. At least this country didn't have the death penalty, offering me the chance to rectify my mistakes.

Morgan and I both showered before our food arrived, giving me time and privacy to make a few phone calls. After speaking with Daniel, I reached out to a former client. My clients often didn't pay me in cash, but they believed in returning favours. The man I contacted earned his living as a criminal defence attorney. Most people loathed them, and I did too, until I'd met Keith Hitchcock.

"Hello, Keith. I hope this isn't an inconvenient time?"

His laughter was warm and comforting. "Not at all, Allysa. How can I help you? I've been waiting years for this call."

"How is Amy doing?" Keith had lost the case, not because he hadn't done his job. The evidence against his client had been enough to fill a double garage. In retaliation, Keith's client ordered one of his friends to abduct Amy. The police failed to locate her. I hadn't. As far as the public knew Amy escaped, but was too high on drugs to remember where she had been held. The police never connected the carnage I had left behind to Amy's abduction. It was difficult to find DNA evidence when the house being used as a meth lab exploded.

"Amy is doing well. She's in love for the first time. It isn't sitting well with me. I reminded the poor guy who I have for clients. You'll see when you have children of your own one day." He cleared his throat and sighed. "I know I'm overprotective of her, but who can blame me?"

"Keith, you need to stop doing this to yourself. Amy survived. In time, her psychological wounds will heal. Allowing any man close to her is testament of that." Jen had shown me first-hand the difference in how quickly the body could heal, but a victim's psyche healed at its own pace. *Sometimes it never does.*

"I take it you're not contacting me for the first time in five years to ask about Amy?"

I stared at my reflection in the mirror. Dark circles replaced the earlier redness underneath my eyes. "I need your help to get a convicted murderer out of prison. Within the next hour, evidence will be delivered to the Marcel Police Department, proving Dan Pimento's innocence in a double homicide. Two hours from now, the men who planted the 9mm in Dan's truck will walk into the police station and hand themselves in. Part of their confession will be that they had carried out the hit on their boss' instruction. Too bad their boss is already in hell and won't rot in a cell. However, she recorded a confession. Before you ask, she died of a heart attack and has already been cremated. If you agree to help me rectify this *gross injustice*, copies of the evidence will be delivered to your door a minute after we end this call."

In the background it sounded like someone called Keith for dinner. "I owe you my daughter's life. First thing tomorrow morning, I'll have my assistant get me the original court transcripts and everything related to the case against Dan Pimento. Where is he being held? I need to speak with my new client."

Gross injustice were the words that sealed the deal. I knew the reason Keith had decided to become a defence attorney and not a prosecutor. "All of it will be delivered to you. Pimento is at Marcel Correctional Centre. Your name is on his visitor's list. I'll cover your fee."

"I'm all in. Won't even bother asking who this man is to you. As for my fee, consider it pro bono. I'm impressed with how organised you are. But it doesn't surprise me considering the lengths you went to in order to locate Amy and bring her back to us. My debt to you will never be settled. If you ever need my help again, you've got my number. Thank you will never be enough."

I ended the call with Keith, unable to stop the tears streaming down my face. The man waiting outside the Hitchcock residence made his way towards the front door as I wiped my eyes.

I never got into this for any other reason than the victims and their families. Along the way I'd made a lot of allies, not to mention enemies. Putting my life in danger didn't matter to me. If anything happened to me, Jake would be there to take care of Daniel. I'd taken every precaution to ensure I'd be around to watch my son grow up, but I wasn't an idiot. Death is a certainty. The trick was to outrun it for as long as possible.

If ever anyone owed me a thank you, it had been Jen. She'd known I executed the men who had raped her. Jen kept her mouth shut and my dad had paid for my crime. It didn't take a psychiatrist to analyse me.

I hoped The Skull Keeper put up a fight. He deserved to suffer for butchering my brother, and for the death of every other victim. *Shower. Food. Find The Skull Keeper.*

Morgan knew more than she was letting on. I'd kept an eye on her in the autopsy room; she'd never touched Jen's face or hair.

Why is she lying?

Forty-four

Present day

People watch true crime documentaries, read a few books and consider themselves couch sleuths. They scream at the murderers for being idiots when they are caught. And roll their eyes when the smallest things are the ones which lead to a criminal being apprehended. All of this, while stuffing their faces with saturated fats and other processed garbage. Those people are the real idiots. None of the wanna-be-detectives has the stomach to commit murder, never mind the intellectual capacity to get away with it.

If they came face to face with what I left of my students, would they still think themselves better than me? No.

It's easy to judge a murderer when you've never seen a decomposing body. I disposed of them as soon as possible. The stench made me queasy. Torture was one thing, but I never wanted that sickening sweet smell etched in my memory.

For five years, no one in Wild Bay considered me capable of committing murder. Let alone seventeen murders. Make that eighteen or nineteen, depending on where the police decided to lay the blame for Terry and Jen's deaths.

There are basic things one must consider:
Blend in. Don't act different or become a weirdo.
Have an alibi.
Cover your tracks and don't leave any forensic evidence.
Don't take a victim from the same place twice.
Vary when you strike. In other words, don't abduct a victim every Wednesday night close to midnight outside a bar.
Don't stick to one victim type, but that's rare. Everyone knows what

they want or hate.

Under no circumstances return to where you dumped the body.

If you commit murder for fame and communicate with the police or newspapers, your days are numbered.

Don't get drunk and tell people what you've done. Amateur move.

No matter what happens, do not get nervous. That's when you will make mistakes.

That's Serial Murder 101 in a nutshell.

Few bother to read the manual; it's all there in true crime books. Then again, not all of them pass high school. Those who do are the ones who stay out of prison the longest, or never see the inside at all. It's true what we were taught as children – stay in school.

I had become a student of death at a young age, without realising it at the time.

If the women had listened to me, they wouldn't have died and I might never have resorted to murder. Something I couldn't put on my resume or bring up in casual conversation.

The Skull Keeper. *Oh, the irony.*

I rid the world of these self-obsessed women. At their young age, they had already thought everything and everyone belonged to them. Through my various lessons, I'd showed them the truth. They didn't feel all that pretty when nothing but raw meat remained of their faces. The manicured nails they had waved at me dissolved along with the flesh of their fingers. Tongues which had never spoken a single decent word didn't belong in their mouths.

I regretted nothing. *Remorse is for those who cheat, steal, and deceive.*

The thing most serial offenders got wrong was that they became cocky. They think they are better than the detectives, MEs, profilers, criminologists, the who-nots working day and night to stop them.

That's any person's biggest mistake – you're no more worthy

of breathing than the person next to you. Unless that person is a paedophile, rapist, narcissistic young woman, or a killer.
Guess that includes me.

The difference was I'd stopped. Fifteen years without taking a life. Jen didn't count. I had plans for her long before I left town. Fate had caught up with her.

Life was going well for me. Until now. There I stood, back in the place I'd hated since birth. The cases were being investigated again. I doubt I'd slipped up, but it was a risk I couldn't take.

Someone needed to die before they uncovered the truth.

Time to clean the angle grinder.

Forty-five

Morgan

The thing about flashbacks – you can't anticipate them. Out of nowhere, your mind fills with images of death. While your brain is preoccupied, you don't realise your soul is being shred to pieces. Again.

The weight is unbearable, crushing down on you until you sink to the floor. Remaining upright is impossible. When people are around, you somehow manage to push back against it. Later you'll pay for defying grief. Grief is the shadow which never leaves. In complete darkness, it envelops you. Tomorrow morning, it follows you wherever you go. It remains by your side for as long as you live.

Tonight, the flashbacks were relentless.

A headache formed as too many images jumped for attention. I refused to focus on a particular one, even though I knew what awaited me later, when Allysa wasn't watching me like a predator ready to strike.

I placed the leftover beef chow fun in the mini-fridge and, despite being desperate to feel the night air on my skin, I didn't dare step onto the balcony. A yacht anchored offshore; the exact make and model I had spent my short-lived honeymoon on. I refused to look at it.

Every time I did, I felt Ray's powerful hands pressing me down, striking my cheek, locking the bedroom door with me inside – alone for hours, sometimes a day or more. If he could do that to his fiancé, what would he have done if we had spent years together?

Ray Wright hadn't been capable of loving anything except control. In his mind, he'd owned me.

Flashes of Terry's laughter, the warmth of his embrace, the

way he had looked at me. The love I felt for him. The last time I had seen him. Desperate for it all to stop, I pressed my palms to my temples.

"Morgan, what's wrong?" Allysa asked.

I shook my head, aggravating the headache. "I loved him. And always will. The guilt of leaving him behind, and him being murdered ... I can't take this pain." The weight forced me to my knees.

She pulled me into her arms and cried with me. When neither of us had any tears left, Allysa pushed to her feet, grabbed two bottles of water from the mini-fridge and asked if my head ached as bad as hers. I said yes and then found us headache tablets in my handbag.

Allysa swallowed the tablets and made herself comfortable on the bed, closing her eyes. "Thank you for loving my brother."

Instead of saying the first thing that came to me, I laid down next to her and also closed my eyes.

Terry. Sebastian. It didn't matter. The man behind the name remained the same to me.

"It was the easiest thing in the world to love him. He was unlike any of the boys and men I knew growing up. There wasn't a person in this town who said a bad word about him. His compassion and zest for life were contagious. For as beautiful as he was to look at, it was his heart and smile which made me fall in love with him. Didn't hurt that he had the sexiest butt ever."

The back of Allysa's hand connected with my stomach. "Hey, that's my brother you're talking about."

"Then I won't tell you what a phenomenal lover he was. The things he did with his—"

"La-la-la-la-la."

I laughed at the sight of Allysa covering her ears. Pulling her hand away from her head, I promised to keep the rest to myself.

"Do you have any photos of the two of you? Did you ever

live together? I realise I have no idea who *Terry* was."

"I lost everything in the fire."

Allysa reached for my hand. "What fire?"

"The police and fire department concluded my mother had burned down the house, barn, and other buildings."

"What happened to your mom?" She squeezed my hand.

I took a deep breath and let it out slowly. "It's believed she poured an accelerant over herself and walked into the flames."

"Oh, Morgan. I'm so sorry."

A tear slipped from my left eye. "Mother always said one day she would find a way to silence the voices."

"Who took care of her after you left Wild Bay? Is it possible she stopped taking her pills?" Allysa rolled onto her side to face me.

I remained on my back, hiding my eyes. If they were the windows to the soul, I didn't want her to see mine. Not in this moment. "Ray hired a private caregiver to live with her. He went out of his way to show me how well he would take care of me as his wife."

"Did you ever speak to the caregiver?"

My head moved from side to side. "The fire department recovered her body from the rubble. So, the schizophrenic was an arsonist and murderer. Yay, look at me having the best DNA. Guess you understand why I don't want to have children."

"When did this happen?"

Oh, come on, Allysa. Give me a freakin break. I bit my tongue and decided to show her the skeletons locked in one closet – the mother closet. Those were the least disturbing.

"About a month after I left town. I know my mother was my responsibility, but after taking care of her for nine years, I was on the verge of a mental breakdown. Trying to earn enough money to keep food on the table, working the farm and leasing parts of it to neighbouring farmers for their cattle to graze. All of this while still in high school. When I met Terry, I realised I deserved to live my own life. Selfish of me in hindsight."

Allysa moved her head closer to mine. "Not selfish at all. We all do what we need to when it comes to our survival and sanity. When did her psychosis present itself?"

Behind my eyelids I rolled my eyes, but appreciated Allysa's clinical approach to pulling the rest of the skeletons out of the closet. We'd both studied psychology so it made sense she wanted to delve into my mother's mind. I assumed her next questions were going to be about the effects it had had on me.

"Typical for women, her first symptoms appeared in her late twenties. It became worse in her thirties. That's when my father took her to a psychiatrist in Marcel. After all the years of her strange behaviour, he had an answer. My mother hadn't told him about her grandmother and her paranoia. I wonder if, in my absence, my mother's symptoms increased and became as bad as her grandmother's."

Allysa pushed herself up against the headboard and took a sip of water. "Did she ever work?"

I moved to sit next to her. "Yes, as a biology teacher at the high school. She had studied for her teacher's degree in Marcel and came back here. She decided on biology instead of chemistry, as she had worried about chemicals and fumes when pregnant with me. My parents started dating when they were still in school. Perhaps if they hadn't fallen in love, she would've studied medicine, as she dreamt of becoming a doctor. What else do you want to know? Their ages when I was conceived? It was long before her symptoms became so bad that she could no longer hide it from my father. And yes, she considered aborting me. No, she was never physically abusive. Verbal? Well, hearing your mother wanted to get rid of you as a foetus isn't great for any child's self-esteem."

Allysa took my hand in hers. "I'm sorry for asking these questions. You've learned so much about my horrible childhood, I want to know you and understand the things that shaped you into who you are today."

No, you don't.

To ease the tension in my neck, I rolled my head from side

to side. "Not all of my memories of her are bad. My mother used to love teaching me lessons, as she called them. From baking to caring for the animals. To her everything was a *lesson*. On her better days, she called me her favourite student."

Forty-six

Allysa

I knew little about real-life friendships outside of the bookstagram community, but I doubted Morgan would be happy when I added another name to our list of suspects. Amanda York.

From an objective point of view, too many things fitted into place. Amanda had the medical knowledge to torture the victims, having studied both biology and chemistry as part of her teaching degree. I knew not all schizophrenics have violent tendencies. But if Amanda had suffered from auditory hallucinations, who knew what the voices may have told her to do?

It's a general misconception that women aren't capable of committing violent murders.

As for moving dead weight around, I knew how to get around the obstacles caused by my lack of testosterone-fuelled physical strength. I was a bit of a feminist – there's nothing a man can do, a woman can't. But I wouldn't be burning my bra any time soon.

Next to me, Morgan kept her eyes closed. Perhaps we were digesting our late lunch, or both lost in our thoughts. Neither of us said a word.

I assumed her mind was preoccupied with memories of her mother. Mine went back to one thing – who sent the package to our house in Colorado?

With Rachel never having taken Pimento as her surname, it didn't make sense. Jen or Sara?

Jen had stalked Morgan and me. Had she found the address

on my Amazon wishlist? Impossible. My security settings didn't allow anyone to see it.

Sara still hated me as much as the day our parents had announced their engagement. Even as a teenager, Sara was more of an in-your-face bitch and not one to waste her time with pranks. If she had thought something, you heard about it. Sometimes the neighbours had as well.

One other possibility – whoever had hired the private investigator. In my line of work, it helped to have eyes in the back of your head. No matter what I'd done, the PI had refused to give me a name. Seconds before exhaling for the last time, he had said a name. That lead hadn't got me anywhere. The name was fake. I'd dirtied my hands for nothing. After Daniel was potty-trained, I thought my days of cleaning up poop were over. Murder was a messy business, and torture even more so.

The list of names of my enemies beat the list of friends one to a hundred. My methods for locating missing persons weren't always pretty. You pissed off a few people in the process, but I knew that going in. If any of them wanted me dead, I would be.

Haters on social media rarely went to those lengths, instead spewing their hatred and cruelty on posts or the odd DM. It was easy enough to block them.

The PI had tracked me down to Texas. No one knew where I spent ninety percent of my time. I always ensured to take enough photos while in Colorado to last me until the next time we went there on a family vacation. Jake understood my reasons. Danger lurked behind screens. A risk I refused to take having Daniel to protect.

I couldn't ask Jake to open the package and send me photos of the contents. Jake knew I took a more hands-on approach to investigating cold cases, but not the depths I jumped into to get answers. Maybe the parcel held nothing of significance. Or Rachel had one of her henchmen send it to me after her death. That woman could reach out from beyond the grave.

Morgan pushed herself up from the bed and closed the

bathroom door behind her. I made the most of the few minutes alone, sending a message to a different contact, calling in a big favour.

Sometimes your enemies are closer than you think.

Forty-seven

Morgan

Allysa kept her eyes on the road. Wild Bay had never been big on working street lights, not even when I lived here. The locals speculated that the various mayors had removed the bulbs as soon as the tourist season drew to a close. The consensus – to cut costs. Ridiculous. How much could a light bulb cost? I didn't care enough to Google for an answer. The dark streets were a reminder of the mischief we'd got up to as children.

Not all my memories of this place were bad.

The best? Terry.

"Boyle asked us to come to the station for more than our official statements on Corey's death," Allysa said.

"With the discovery of Jen's body, the locals took to the community Facebook group to voice their fears that The Skull Keeper is back. If you ask me, there's a lot of pressure on Will to solve this case before the next school holiday."

Back when The Skull Keeper left victims all around town, Facebook hadn't been a thing yet. It took years for the app to be downloaded onto the locals' phones. Not everyone had access to the internet back then.

We'd come a long way in allowing strangers and acquaintances into our lives.

Growing up I'd heard stories from the older generation that the local hair salon or barber was the place to visit if you wanted the inside scoop on your neighbours.

Had the fake gossip falling faster than cut hair, carried more weight than the plastered-on smiles and staged photos people now posted to social media? I gave a mental shrug and focused on the real reason for Will's late call. In his defence, it was 7 p.m. Our late lunch or early dinner had confused my circadian rhythm.

"If he thinks he's going to pin seventeen murders on Sebastian, I'll help you gut him. And it doesn't solve Sebastian's or Jen's murders. I wonder who they're investigating for Donna's..." Allysa faked a sneeze, blaming her allergies.

"For Donna's what? Last I heard, she committed suicide. Of course, there will be a preliminary investigation, but I doubt anyone will dig too deep. Everyone knows what she was and who cares if one of the vilest humans to ever walk these streets ended up murdered? Live by the drugs, die by the bullet."

Allysa and I didn't talk while walking into the police station. Will typed away on his phone and pushed it into his pocket as soon as he saw us approach. "Thank you for coming down to the station. Please follow me."

He led us in the opposite direction of the stairs leading to his office. This wouldn't be my first time in an interrogation room. The police had gone to great lengths dissecting the events of the night Ray had died. Silly, because I thought that was the medical examiner's job. I had been so drained after being questioned for hours, I wanted to check my chest for a Y-incision.

Will closed the door and asked us to take a seat. I wondered if anyone was watching from the other side of the two-way glass. As a courtesy, I waved in case someone stood in the adjoining room. A few times I'd observed an interrogation from that side; all part of my research.

"If I had the authority to kick you both out of town, I would. Since your arrival, the murder rate is edging closer to when The Skull Keeper was active." Will pulled the steel chair away from the desk and turned it around to straddle it.

The chair underneath me didn't move. Bolted down. When Will had interrogated Terry, the chair hadn't been held in place. Terry had told me everything after the police let him go. The things Terry hadn't said, I had asked. It was the first time I had access to someone who was a murder suspect.

"We will leave as soon as my brother's murderer is behind bars. Stop wasting your time talking to us and do your job. If you've still got a thing for Morgan, I recommend you see a marriage counsellor. There are far better ways than this to spend time with a woman you once dated."

I rubbed my temples with my thumbs and stared at the reflective surface of the table. Allysa always spoke her mind, as did I. "Willy – sorry – *Detective Boyle*. Sir. Allysa doesn't realise that you had lost all interest in me as soon as Holly started flirting with you. Did your name ever make the list of suspects in her disappearance?" I looked past him; straight at myself. "Whoever is behind the glass, make a note of that. If you need me to speak to you after this little chat, let me know. Please have coffee ready for me. Milk, no sugar. Thanks."

Will cleared his throat; the sound of phlegm unmistakable. "Where were you this afternoon?"

"There are six hours in an afternoon. Be specific. Also, should we have an attorney present for this impromptu chat? At least this time around you aren't making yourself comfortable on the bed I'm sleeping in at the guesthouse." My expression remained emotionless. "Who died?"

Will stared daggers at me. "What makes you think someone died?"

Allysa sighed and pushed her fingers through her hair. "Listen, *Detective*, either you get to the point or we're leaving. And no, we won't be leaving town. Not until I have the answers I came for. Also, I need my brother's remains. He deserves a proper burial."

"Did you consider the possibility of The Skull Keeper working with an accomplice? Perhaps the accomplice is carrying on where he left off, without the necessary know-how to replicate the murders to a T, an S, and a K." The tapping of my fingers against the table became rhythmic.

"I know that song." Allysa turned to me; laughter visible in her eyes.

I snapped my fingers. "Let's get back to Holly Green's disappearance, shall we? Not long after she disappeared, TSK's first victim was found. Is it possible that Holly had been the actual first victim? Did you ever consider the possibility?"

Will pushed to his feet and paced the room. "I'm the one asking questions."

"Are you? Because it seems to me you called us down here to find out what we've uncovered since the last time we spoke. Detective, two civilians can't do your job for you." Allysa turned to me. "When did your friend disappear? How long after that did you find the first official victim on Corey's farm? Was it his farm?"

I didn't miss a beat. "Not on paper, but Donna wasn't one for farming. She had inherited it from her parents. We referred to it as Corey's because he did all the work. Donna should've rented the well from him, as that's where she stashed her stash." I laughed at my joke.

Allysa smiled and shook her head.

"To answer your other questions, *Mrs Ross*, if memory serves me right, Holly went missing about a month before Judo found the first victim."

"Who is Judo?" Allysa took over Will's job.

"My horse. We were on a morning ride when he got spooked and I noticed the body. The killer hadn't even tried to hide her. The body would've been visible to anyone passing by on foot, horseback or on a tractor. Perhaps it had been dumb luck that I found her. I wouldn't have if driving past in my car."

"Please think back to the time your best friend disappeared. Did anyone have reason to cause Holly harm?" Allysa asked.

With my chin resting in my palms, elbows on the desk, I willed my eyes from left to right as if thinking. "Why yes, one person comes to mind. Earlier that day, Holly had mentioned she planned to end her relationship with the man she'd been dating. He was a few years older than us. And he is—"

Will slammed his palms on the table. "Enough."

"Funny you say that, because that's exactly what Holly had

told me she'd had of the *mystery* man." I smiled and winked at Will.

Underneath the table, Allysa patted my leg. "Let's get back to the reason you called us down here. To do your job, *Detective*. I didn't see Amanda York's name on your list of suspects."

I pursed my lips and tried my best to appear on Allysa's page.

"Amanda York?" Will resumed straddling the chair. "Women aren't capable of such horrific crimes."

Allysa and I glanced at each other and tried our best not to laugh.

I spoke first. "You consider poisoning someone you're supposed to love and cherish over a prolonged period, not horrific? Don't get me wrong, I never considered my mother of being violent, but you're very judgemental. Dare I say you're a bigot or a sexist? Why yes, that's what you are. Among other things."

"Amanda is dead. We found her body inside the house." Will rested his arms on the back of the chair, thinking he was running the show.

I tilted my head to the right. "Did you conduct a dental verification to confirm her identity? No one contacted me to give a DNA sample."

My shoulders lifted and eased back down. Will opened his mouth, but I held up a hand. "Let me guess, there wasn't any money in the police's budget for a forensic orthodontist. Therefore, *Detective*, you can't say with certainty that the crispy critter you recovered had, in fact, been my mother."

Forty-eight

Allysa

Boyle stared at Morgan, shaking his head. His mouth open wide enough I considered sticking my fist in. "You're talking of your mother. The woman who gave birth to you. Raised you. Loved you."

"I'm not sure whether she had ever loved me or did the handful of pills she took every day trigger a maternal response in her brain." Morgan stretched her arms above her head. "*Detective Boyle*, why are we here, in this tiny room that reeks of body odour and incompetence? Maybe the smell is yours."

Boyle placed his glasses on the table and rubbed his red eyes.

I seized the moment to speak my mind. "We're not suspects, otherwise you would be questioning us in separate rooms or one at a time. Is there even another interrogation room in this tiny building of yours? Don't bother answering. Educated guess – there's no one on the other side of the two-way mirror to observe this get together. Reason being – you don't have shit. You're hoping we've uncovered more, in a matter of days, than you have in twenty years. Sorry to disappoint you, but we don't have a suspect tied up and stuffed in a closet back at the guesthouse."

"To be frank, I lost a dear friend today, so let's cut the crap. Any of my other reasons for calling you here are none of your business. The fact remains – you came to town and so did death. You're both people of interest in the murder of Jen Burke. I might not have proof yet, but I doubt Donna Perk committing suicide after talking to you on the beach, Allysa, is a coincidence." Boyle pushed to his feet. "What did you and Donna discuss during your meeting?"

I rested my arms on the table and leaned forward. "Not a meeting, rather a chance encounter. After all, she had been my brother's employer and the one to tell me of Sebastian's murder."

"Then why did she pull a gun on you?"

I laughed. *Shit*. "I asked her to."

"What?" Morgan and Boyle both asked.

"When I studied psychology, our professor mentioned the possibility of triggering repressed memories when under extreme duress. It's not as if you would've helped me, Detective, seeing as you're an officer of the law and supposed to serve and protect. None of that allows you to aid in my quest to recover my memories."

"Quest sounds like you're in some kind of adventure or fantasy novel. If Will gives me his gun, I'll gladly help you. What are best friends for, if not holding a gun to each other's heads?"

I rolled my eyes at Morgan; grateful she didn't call me out on the lie while in a police station. "Next time, okay?"

"If you don't, I won't play with you at recess."

Boyle reached behind his head and massaged his neck. A miniscule part of me felt sorry for him. But he'd decided to put Morgan and me in the same room. The consequences were on him.

"You can spin it however you want. The point is, Donna held a gun to your head and that same night she died." Boyle continued working his hand up and down his neck.

"Did your witness tell you that at one point I turned around and lifted the gun to my head?"

His hands stopped. "No."

I threw my hands in the air, palms facing the fluorescent light above. "There you go, silly. Donna tried to help me. As difficult as it might be to believe, she felt terrible for telling me about my brother's murder. The days before and after

Sebastian disappeared are a blur to me. Losing my brother, a few years after losing my mother ... you can't understand the impact such traumatic events have on an adolescent brain." We weren't in court. And even if we were, perjury was the name of this game.

"Who did you lose today, Will?" Morgan asked.

Boyle returned the glasses to his face. Perhaps contact lenses, or a different career, would make him look younger. "Jessica Linetti."

Morgan pressed a hand to her mouth. "No."

Boyle nodded. "I'm sorry. At least her death appears to be from natural causes. None of us realised it at the time, but the strain and emotional devastation we endured during those five long years TSK killed poor innocent young women ... I guess it caught up with her. Again, I'm sorry Morgan, I know she'd been one of the few people to visit your mother."

"She had the same soft spot for Corey as she did for me. Corey and I saw her as the ideal mother. It's a pity Jessica never had children of her own. I shouldn't have broken contact with her when I left town. If I didn't know her better, I would've thought her cold behaviour towards me in the morgue and at Corey's house was because I'd left and never made time to call on her birthday."

"Jessica wasn't like that. When she arrived at the scene where Jen Burke's body was discovered, all the life and joy drained out of her. We all felt it. It's as if the past fifteen years was nothing but a dream. Now we have more deaths to haunt us and a murderer we can't stop."

Morgan reached across the table and waited for Boyle to take her hand. "That's why you called us down here. Why you called *me*. Jessica had loved me as her own daughter, and she was the closest thing to a role model I had. Will, have you considered The Skull Keeper might be part of the investigative team? Allysa and I haven't even started questioning the locals. No one has recognised me. Someone close to this investigation murdered Jen. TSK is part of the investigation. How else does he know how to avoid leaving any evidence?"

Boyle gripped Morgan's hand. "I need you to leave town for your own safety."

"I'm not afraid of a copycat." Morgan released his hand and sat back in the chair. "Allysa came here for answers, and I need to know what happened to Terry."

Boyle didn't have a reason to keep us. Morgan and I promised to be discreet when we started talking to the local people the following day.

Before we left the tiny room, Morgan gave Boyle a hug and whispered something to him. His face filled with grief and sorrow. I didn't need to hear what Morgan said; I knew my friend's heart. I'd never believed in auras, but I assumed Morgan's emotions would be a tornado of various colours. With her, things were never as it seemed.

One moment she wanted to strangle Boyle, the next she hugged him. Maybe she didn't consider it important enough to mention Doctor Jessica Linetti's role during her childhood.

Side by side, we stood outside the police station and breathed in the salty air. Morgan lifted her eyes to the moon and sighed. I hugged her from the side.

"Let's go for a drink. I need something strong." Morgan rested her head on my shoulder.

"You don't drink alcohol."

Morgan wiped her eyes. "Tonight, I do. Jess loved a good whiskey, that's what I will have in honour of her memory."

"Let's walk to the closest bar. The fresh air will do you good. After my day, I need some exercise and endorphins as much as you do." The sight of my dad in his orange prison-issued overalls played in front of my eyes.

Morgan snorted a laugh. "Liar. You want to take me for a walk because you miss your dogs. I swear, if you try to put a leash on me, I will bite your arm off."

It wasn't the time to give her a biology lesson; Morgan knew enough about forensics to know it's impossible for a human to bite an arm off. Perhaps her love for the subject had started because of her relationship with Dr Linetti. "I love you, Morgan. I'm sorry about Doctor Linetti."

"Death will come for us all. Is it wrong to say I'm glad hers wasn't violent? I guess not, considering what we've seen. I love you more. Hashtag fact."

We walked past the rental car and down the dark street. I didn't know which way we were heading and didn't pay attention to the vehicles parked next to the road.

Big mistake.

Forty-nine

Morgan

Everything hit me at the same time. Thirst. A pounding headache. The weight on my wrists and ankles. The smell was unfamiliar, but it carried a hint of freshness. I willed my eyes open. A faint yellow light illuminated the room from above.

Not my room at the guesthouse and I didn't remember hooking up with someone at the bar Allysa and I had been heading to. I'd never cheated in a relationship before and wouldn't on Wyatt.

The pressure on my wrists and ankles? Chains fastened with locks. My eyes followed the length of the chain until it disappeared underneath the bed. Without making a sound, I forced my body upright, ignoring my brain's plea to keep still. I moved my legs over the edge of the mattress. The carpet underneath my feet was worn, but without dust or visible stains. To my right, a door stood slightly ajar. I tilted my head to get a better view.

Who abducts a woman and keeps her in a room with an en suite bathroom?

The most pressing question – where was Allysa?

I pushed to my feet and stared down. The black jeans and tank top remained against my skin. Perhaps my shoes had come off during the fight? *Did I put up a fight?*

The most reasonable explanation was that someone had drugged me. It also explained the thirst and the feeling of nails being hammered into my skull.

A bottle of water stood on the bedside table. I checked the seal, even turning the bottle upside down and squeezing it.

Not a drop slipped out. At this point I didn't care for more sleep. Twisting the cap off, I filled my mouth with water. It tasted like water so I swallowed.

Authors don't get enough sleep and neither do avid readers. Trying to be both left me bone-tired. No one knew about my assistant who helped with social media engagement and follow trains. It was exhausting being two different people.

I pulled on the chains to see how much movement my captor allowed. The door to the en suite bathroom gave me hope it would be enough. It took an immense amount of trust for me to allow someone to tie me up in the bedroom. Terry and Wyatt were the only men I'd ever allowed myself to be that vulnerable with.

Wyatt. I wondered how long it would take before he realised I was in trouble, and if he even would. We cared about each other; despite neither having said the L-word. After all these years, my heart still belonged to Terry.

As for Ray? I hoped he burned in hell. *Thank you for the money.*

Money didn't help in a situation like this, unless this was a kidnapping for ransom. My thoughts filled with fear for Allysa. I hoped I was the target, but knowing the truth about her, the odds were fifty-fifty. Unless... *Impossible.*

The room wasn't much bigger than the one which I had slept in for twenty-three years. Standing in this room, chained to the bed or something underneath it, I decided it was time I bought a house; one with a closet bigger than this bedroom. If I survived whatever awaited me.

Far too many years I'd spent travelling the world, which had served my wanderlust, but I needed roots. A husband. No children; not with my genes. Maybe dogs, seeing as Allysa loved hers. I wanted a writing cave with floor-to-ceiling bookshelves. A view from my office overlooking either a lake, river or perhaps the ocean. I'd always liked water. Life-giving, and keeper of secrets.

A thick coat of black paint on the window obscured

my view of the outside world. No longer wet, but a hint of 'recently painted' lingered as I pressed my nose against the glass. I scratched at the paint, wishing I'd kept my nails longer, but didn't because of typing every day.

I missed writing and getting lost in the lives of my imaginary friends. Their lives were exciting and sometimes, when I was in a good mood, the story ended on a happy note for them.

Unlike my life.

I was an idiot to think I could find lasting happiness. Many people go through life with nothing bad or heartbreaking happening to them. Not me. One gut punch after the other was all I'd ever known.

That's okay, I'd made peace with existing instead of living.

No time to dwell on what my life could've been, had a schizophrenic not given birth to me. Or watching my father pull the trigger.

We're shaped by the things that happen to us. The cards fate pushed into our hands even before birth.

Half schizophrenic plus half coward, equalled the worst nightmare for whoever abducted me.

I refused to die here and would leave walking through my abductor's blood.

After searching every corner, object and any other potential hiding places, I concluded there weren't any cameras.

My captor's first mistake.

"I'm ready to play you piece of shit!" The sound of my laughter filled the room. No one held the power to break me, no matter what.

To die here might be a fitting end.

But first, I'd fight.

Fifty

Allysa

Typical of Morgan to try her best to enrage our captor. Either she wanted to die sooner rather than later, or find out why we'd been abducted.

I clung to the fact that I'd promised Jake to be home by Friday. If I didn't arrive in two days, he'd know something happened to me. Soon someone would notice our rental car still standing in the parking lot outside the police station.

I hoped. I prayed.

Morgan's fate, and mine, rested in Detective Boyle's hands. With any luck, his obsession with Morgan and his fear of her spilling his little secret would work to our advantage.

I doubted any of our thousands of followers would realise neither of us had posted our daily post or reel. There were a few who might reach out and send a DM, but then forget about us and unfollow us when we didn't respond within their desired time frame. We were all guilty of forgetting others had lives outside of the bookstagram community. Illness, death, work and various life responsibilities happened every day. Yet we created expectations by being available twenty-four-seven. Or appeared to be, with the help of post-scheduling apps.

I hated being two people.

"Hey butthole, I'm waiting." Morgan's voice carried into my room.

I grinned. Neither of us had a drop of patience or the ability to wait. The sheer volume of books we pre-ordered a testament to that.

I wanted to tell her I heard her and that I was okay. As okay as anyone could be in our situation. Instead, I kept my mouth shut, focusing on the sensation of the metal links chafing my wrists and ankles. Soon the metal would work its way through my epidermis and start cutting into my flesh. Underneath my bare feet, the laminated wooden floor didn't feel cool. My shoes were nowhere in sight. Not even in the en suite bathroom.

Half of the water bottle's contents swirled in my stomach. I remained alert. If our captor wanted to keep us sedated and compliant, the easiest thing would be to inject a tranquilliser into the water. I wasn't an idiot. My tongue sticking to my palate didn't override logic. Before the first dropped passed my lips, I had scrutinised every part of the plastic bottle laying on the bed. I didn't care to put it back on the coaster.

The cleanliness of the room, bedding and bathroom surprised me. The cream-coloured pillowcase smelled of laundry detergent, reminding me of a lavender bush.

"Hey, Tiny Dick, I know you can hear me!"

I assumed Morgan was pounding against something solid. The racket became unbearable as it increased the ferocity of my headache, but I didn't dare cover my ears. If *Tiny Dick* responded, I wanted to hear.

With my eyes closed, I focused on my other senses. The banging intensified. Morgan was being held either in a room next to mine or across from it.

The piece of paint I scratched from the window allowed me a glimpse outside. Morgan could scream until she burst like a bird in an animated movie; no one would hear her. Trees created a wall as far as I could see. Below my vantage point, a derelict paddock remained. If I had to guess, we were on the second floor of a house.

Not being locked in a basement or a dark room didn't mean we were in less danger.

With the chains trailing behind me, I marched to the bathroom. I hoped the toothbrush was as new as the tube of toothpaste. Bottles of shampoo, conditioner and face wash stood on the shower floor. No razor. "Morgan?"

No reply.

"Morgan?" I tried again.

"Lysa, you're here. Dammit! I've been hoping you were able to away. If we're both here, it means more than one person took us."

I didn't need to see Morgan's face to know she was busy analysing our abduction. The same way she did when faced with a plot hole in one of her novels. Morgan never discussed the details of her stories with me, but she often mentioned struggling with a scene or needing to conduct more research. We weren't fictional characters in one of her thriller novels. CJ Green couldn't write us out of this situation.

We needed to survive on our own.

As much as I didn't want to be here, there wasn't anyone else I wanted by my side when facing a predator. Morgan Wright was more than she claimed to be; hiding behind the pen name CJ Green, wasn't her only secret persona. *I need proof.*

"Allysa?" Morgan's voice carried through the air vent above the toilet. "Are you there?"

"Yes. The last thing I remember is us heading towards the bar after speaking to Boyle."

Morgan's laughter was faint, but unmistakable. "We didn't speak to him. We showed him the reason two suspects should never be questioned together. I guess you can say we taught him a lesson."

"Enough!" The male voice caught me off guard. "Things will get real nasty if you don't shut up. You don't want to see what happens when you disobey me."

I spun towards the bedroom door. Morgan succeeded in getting him to make his presence known. She never failed to draw attention, even when she hated being in the spotlight.

"Hello, Tiny Dick. Oops, I guess I shouldn't call you that, seeing as you're the one in control. My bad. However, you can't be much of a man if you have to drug two defenceless women and abduct them. Did Mommy not love you enough? Or did Mommy love you too much? Did Daddy slap you around? Or did Daddy leave when you were too young to remember him? It doesn't matter, whatever happened, it seems you can't get a date. Maybe Allysa and I can give you pointers? She's better at keeping men. I'm better at bedding them. Thank you for the clean room and the chain being long enough that I can use the toilet. If you don't mind, please schedule my mani and pedi for tomorrow morning around ten. Whatever you used to knock us out has left me thirsty and you can't use the loo with wet nails. Well, you can, but then the poor nail technician needs to start again and I guess that means you'll have to pay her double. Also, I don't eat breakfast, but need at least two cups of coffee before I'm semi-coherent in the morning. I assume for what you have planned, you either want us passed out or wide awake. If it's the latter – milk, no sugar. Thank you, Tiny Dick."

I laughed into my hands. Trust Morgan to try to control any and every situation. I once heard authors incorporated a part of themselves into every character they wrote. Morgan was being one-hundred percent Sabine. Playful, strong, and if someone threatened those she loved, she'd rip their face off. I'd often been on the receiving end of Morgan's verbal diarrhoea when watching one of her videos. It was fun hearing it directed at someone else.

Despite a spider petrifying both of us, the man on the other side of the door didn't stand a chance. Even chained and locked inside the room, I knew without a doubt, Morgan and I would walk out the front door, leaving his body to rot.

The first of the three deadbolts on the bedroom door turned.

I took a step back, waiting for what came next.

Fifty-one

Morgan

The hair on my neck stood up. My nails dug into my palms as I pounded against the wooden door. It didn't budge. I had written a scene like this in Predator; this wasn't a standard bedroom door but a fire door. No chance of breaking it down without the right tools.

The chains didn't budge, no matter how hard I pulled. To an outsider, I would look like a chained wild animal desperate to get to her young. Not that I had a maternal cell in my body. Yet the sound of Allysa's screams awoke something primal in me.

"Leave her! Come get me. If you're man enough." Pain radiated through the sides of my hands and shot up my arms. I fell on my back. Hard.

The carpet scratched the exposed parts of my skin. I moved closer to the bed; my arms being dragged above my head. *What the hell?*

The bedroom door opened. "You claim she's your booksta bestie. Prove it. Be a good girl. Or else I'll serve her to you with mashed potatoes and broccoli. At first, you'll refuse, but after a few days of going without food, you'll beg for seconds."

I willed my body to move and pushed to my feet, focusing my eyes on him and not Allysa. "I prefer thigh over breast."

The man laughed until his lungs spasmed. Followed by a pack a day kind of cough. Even from where I stood, the smell of stale cigarettes hit me. I loathed it, but craved nicotine. If he offered me one, I'd stab it out in his eye. Times like these people deserved a crutch. Or as most people like to call it – a bad coping mechanism.

"Remove the knife from Allysa's throat or I'll show you your tar-stained lungs." I tilted my head to the side and tested the range of motion the chains allowed. Not enough.

"This isn't one of your novels where the heroine and her sidekick escape death." The man wore black. His face hidden behind a mask associated with bank robbers and home invaders.

"Look at the two of us twinning in our all-black clothes. The balaclava is a little excessive, don't you think? Unless you're ugly, if you are, please keep it on. The fact that you're hiding your face tells me you plan to let us live. Sorry to be the bearer of bad news, Tiny Dick, but you're the one who will die." I shifted my weight from one foot to the other, ignoring my sweaty palms and the rapid beat of my heart.

"Morgan's right." Allysa's speech didn't sound normal. Her words came out slow and slurred.

He lifted his arm and shot me. *The audacity.*

A hint of copper filled my nostrils. I opened my eyes. My legs and torso were no longer covered. This room was much darker than the one I'd woken up in earlier.

Tiny Dick upped the game. The bastard had shot me with a stun gun.

I waited for the bile to settle and the dizziness to subside before lifting my head. The headache was worse than before. I must've hit my head when my muscles contracted from the electric current or voltage. *The science behind it hadn't mattered when I had pressed the trigger and taken my targets down.*

Despite being unable to touch my head, I knew there was a bruise on my right temple. The sharp, throbbing pain reminded me of the times Ray had punched me.

"You pissed your pants. Not such a badass after all, are you little girl?" Tiny Dick's voice came from behind me.

Across from me, Allysa sat chained to a wooden chair.

If we could stretch our legs out, our toes might've touched. I doubted my bladder failing me was the reason she also lost her clothes. It took a few minutes to realise this room wasn't as warm as the bedroom, or cell, depending on how you looked at it.

The man placed his hand on my shoulder. "Call me *Tiny Dick* one more time and I will show it to you. Nice and slow. As often as you can take it. You said yourself you're better at bedding men than your friend is. Guess I'll be the judge of that."

I swallowed hard. "I won't call you *that* again if you promise not to refer to us as *girls*. It's demeaning and sexist."

"I butcher pretty things like you for fun. Do you think I care about your feelings? Sorry to break it to you, sweetheart, I don't. If you feel the need to call me anything, let's go with Scully. In time, I'll show you my collection, but that's a right you have to earn."

Allysa stared at him, hard. I opened my eyes as wide as possible, desperate for her to keep quiet.

Scully cleared his throat. "I killed your other friend, hoping it would scare the two of you out of my town. You're pretty close with Detective Boyle, seeing as he spent time alone with you in your rooms at the guesthouse. I guess best friends share everything. Even the dick of a dirty detective."

"Why don't you bring Boyle here? He'll tell you what happened behind closed doors." Allysa tried to change position, but the chains keeping her wrists to the armrests of the chair and the one around her waist, made it impossible.

"He gave you the case files of the women who belong to me. No way he did it without getting something in return."

I lowered my left shoulder, desperate to escape the warmth of Scully's hand against my skin. "I blackmailed him, silly. You have no idea who I am."

Fifty-two

Allysa

Chained naked to a chair, wasn't the time to reconsider my decision against going for breast augmentation. Morgan's body didn't look thirty-eight. Mine felt much older, despite my rigorous exercise regime. The effects of whatever he'd injected me with lingered. Scully hadn't considered the possibility of Morgan hitting her head, never mind doing so hard enough to lose consciousness. Rookie mistake.

Years of hands-on experience had taught me the importance of knowing any weapon as intimately as I did myself. *Research is key. Practise makes perfect.*

"You murdered Jen?" I asked, despite the way Morgan glared at me.

Scully nodded, stepping between the two chairs. I tried to kick him, but my ankles pressed against the chair's legs. Solid wood and thick chains kept my body immobile, but my head and neck were free to move around. I rolled my head from side to side, desperate to feel a sense of control.

How many days did he plan to keep us? And how much of the tranquilliser could our bodies take?

We were going to find out. One way or another.

"A thank you wouldn't hurt. The bitch stalked both of you on social media. The way I see it, I did you a favour." Scully scratched his head through the thick material covering his face.

"That thing is soaked with sweat. Take it off. We won't laugh and promise to still fear you. Make yourself comfortable." I smiled when he turned to me.

"Why did you leave Jen's phone when you kept, or got rid

of, all your other victims' phones?" Morgan asked.

I realised how little I knew about the details of the murders. Morgan had kept the case files in her room in the built-in safe. I'd read them once and then, seeing the horror which had been inflicted on those poor women, blocked out certain details. All I could think was that at least Sebastian had been dead before his body was mutilated.

I closed my eyes, trying to remember what The Skull Keeper took from his victims first. *Eye? No. Tongue? Yes.*

My teeth pressed against each other so hard my jaw ached. It worsened the headache.

Morgan's face changed to something I hadn't seen before. Perhaps this expression she kept for men. "Scully, do you have anything for pain? My head is killing me and my body aches. If you don't have any ibuprofen, I'd appreciate an ice pack for my muscles. Be a doll and rub my temples. Please."

Despite his hulking form, he moved fast. The back of his hand connected with Morgan's cheek. Blood and spit rained down on the floor.

"She has a concussion! Don't hit her." I fought against the restraints until every part of me hurt.

Never in my darkest dreams had I considered I would witness someone I loved being hurt. I'd done everything possible to protect Jake and Daniel from my work.

Morgan's gaze remained on the floor, no matter how many times I cried out her name.

This wasn't what I had planned for us.

Our meeting up in Marcel, and uncovering the truth behind Sebastian's disappearance, was meant to be a mystery for us to solve together. We were supposed to grow even closer. I trusted her with my life and now we were at the mercy of a killer.

"You saw what I'm capable of. A little slap is nothing compared to what comes next. I've always dreamed of playing this game with two friends. Let's see how well you know each other." Scully disappeared behind the door.

My senses heightened to the point where my body trembled despite the restraints. "Morgan?"

"Yes, bestie?" Blood dripped from the corner of her mouth as it lifted towards her ear.

"How can you smile at a time like this?"

Morgan shrugged; pain visible on her face. "This isn't my first rodeo. I'm a lot stronger than I was at fourteen. And this time around it won't end with me agreeing to sell drugs to pay off my father's debt if it meant they would stop torturing my mother."

"What?" The word uttered before my brain comprehended the magnitude of what Morgan said.

"My father used to say I was born stubborn. A fourteen-year-old girl doesn't jump at the opportunity to sell the very things which destroy lives. I never cared who bought from me if it meant I was one sale closer to getting those men out of my life and away from my mother. They set targets as if I were a sales rep. If I hadn't met it, they punished her. It's cruel to torture a woman who hadn't always known what's real and what wasn't. I stopped giving her meds whenever my sales were low. She didn't need to suffer because I'd failed her."

The woman sitting across from me was a complete stranger. But over the course of the preceding days, we'd learned more about each other than either wanted to share.

It's impossible to know the details about anyone's life if you weren't there to witness the emotions, turmoil, fear, or rising from the ashes.

Scully appeared behind Morgan with a syringe in each hand. "Here you go."

He injected Morgan first. I bit my tongue, despite wanting to tell him that wasn't the way to administer a sedative.

Scully threw the syringe towards a corner of the room and turned to me, scratching his head with his free hand.

He injected me and sat down on the floor, crossing his legs. "This game is called: How well do you really know your best friend?" Glee filled his soulless eyes.

Fifty-three

Morgan

Scully's laughter filled my throbbing skull. I wanted him to drip acid in my ears. Anything would be better than the sound of his laugh-cough or cough-laugh. He needed to cut back and buy a portable oxygen tank. I made a mental note to never touch a cigarette again. Not even the occasional one.

"A few weeks ago, Allysa posted some random facts about herself as a bookstagrammer. CJ Green did the same two days later, as an author. Did either of you care to read each other's posts or did you just share it to your stories, loving on each other for all your followers to see?"

"We know everything about each other," I said.

Scully nodded. "The thing is, Morgan Wright, do you *remember* what someone tells you? Do you keep that information locked away deep within your soul because you truly love and care for that person, or is it just an act?"

He rose and stretched his arms above his head the same way I often did. "I don't believe in friendship. People are self-centred and egotistical. They give you the time of day when it suits them. When you outlive your purpose or do the smallest little thing to upset them? Unfollow. They will lie and deceive expecting the same—"

"Did you play alone a lot when you were young?" I turned my head and spat blood on the floor; grateful a tooth didn't follow. "I assume you played with yourself often during puberty. I'm sorry you didn't have any friends, Scully. If you want, Allysa and I will be your friends. We've never done any of the things you mentioned to each other because we were burned by others throughout our lives. Seeing as you're from Wild Bay, I'm sure you remember Holly Green?"

Scully nodded, but didn't say a word. To my surprise, he gave me a sip of water and then offered the same bottle to Allysa. There were worse things in the world than having your friend's blood on your lips and perhaps a little in your stomach. I hoped Allysa didn't dwell on the latter.

"The best day of the first eighteen years of my life was the day the police officers came to inform me of Holly's disappearance. I cried. They mistook the reason for my tears so I rolled with it. Holly Green was a bitch. I'm happy to say I've met no one like her since. And I didn't bother to make friends until I met Allysa." Rage burned me from the inside out. I never allowed myself to dwell on the hurt. There were better ways to deal with it.

"What did Holly do to you?" Allysa asked.

I looked past Scully at the woman who was more of a sister than my friend. "A better question is, what didn't Holly do? I should never have told her the details of my father's suicide. How was I supposed to know my *best friend* would use it as a weapon to further destroy my battered self-esteem? You don't want to know what Holly said about my mother."

"Did you kill her?" Scully asked.

I lifted my eyes to his and tried to grin. "No. You did, Skull Keeper."

Fifty-four

Allysa

The silence became unbearable. I glanced between Morgan and Scully; defiance radiated from her. Scully scratched his head again, and I considered telling him he didn't need to wear the balaclava. My instructions had never included playing dress-up, or Morgan and me being naked.

I knew Morgan was withholding information from me regarding The Skull Keeper. As much as I loved her, finding my brother's murderer outweighed her enduring a little torture. The things that were to be done to us weren't considered torture in some parts of the world. It would be enough to make our story believable when we escaped, but without leaving permanent, disfiguring physical scars.

Emotional scars? Morgan and I had both suffered enough during our childhoods that this would be a mere blip on our life radars.

Scully turned to me and shook his head. No sound came from behind his mask.

"My head hurts. May I return to my room to lie down for a while?" Morgan asked. "I hope you'll have our clothes ready for us. We can be participants in your game later."

We didn't have much time left if Scully stuck to the script. Neither did he. The plan never involved him walking out. His employer knew this when I'd asked for a favour.

What could bring two friends closer than surviving captivity? Morgan would be my best friend forever when I killed to save her life. *And owe me the truth.*

With his back to us, Scully prepared for what came next. I

hoped he stuck to the script, because I no longer felt like the director. Naked and tied to a chair; I'd written the opening scene, but the power was no longer in my hands.

I braced myself as goosebumps rippled across my skin.

"Excuse me, please turn up the heat. It's getting too cold for my liking." Morgan shivered.

I stretched my fingers and curled my toes; desperate to get my blood to flow.

Scully stepped out of view and returned with two buckets. I inhaled as deep as possible; at least the same smell which had assaulted my nose outside Corey's house didn't fill the room.

Morgan screamed.

Scully turned to me, lifting the other bucket. I kept my eyes locked on his, taking a deep breath and bracing myself.

A thousand needles pricked my skin simultaneously. I pursed my lips and shook my head like a wet dog, trying to get the ice water off my hair and face. It didn't help.

"First question: What is Allysa's favourite colour?" Scully asked Morgan.

Her teeth chattered, but she managed to say, "Turquoise."

"Allysa, same question?"

"Black." If all the questions were this easy, he'd be dead in no time.

Scully turned to Morgan. "Who is her favourite cartoon character?"

Morgan took a deep breath. "Hear me out before you do anything. Allysa's favourite is SpongeBob SquarePants, but as a child she loved Taz, the Tasmanian Devil."

He turned to me. "Morgan is right. She's the second person I've ever told about Taz. If you asked my husband, he might not even remember."

Scully nodded and gestured for me to answer. "Taz is her favourite, but she also loved Pinky and the Brain."

"You're Pinky," Morgan said to me.

I rolled my eyes before trying to shake more water from my hair.

"Dogs or cats? Allysa, you answer first." Scully crossed his arms over his chest, staring at my wet body.

"Neither. Morgan isn't one for pets."

Scully nodded and waited for Morgan. "Always dogs. Allysa is deathly allergic to cats."

"If you get the following question right, you can go back to your rooms. Other than psychological thrillers, which other genres does the other enjoy reading?"

Morgan answered first, "Domestic thrillers and true crime."

"Romantic suspense thrillers and true crime."

Scully removed a bunch of keys from his front pocket and stepped behind Morgan's chair. "We're done. For now." He held a black pillowcase above her head. Fear exploded in Morgan's eyes before the material consumed her face.

We weren't done yet. Those were the warm-up questions. Next, he should've asked the ones I didn't want to ask Morgan outright.

Why is he not following my instructions?

Fifty-five

Morgan

A loud noise jolted me awake. Terry visited had me in my dreams; distorted memories of the last time I had touched him.

I took deep and controlled breaths until my heart stopped pounding against my ribs. Whatever the noise was which woke me up, I didn't hear it again.

The duvet didn't press down on me as much as my conscious. I kicked it off, aware of the pressure still around my ankles and wrists. Scully hadn't redressed me while I'd slept.

No nausea as I pushed myself upright. Dizziness didn't force me from side to side like when on a yacht. I always hated sailing; I was a land lover without sea legs. Perhaps the reason Ray had decided on it for our honeymoon. *Sadistic bastard.*

The smell coming from the bedside table forced my eyes in that direction. A tuna and mayonnaise sandwich and a glass of orange juice stood next to a full bottle of water.

I took slow bites and even slower sips, despite being famished. My swollen and tender bottom lip didn't deter me from eating or drinking the orange juice.

After relieving my bladder and brushing my teeth, I walked to the painted window. The chains securing my right wrist did a better job than my nails, allowing me a glimpse of the outside world.

The tree tops were illuminated by a soft yellow glow. A brand-new day in this three-star hellhole. I'd set foot in far worse places. The cleanliness of the room added to my positive outlook, despite the very bleak situation Allysa and I were in.

Scully didn't scare me, even though he had a mean backhand.

The reason for my lack of fear?

Scully wasn't The Skull Keeper.

If not for his nasty cough, I may have suspected Will of orchestrating our abduction in order to get his hands on the proof I had that he'd been in a relationship with Holly when she had disappeared. And that he'd been the last person to see Holly Green alive. Will had always hated smoking, not even touching the occasional joint. Back in the day, he'd bought more than his fair share of ecstasy from me.

I showered, hoping to find my laundered clothes on the bed. Even if it meant Scully watched me. *Watching is better than touching.*

As I turned the taps to close off the water, I heard another shower running and assumed Allysa was following my morning routine, minus the caffeine. Unless Scully favoured her.

With the towel wrapped around my chest, I sat on the bed. I never left it for housekeeping to make the bed, no matter which hotel I stayed in. There are basic things one should do for yourself. Despite my bank balance, I never saw myself as better than anyone else. Nothing like the tourists who descended on Wild Bay during the holiday seasons. People should be nicer to those who handle their food and drinks. I had spat in a few drinks during my waitressing days. Some clients I gave a little something extra. Not urine – liquid cocaine.

"What does a woman need to do to get coffee? Please, Scully. I'll forget my name and won't be any fun for round two of your game. Please." One thing I would never regret was begging for coffee. After the days I'd had since arriving in Marcel, I deserved more than just coffee.

I tried to pull the links from my skin to ease the pressure, but true to form, the steel didn't budge.

"Scully, please. Morgan and I need our coffee. We promise not to complain if it isn't the good stuff we're used to drinking every day," Allysa said from her room. She didn't add we both consumed an average of six cups per twenty-four-hour cycle.

Even a Powerade would make me smile, but if Scully didn't

have coffee, I doubted he'd bought anything to replenish our electrolytes.

"Allysa, how did you sleep last night?" I called out, not knowing whether she came to the same conclusion I did – we may have slept more hours than normal.

I wondered what other authors and avid readers did at night without a book to keep them busy. That was a world I refused to live in. At least I'd always have my imaginary friends to play with. *Not the same as my mother.*

"Right through the night. For the first time in forever, I didn't wake up in the middle of the night and stare at the ceiling."

The corners of my mouth lifted, stopping short of tearing open the cut on my lip. "I keep on telling you not to read certain true crime books before bedtime. Do you ever listen to me? No."

"Scully, may we have our clothes back? I'm cold. If you want to ogle our boobs later, I promise we will take them off before round two."

Allysa and I shared information, hoping our captor didn't catch on. The wanna-be-Skull-Keeper struck me as the bluntest sword on the battlefield. Scully, or whatever his real name, was a butter knife.

As for me? A Damascus sword. Sharp enough to slice falling silk in half. Strong enough to split stones without ever going dull.

Fifty-six

Allysa

What kind of captor brought food but didn't return clothes? If he wanted to rape us, he could've done it at any time. What's-his-name wasn't following my instructions.

I didn't intend to offer him a chance to explain himself before killing him. For Morgan, our friendship, and the truth.

When I woke up, my hands still trembled. I hated when things didn't go according to my detailed plans. Before getting in the shower, I stretched, trying to relieve the muscle spasm in my back and neck. A clear sign I'd spent the night angry, despite getting more sleep than I had in years.

A recent addition to my room was a digital clock. Nothing fancy, but at least I knew the time. The red numbers mocked me; reminding me time wasn't on my side. Jake expected me home by tomorrow. If I didn't get the answers to my questions within the next six hours, I wouldn't make it in time.

Scully never bothered to check the window to ensure I hadn't scratched at the paint. Why would he, when burglar bars were bolted into the exterior wall and covered the entire window?

Him deciding when to end the game didn't sit right with me.

Morgan's voice entered my room. I craved coffee as much as she did. Morgan Wright. The last woman to love my brother. She knew the identity of whoever murdered him. It was time she told me.

Not only was Morgan withholding information, but she'd also realised Scully wasn't The Skull Keeper. Only explanation for it – she knew the name of the man who had tortured and butchered seventeen women. Not including Sebastian and Jen.

Did the real Skull Keeper have an accomplice who mimicked his work when murdering Sebastian and Jen? A copycat? An apprentice?

What plausible reason did Morgan have to protect this person? Too many questions. Zero answers.

We needed to get back into the basement so that Scully could ask my friend what I couldn't. I wrapped the duvet around my body and paced the length of the room.

It happened without warning.

I stared up at the ceiling. The back of my head bounced on the wooden floor. My arms moved above my head. The bed came closer as the pain in my shoulders burned into my ribs. The duvet bundled at my waist and legs, leaving my thirty-eight-year-old boobs exposed. Not the most flattering position. Lucky for me, my husband loved me no matter what pregnancy, breastfeeding or ageing had done to my body.

The bedroom door opened. The masked man entered and stared down at me without saying a word. The telltale sound of wheels rolling over a wooden floor filled the silence. He threw something onto the bed and closed the door before I could ask him why the hell he wasn't sticking to my plan.

The chains eased their hold on me, allowing me to rub my aching shoulder muscles.

I pushed to my feet and, again, covered myself with the duvet. Pointless as Scully did whatever he wanted. Whenever he wanted.

I wondered how the restraints' mechanism worked. How was he able to do that while standing outside the door? *Has everything really gone electronic?*

My suitcase stood next to the bedroom door; my handbag lay on the bed. This had never formed part of the plan.

I covered my face with my hands.

No control.

Morgan and I were at the mercy of the masked man.

I rummaged through my suitcase and handbag to check that everything was still in its place. One thing our captor forgot to give me – my phone. Wishful thinking on my part. The moment I lost control, in any situation, I hoped against my better judgement.

I drew the curtain back and squinted through the small hole I'd scratched open the day before. Someone drove our rental car in to a dilapidated building; I assumed it once served as a barn. *Who is the driver if Scully was here minutes ago?*

Morgan, knowing the identity of my brother's murderer, angered me to the point of wanting to strangle her until she gave me the name. And then continue strangling her until her lungs stopped fighting for oxygen. *Nobody lies to me.*

With my forehead pressed against the black coated glass, I thought of one thing. It terrified me.

Morgan and I were in trouble.

The kind of trouble her smart mouth and my years of hunting evil couldn't get us out of.

With the rental car here and our belongings cleared out of our rooms at the guesthouse, Detective Boyle would no doubt come to the conclusion we decided to leave town.

A tear slipped from the corner of my eye. *I'm never going to see my family again.*

Morgan was to blame for all of this. Her refusal to tell me the truth had forced my hand. And now that same hand was tied up in a remote farmhouse.

I stared at my suitcase, thinking about the events of the past few days.

Who did Morgan love more than our friendship meant to her? The most obvious answer was her mother, although it didn't sound reasonable, considering the way she spoke about Amanda York.

Sebastian. Maybe Donna had identified the wrong body as Terry Holt's.

If Sebastian was still alive, that meant ...

Sebastian Pimento, aka Terry Holt, had murdered seventeen

women. My stomach turned in on itself. I fought to keep my breakfast down.

Where did Morgan fit into it?

His accomplice?

How else did she know about Holly being the first victim?

Fifty-seven

Morgan

I'd never been happier to see my suitcase, even more than when my luggage went missing at Edinburgh Airport. That day I'd had my carry-on with my laptop and I wasn't naked. *My laptop.* I searched for it, throwing all my clothes onto the bed. The bottom of the suitcase stared back at me. It also wasn't in my handbag, neither was my phone hiding in there. Whoever took it also stole my knives. No biggie. I'd hidden a few other tools with greater care.

I had locked the case files in the built-in safe in the bedroom at the guesthouse. However, if they could clear out the room and steal the rental car right in front of a police station, I doubted a safe would prove an arduous task. Together with the case files, *they* also had my notes.

There was no way that one heavy-smoker orchestrated this without help. The questions during Scully's game had proved what an idiot he was. Any of our thousands of followers could've seen the posts, or anyone who followed the hashtags accompanying our posts.

At the bottom of the black pile I found my favourite jeggings and grabbed a sleeveless shirt. Underwear wasn't necessary in case my bladder embarrassed me again.

That was the problem in situations like this: you could never anticipate what would happen next. Much like writing a novel when the characters took over and exposed plot twists too early on. I didn't know about other authors, but I had a love-hate relationship with most of mine.

I stared at my reflection in the mirror, pushing my

damp hair behind my ears. Whoever had gone through my belongings forgot to pack my hair dryer. Probably thought I might become suicidal, forgetting the chains restricting my movement beyond the bedroom door could be as useful as any cord or shoelace. *Idiots.*

"Okay, *boys*. I'm dressed. My tummy is full. You can bring my coffee now. Be darlings and ensure my friend gets a mug as well. Remember, Scully, milk no sugar. For both of us. Thank you!" I hoped Allysa caught on, unless she'd come to the same conclusion on her own.

Part of me wished they kept us locked in the same room. Maybe they didn't for our own safety. I'd stab anyone in the back if it meant I'd live to see another day. Allysa was no different.

After all, she had stood back and watched her father go to prison for a crime she'd committed. Crimes, to be exact. Plural. Double homicide.

I knew Allysa a lot better than she knew me. She didn't know what I was capable of.

The day dragged on. Absolute torture without caffeine or a good book to read. I paced the room, plotting my next thriller novel in my head. Without my laptop, it was the best I could do.

I decided to write about two best friends who went on a vacation and then ended up being abducted. *Real life makes for great inspiration.* Many authors draw inspiration from actual crimes. Nothing beat experiencing it for yourself. Although, there were certain crimes I never wanted to experience again.

I closed my right eye and studied the outside world with my left. For a moment I imagined how The Skull Keeper's victims observed everything being done to them after they lost an eye. If Scully was The Skull Keeper, he would've removed our tongues the day before. Rookie mistake for a copycat.

The amount of research that went into each of my novels read like a textbook. Scully failed to get the most basic things right. I expected better from him. It was difficult to switch off the thriller author in me; I always contemplated murder, mayhem, and torture. The days spent with actual homicide detectives, the sheer magnitude of crime scene photos I'd studied, the autopsies I'd witnessed, swirled in my brain non-stop.

When I was stuck writing a scene, I'd go and sit in a coffee shop and watch people. I studied them through a killer's eyes; potential victims stand out like a foreign accent in any country.

You just needed to wait for the right time.

I touched the metal object in the seam of my top. Soon the perfect opportunity would present itself, but first I wanted to know what Allysa's end game was.

Only an idiot wouldn't do their homework. She enjoyed abducting people. Not random people, but criminals. Predators the police failed to apprehend. Those responsible for the cold cases remaining unsolved.

Why hadn't she closed her eyes before Scully splashed the ice water over her?

Simple. She'd known it was going to happen.

Fifty-eight

Allysa

Ask anyone what their opinion was on the worst way to die and you'd get a range of different answers. In my opinion, it wasn't burning to death. I'd inhale as much smoke as possible and ensure I lost consciousness before the flames got to me. Fire's nemesis was my biggest fear.

I coughed; my lungs desperate to get rid of the water. Waterboarding was more fun when you weren't on the receiving end.

"Where is the body?" he asked again.

I answered with more coughs.

Morgan tried to move closer, but the chain around her neck yanked her back. He turned to her and grinned. "Don't worry, you'll get your turn."

"Where is Scully?" Morgan asked.

The tuna and mayonnaise sandwich I'd eaten earlier exited my body, ending up on my lap.

He marched towards me and tossed a towel at my head. "Clean yourself up. I don't have time for this shit. Where. Is. His. Body?"

I didn't look at him while wiping breakfast from my pants. "Who is this *he* you keep referring to? You need to be specific."

"Hey, dipshit. Why don't you take this thing off my neck and then you try your macho act on me? Woman to piece of shit."

How Morgan realised this man wasn't the one from the day before left me dumbstruck.

In my defence, a black pillowcase or something similar, had

covered my face when I was brought down to the basement. Perhaps her years of studying people attuned Morgan to basic mannerisms, or the way people walked.

The man was the same height and build as Scully. When he opened the bedroom door earlier, he'd even worn the same balaclava. But our previous captor never punched me, and Scully had never shown us his face.

"You should be more careful about who you befriend. Allysa Ross is bad news and you're collateral damage. Not that I object to pulling a double. I've broken bitches uglier than you. Never at the same time. This will be fun."

"Do not call women bitches. It's easy to swing your dickheadedness around when you've got us tied up like dogs." Morgan lifted both hands in the air. "Not even dogs should be chained down. Oh, look at you. You're such a big and scary man." Morgan's laughter filled the basement. "I'm not collateral damage, dumbass. I watched while she killed him. Getting rid of his body wasn't a one-woman job."

"Morgan, stay out of this. Let my friend go and I'll draw you a map to where I buried his body parts. Don't worry, I dug deep enough. Your boss will get every piece of his son back. Minus hair, skin and his dick. I, uhm, removed those while he and I chatted about his sins."

The man smiled. It looked genuine. "Just between us, I think it was a nice touch that you sent his cock to his parents. The little bastard didn't have the balls to take over the family business."

I matched his smile. "I'm glad you approve of my methods. It didn't bring closure for Alex's victims. At least he'll never hurt another woman. Why isn't Mister Bing here? I expected him to come for me himself after I executed his precious son."

Everyone is someone's child. Nothing would stop me if anyone touched a hair on my son's head. Unlike Alex Bing's parents, Jake and I never indulged Daniel or raised him without rules and guidelines. We weren't handing Daniel stepping stones to become a serial rapist.

Morgan laughed again. "Wait, what? His surname is Bing? Oh my word, the children must've teased him at school." She stared at our new captor. "And you take orders from a *Bing*? How do you keep a straight face saying his name? Please tell me, I'm serious. That's a skill I need to master."

After what felt like minutes, Morgan drew a deep breath, clutching her stomach. "For the record, *we* killed your boss' son. Allysa, we've spoken about you hogging the scythe. We're partners in playing The Grim Reaper and taking out trash."

I stared at my best friend. The woman who always had my back. Despite everything she'd kept from me, Morgan didn't deserve to die like this. Not for my actions.

What was more important – her life or hearing the truth about who murdered my brother?

"You're not Scully, the man from yesterday. So, Big Baddy, what's your name?" Morgan asked. "Even as an author, I name my characters right from the start. It may change later on, but everyone deserves a name."

He turned to Morgan and shook his head. "I can't decide whether you're fun to have around, or if it will be better to just end you now."

Morgan lifted her arms at the elbow and shrugged, waiting for him to answer.

"Death or Reaper, seeing as you brought it up."

The chain rattled behind her as she shook her head. "No. You look like a Bob to me. Lysa, you know what we should do? Weigh him down and toss him into the ocean. Bob can live under the sea."

My stomach protested after all the coughing, but I laughed with Morgan. "Bob, I'm hungry and we still haven't had a drop of caffeine. Please, may we have some pineapple with our lunch?"

"This is the reason I've avoided taking two women at the same time. You either piss yourself from fear or get all giggly."

I stared at Bob, realising how much Morgan's presence meant to me. I'd never hated and loved someone at the same time. "What else have you got for me, Bob? A little water can't be it. Let's get to the good stuff, Bob."

Fifty-nine

Morgan

What the hell had Allysa got us into? Herself, to be precise. Nothing about this made any sense.

Who was this Bing person?

I played typical nonchalant Morgan, but I wanted to pee myself again more than once.

I didn't want to die.

There were too many things and places left to explore. I wanted to write more books. The list of unpublished books saved in a folder on my laptop ran through my mind.

More than anything, I needed to know whether I could love again, or if that emotion had been yanked from me the last time I'd seen Terry.

Even though Scully had slapped me, stripped me naked, and poured ice water all over me, I figured our chances of surviving were better with him than Bob. *Where is Scully?*

Bob's rage focused on Allysa. At least Scully had paid me equal attention. Was Scully a fan? Unless he made an appearance again, I doubted I'd ever find out where his game was headed.

I hated unsolved mysteries, especially when I was part of one.

"Where's Scully? I'm going to start a riot and demand you step down from office in order for Scully to retake his rightful place as master of this court." The thick metal around my neck allowed me to talk and laugh, but controlled my range of movement.

"Who is Scully?" Bob asked.

I rolled my eyes at him. The basement not as gloomy as yesterday, but still cold. "The man who played with us yesterday. His questions were fun. Allysa and I answered them all correctly."

"Your fat lip caused by your smart mouth, then?" Bob snorted a laugh. "What makes you think I'm not him?"

I dragged my hands down my face, grateful I didn't touch anything down here except the metal collar. "You don't reek of second-hand smoke and you don't cough. Not hard to figure out that you're your own man, *Bob*."

Bob walked out of the basement and locked the door behind him. Either he was a pro or he forgot Allysa and I couldn't go anywhere with our ugly neck jewellery. *Not yet.*

I played with the hem of my tank top, reassuring myself of the little control I held in this situation.

"Morgan, I'm sorry for getting us into this mess. Shut your damn mouth and do whatever it takes to get out of here alive." Allysa slid off the table where Bob had restrained her. "He is carrying a 9mm holstered at his lower back."

I nodded; I'd seen it too. "Who is this Bing whose buzzer you pressed? Or is it more of a message alert tone type bing?" Not my best joke, but I tried to lighten the mood.

"It doesn't matter. You have to get out of here and tell Jake what happened to me. I don't want him and Daniel to end up like the families I've been helping." When I lifted a brow, Allysa added, "Through the cold case account."

"Stop lying to me. You killed Bing-ding-dong's son. I know you, Allysa Ross. You had good reasons for it. Spill." When the word left my mouth, I realised it might be a little too soon for her to discuss or hear anything related to water.

Allysa hunched over as her bare feet met the cold concrete. One cough and she straightened her spine, looking right at me. "Is your suitcase in the room?"

I nodded.

"Morgan, this situation is serious. Our rental car is no longer outside the police station. It's in what looks like a barn.

Boyle won't realise we're missing. And as much as I dislike him, he was our only hope of getting out of here. Whoever murdered Jen didn't do us any favours. If he didn't kill her, she would've witnessed our abduction and alerted the authorities. Sometimes it helps to have a stalker."

"What about Sara? She hates you, and I didn't make the best impression on her. Can she be behind this? With the genes she got from Rachel, I doubt anything is beyond her, not even torture." I tapped a finger on my lip. "Hold on. How did this Bing person know you're here? I don't think Bob and Scully are colleagues. Scully abducted us and played his little friendship game yesterday, but today Bob wants to hear what you did with the young Bing's body."

Allysa opened her mouth, shutting it at the sound of the deadbolts sliding back on the basement door.

Bob glanced at us, dragging something heavy into the room. "You've been asking about him so much, well here's your Scully."

A knife's handle stuck out of Scully's left eye socket. Blood had dried around his throat, no stains visible on his black clothing from where I stood.

The smell? I preferred his body odour and the cloud of stale cigarette smoke which had surrounded him.

"That's just nasty. Better you than us needing to clean him up. Have you wiped someone else's butt? I haven't and today will not be my first time. Allysa, you do it." I winked when Allysa stuck out her tongue at me.

A dead body is a fascinating thing. To me, it seemed to live on for a while as it went through the stages of decomposition. Most people believe the stomach empties itself completely. It doesn't. The sphincters stop their work the moment the heart stops beating, but if there is anything in the bladder or bowel, it will be expelled. It's more seeping out than full-on defecation, like when someone eats too much curry or a bad taco.

I'd learned a lot watching autopsies and it wasn't the type of things to bring up in random conversations. Few people would appreciate discussing corpse-poop over dinner or coffee.

Another reason I loved Allysa – she was always open to discussing anything, as long as I brought it up after her first cup of coffee and a morning nap, depending on how she had slept the night before.

"I must admit, I imagined him a little less attractive."

Allysa gagged. "You're looking at a corpse, and that's the first thing out of your mouth?"

My shoulders lifted and sagged. "Don't act shocked by, or disgusted with, my dark sense of humour. Okay, Bob, you've made your point. Allysa and I accept the fact that you're capable of murder and will appear a little more petrified to stroke your ego. I'm thirsty. Is it time for me to be waterboarded or are you only worried about keeping my bestie hydrated?"

While Bob dragged the poopie body out of the basement, I looked around the room, hoping to see an air vent. No luck. The smell remained. It was my turn to gag.

"Morgan, we don't have much time. I've seen how these guys operate. Waterboarding is their idea of a casual chat; a getting to know each other and asserting dominance type thing."

I nodded. "It makes sense. We're chained up in a dungeon of sorts. Bob and his colleagues are into BDSM. I refuse to call him master and call dibs on *pineapple* as my safeword."

Allysa pursed her lips, failing to hide her smile. "No, shit is about to get real. I'm sorry for getting you caught in the crossfire."

I swatted her apology away like a fly. "Don't sweat it, bestie. This is great material for my next book. You and I are survivors. We'll be fine."

Allysa shook her head, moisture dripping from her eyes. I doubted it was from the waterboarding. "If you make it out, tell Jake I'm sorry. And tell Daniel I love him."

Bob strolled back into the room. "Playtime is over. *Bitches.*"

My short nails dug into my palms. "We can strike Scully's name from our list of TSK suspects. No way did this buffoon take out a serial killer when the police don't even have one solid lead."

Sixty

Allysa

I felt it coming, but was powerless to stop it. I tried to take deep and calming breaths; my lungs refused and burned even more. When I went through the contents left in my suitcase, I'd never thought to check for my pills. The same ones I'd seen Morgan take, but we'd never discussed it. People rarely admit to requiring chemical assistance to get through the day. The inevitable panic attack etched closer. I fought back with everything in me.

Death isn't devastating to the person who dies. The ones you leave behind will never live without the cloud of grief hanging over them. I didn't want that for my husband or son.

The navy tank top stuck to my chest. I shivered no matter how hard I tried not to. Bob threw something on the table and told me to get dressed. He didn't offer me privacy.

Morgan made a valid point – Scully wasn't The Skull Keeper. It still didn't get me anywhere closer to the murderer's name.

With my back to Bob, I pulled a dry tank top over my head. I refused to die without hearing the name of my brother's murderer. *And the seventeen victims*, a voice whispered in my head. It was selfish to no longer care about seventeen other families who had mourned the loss of their daughters for fifteen to twenty years.

Even if I learned the truth about whether The Skull Keeper had killed Sebastian before drawing my last breath, it didn't matter. My brother would still be dead.

Dry clothes didn't bring immediate relief from the cold. I

rubbed the towel against my soaking hair, studying Morgan's movements. She kept touching the bottom of her top. I saw her do it earlier.

I didn't regret killing Alex Bing and I never would. His victims no longer had to look over their shoulders or uproot their entire lives because he'd been sadistic enough to rape the same victim more than once. Often months after the first attack. Alex had been a parasite, waiting for his victims to regain a sense of themselves and then strike again. The second attacks were more violent than the first. The psychological impact devastated the victims. Some had taken their own lives. He was responsible for their deaths, making him a serial killer and rapist. The one thing his daddy's money and black-market connections couldn't do? Keep Alex safe from me.

"I tell you what, Bob. Come with us while we track down a serial killer. As soon as said killer is apprehended and in police custody, you can do with us whatever it is you have planned. Okay?" Morgan asked.

Bob shook his head. "The file your decomposing friend compiled on the two of you is a very sad read. Two little women who think themselves stronger than a serial killer who has evaded the police for twenty years." Bob laughed; the sound chilled me to the core.

"Jen wasn't our friend," Morgan said.

Does she ever stop talking? "Bob is referring to Scully." I offered.

Bob bent down and opened a black duffel bag that laid at his feet. I knew it didn't hold anything good, despite not being able to see the contents. Also, not lunch or coffee. Was it too much to ask for one last cup of coffee before we died? Even prisoners on death row receive a last meal. Convicted felons have more rights than the abducted.

Life isn't fair.

Bob pushed to his full length, gripping similar objects in both hands. He repositioned the wooden chairs to face towards each other. In a move I had practised countless times,

Bob reached behind his back and under his shirt, lifting the gun's barrel to Morgan's head. *He's faster than I am.*

Bob tossed something at Morgan's feet. "Place the flexi-cuffs around your ankles and then your wrists. Pull them tight with your teeth." He waited for Morgan to do as instructed. "Now, extend your arms. I don't trust you." Morgan lifted her joined arms with a sly grin on her face.

Bob turned to me, ordering me to do the same. As my teeth gripped the plastic, I realised we no longer stood a chance.

My first mistake hadn't been killing Alex Bing, it was asking Morgan to help uncover the truth about Sebastian's disappearance. With her way of figuring out plot twists and loopholes, it had made sense to ask her to meet me in Marcel. Morgan loved solving murder puzzles.

My second mistake – telling Donna I knew her new boss.

This had led to my third mistake – thinking Bing wouldn't send his henchmen when I didn't have the evidence of his crimes with me. No one would be dumb enough to travel with such crucial information.

Scully, the dead idiot, should've stuck to the script. I didn't care that he lay rotting somewhere in the house. In his line of work, it was bound to happen.

Mistake number four? Asking the wrong person for a favour. In the unlikely event I walked out of this house, I needed to reconsider who I helped and called in favours to. My supposed ally had contacted Bing.

Bob fastened a black belt around my waist. It took my brain a few seconds to register what it was.

"I'm going to remove your neck shackle and you're going to hop to that chair. If you don't…" He waved the remote in my face.

I hated making mistakes or being told what to do. Nevertheless, I hopped towards the damn chair as if my life depended on it. It did.

Morgan stared at the stun belt as he fastened it around her waist. "Not very flattering, but at least it's black."

Bob double-checked the ropes securing us to the chairs. We weren't going anywhere. Not by choice. "Okay, let's pick up where my predecessor left off. The rules of the game have changed."

Sixty-one

Morgan

I hated the feeling of my stomach twisting into a knot. The nausea. My heartbeat was uncontrollable. My breaths were coming fast. The one thing with the power to calm me either lay somewhere amongst my belongings or had been left behind in the bedroom at the guesthouse. I needed my anxiety meds. *Now.*

When Allysa went to visit her father in prison, I'd snuck into her room and found the same prescriptions in her vanity case. Ironic, the things we had in common but never discussed.

Most of the time writing, and pouring my emotions into my characters, helped to control my depression and anxiety more than the tiny white pills did. Without my laptop, my imagination would have to do. I focused on the book I was busy writing and tried to imagine what the characters were getting up to without me.

An eardrum-exploding sound filled the silence.

Bob stepped closer to my chair, tossing the hunting knife between his hands. Not once did he break eye contact. "Keep still. I don't want to hurt you." The sound of his laughter made my stomach clench even more.

I steeled my expression, refusing the give him the satisfaction of seeing my fear. Seventeen faces filled my mind while Bob cut my shirt off and tossed it onto the floor. He checked the stun belt and did the same to Allysa. She wore a dry sports bra while I sat with my breasts exposed to the cold air. Bob stared at my breasts, tilted his head, and then shook it. He stepped out of sight and returned with duct tape.

After he was satisfied with the makeshift covering, he tossed the silver roll next to our discarded shirts.

My chest resembled something straight out of a DIY BDSM manual. I'd seen some weird stuff doing research for my novels.

Bob pulled a few tiny black items out of his pants' pocket and studied it. "I found these in Morgan's room at the guesthouse, but none in yours, Allysa. Care to explain to your friend why you placed miniature cameras and listening devices in her room?"

"I wanted some tips on phone sex and, whenever I asked, Morgan changed the subject." Allysa tried her best to appear bored.

I rolled my eyes at her. "Google it. Or join a support group for the not-so-kinky. There are things friends shouldn't discuss. We're not in high school anymore, Lysa. Figure it out or call one of those numbers where you pay for it. Let the professionals teach you to talk dirty."

Nothing but calm and a slight irritation visible in my demeanour. On the inside, a million explosions erupted at the same time.

This latest stunt of hers deserved a fitting punishment. I'd block her on Instagram and Facebook. TikTok remained on my to-do list, but I'd never gotten around to joining the app.

Allysa was the closest thing I'd ever had to a sister. I doubted I'd ever trust anyone else to get as close to the real me as I had allowed her. Every detail she'd learned while on our vacation of a lifetime wasn't to be disclosed to anyone else. I'd rather kill her than allow anyone to hear the truth about who and what I was.

The siblings in my novels often bickered. Perhaps we could come back from this. If we survived Bob. In order to do that, I needed to kill him. Imagining Bob as our abusive older brother might endear me to Allysa and get me through the next few hours or days.

Our fates were in Bob's hands.

"Are you sure Detective Boyle didn't install those in her room?" Allysa asked.

Bob shrugged his over-muscular shoulders. "Who? Oh yes, the detective working the serial killer case you two thought you could solve."

Laughter filled the room, followed by a sound which made both Allysa and I jerk, despite having our movement restricted. It was a natural response, not a sign of fear.

"Two hot chicks can't heat up a cold case. You sure are dumber than you are pretty."

"Ah, Allysa, Bob thinks we're pretty and hot. Thanks, Bob. Best compliment either of us has received in days." Sarcasm. The one thing to shield me against the reality of what would happen if Bob used his new tool on us.

Awesome, a whip.

Not forgetting the device strapped to my waist.

There's a reason many countries frown upon its use on prisoners. Before having a stun belt strapped to my flesh, I'd agreed with the countries opting to use it on violent criminals. If nothing more than to keep them in line.

The duct tape made my boobies itch. I focused on that rather than Bob's sudden movement.

Again, the sound.

This time next to Allysa's head. She shut her eyes, even though I knew she didn't want to. Allysa was all about coming across as strong and fearless, despite having a heart of gold when it came to victims, their families, and the people she loved.

"Blondie, you're up. First question – what is Allysa's mother's name?"

I hated it when people called me blondie. It's not like I went around calling people brunette, shorty, fatty or anything else demeaning. I knew the answer, but curiosity got the best of me. "Alicia."

The tip of the whip kissed my left shoulder. I screamed too many swear words to remember them all.

"Your turn, *murderer*. How did Morgan's husband die?" Bob readied the whip, turning to Allysa.

"Murderer? You're not allowed to judge. Not when you have two defenceless women at your mercy." I kept my mouth shut when the whip impacted with my stomach.

Allysa closed her eyes. "He spontaneously combusted after spending twenty-four hours non-stop with her. She may be good in bed, but you've heard her. Morgan never stops talking."

I cringed at the sight of the red welt left on Allysa's sternum.

Bob draped the whip across the back of his neck. "Both of you, stop fucking around. I don't have anywhere else to be, but you have an appointment with death. It's up to you whether you'll be on time or late. I'm a very patient man."

"Something the three of us don't have in common." I smiled up at him, showing my teeth. "Allysa, I can't bear to see you suffer. Let's play his version of Scully's game and get this over and done with. I'll tell him where Bingy-boy's body parts are."

Sixty-two

Allysa

Morgan tried to negotiate with a hitman. If not for the whip licking at my skin and drawing blood, it would've been comical. Every time she said something he didn't like, I paid the price. Morgan wasn't a people person. At all.

"Do you want to go from Bing to cha-ching?" she asked.

I inhaled and let out an exaggerated sigh. The sigh contained more pain than I intended, but my lungs still burned and cuts and welts covered my upper body. "Morgan isn't part of this. Let her go, and I will tell you where you can start looking for Alex's body."

Morgan matched my sigh. "Attention hog. Can you see this chunk of steroids trudge through the Everglades poking around, trying to find a piece of his boss' son?" Morgan broke into song. "Here a femur, there a humerus, everywhere a bone bone."

I wished things could've worked out differently for us. Morgan Wright was the best friend I ever had and I'd miss her sense of humour. As disturbing as it was. "I buried him across the Mojave Desert."

"Last time I checked, Florida isn't in the Mojave Desert or any part of Florida desert terrain."

How does she know?

"When did you last tell the truth, Allysa?" Morgan tilted her head.

I matched her posture. "That's rich coming from you, *Mandy.*"

Morgan closed her eyes; her chest expanded and lowered

much slower. "I am rich. And calling me Mandy is a very low blow. Not cool, supposed friend."

Bob screamed, clutching his head with both hands. "Shut up! If I didn't need answers, I would cut out your tongues."

Morgan lifted her chin in his direction. "Ah, you're one step closer to being The Skull Keeper than Scully tried to be. Good job. Name your price. And don't give me any of that *I'm loyal to my boss* bullshit. Every person has a price, and we both know you don't have a moral compass. How many millions and in which currency?"

The whip silenced both of us. Our animalistic screams shook the foundation of the house. Bob dropped his arm to his side. The instrument of unimaginable pain fell at his feet. He stormed out of the room without saying a word. The deadbolts sliding into place was the only sound.

I waited for Morgan to lift her head. She didn't. "Morgan, I need you to talk to me. We need to get out of here."

She gave a slow nod. "Not yet."

"What do you mean, *not yet*? We're going to die if we don't work together. It's our only chance of survival. You said it yourself – we're survivors. I refuse to die like this."

Morgan lifted her head; I winced at the sight of the deep gash on her neck. "Do you have any idea how much plastic surgery it's going to take to make me bikini ready again?"

Psychopath? Sociopath? Did Morgan have CIPA? (Congenital insensitivity to pain and anhydrosis).

Blood trickled from her lacerated skin. From where I sat, it was impossible to count the cuts. It never occurred to me to count the lashes Bob gave me. Throughout his rage-fuelled tantrum, I kept thinking about Jake and Daniel. And all the things that led me to this point – on the precipice of death. My toes already dangled over the edge.

"Bob better come back with coffee, otherwise I'm calling his manager."

I wanted to pick up the whip and lay into her. "Do you not realise the magnitude of our situation?"

"Lysa, there are things in life we can control, like what we eat, or deciding which book to read next. Whatever Bob has planned for us will happen. And then I'll kill him. Ray did worse things to me. He had mastered the art of psychological torture. A little physical pain is nothing."

"What's nothing?" Bob asked.

I never heard him approach or open the door open.

Morgan leaned her head back in the chair. It didn't look comfortable, despite her acting like this was a day at the spa. I hated having strangers touch me, even when I paid them to work the kinks out of my back.

"I smell coffee. When you step in front of me, you better be holding coffee mugs. Caffeine me up, Bob, or I won't tell you where in the Everglades the alligators and crocodiles feasted on young Mister Bing." Morgan closed her eyes and smiled. "Fun fact to stretch your peanut-sized brain – the Everglades is the only place on this entire planet where gators and crocs coexist."

Morgan opened her eyes and stared at me. "It's kind of like our friendship, don't you think?"

"Who the hell knows these kinds of things? And what does it even matter?" Bob stepped closer, holding two mugs.

The smell hit me. Hard. It intoxicated me. I craved my caffeine fix like a junkie craves their next hit.

"Apart from not having the slightest clue as to what I am, you also didn't do your research. I'm an author. Psychological thrillers are my thing. Snowflakes call them dark. In my opinion, my books are based on more reality than fiction. I do a hell of a lot of research, and you'd be surprised at the wealth of information contained inside my head."

"I prefer movies," Bob said.

Morgan and I snorted a laugh and said in unison, "Books are *always* better."

Bob held the straw to my mouth. The perfect temperature, but it could've been stronger. Someone had neglected to teach him how to make a woman happy. At least a coffee-addicted one. Beggars can't be choosers; I drank as fast as my throat could swallow.

Morgan drank the mug's content with the same appreciation and speed.

"Okay, enough with the games. It's time for the final round. Not sudden death, but still a death round." Bob flung both mugs at the wall behind me. "All I ask is that neither of you pass out. Let's not delay the inevitable."

Sixty-three

Morgan

Allysa and I stared at each other. Did the possibility exist that by the time we walked out of here, she'd know me as well as Terry had at the end?

She offered me a sad smile; I returned it. We may have cracked jokes, but it was a defence mechanism for both of us. That's how well I knew her. It didn't happen often that she managed to keep her actual feelings from me. I saw behind the mask she wore in front of others.

My personal motto? Survive at all costs.

If it comes down to it, I might have to kill her.

Bob lifted his hands, showing us the remote controls. "In case you didn't know, those are stun belts around your waists. Should either of you piss yourself, that's your problem. If you shit yourself, your friend will clean you up. I can do this for days. Make it easier on yourselves and tell me what I want to know. I promise to kill you as quickly as possible. 50,000 volts are heading your way. Are you ready?"

I cleared my throat. "Bob, you forgot to add that the shock lasts eight seconds. When torturing someone, it's a good idea to explain to them in great detail what to expect. Knowing what's going to happen is more terrifying."

Bob didn't know the torture game as well as he thought. It wasn't my place to teach him, but I wanted Allysa to know what was coming. Which might've been dumb of me considering what she was; a vigilante.

Our friendship didn't make sense.

But sitting in a basement, unable to move, I realised what

drew us to each other. On a subconscious level, we were like a great white shark and an orca. Hard to say which one of us was the ultimate apex predator.

Maybe I'd make things interesting *if* we survived. In order to do that, I needed to get back to the room upstairs.

Bob shifted his attention to Allysa. "Against my better judgement, I'm going to ask, why is someone like you friends with her?"

Allysa smiled and met my stare. "Because Morgan isn't like other people. She understands me in a way few others ever have."

"A murderer and an author. Weird." Bob shrugged.

"No, not weird. And don't call Allysa a murderer. She rights the wrongs the police and courts can't, because money talks and she is deaf to it. The world needs more people like her. Do you have friends who aren't aware of how you earn a living? Does your wife know?"

Bob turned to me, rage simmering in his eyes. "I'm not married."

I snorted a laugh. "Oh, my dear stupid man. I tried to avoid lecturing you, but you're just so dumb. And I struggle to turn my back on those too ignorant to listen and learn. Look at your ring finger. Do you see the indentation? See the faint tan line? Either you got divorced in the past month, or you removed it to not give us any personal information about yourself. Word of advice – don't torture people in a well-lit space. Scully kept the lights low. Point for him. You think it's a done deal and that we're as good as dead? It isn't over until your victim draws his or her last breath. From the moment you take them to the instant their soul leaves their body, nothing is final. Now let's get this party started. Don't you dare play electronic dance music or I'll break free from these flimsy restraints and beat you to death with my joined hands. It's metal or nothing."

"You talk big for someone who writes books for a living."

The tip of my tongue played over my exposed teeth. "Sorry, Bob, but you're going to fail this test. An F for you."

50,000 volts shot into me. My body thrashed against the restraints.

Every muscle contracted.

My organs tried to explode.

The heat unbearable.

Sixty-four

Allysa

Bob turned to me once Morgan's body stopped convulsing. "Where is Alex's body?"

"Scattered throughout the Everglades." There was no point in lying any longer. *How does Morgan know?*

Bob waved the remote control. "Bullshit. You want me to believe you abducted him in New York and then drove to Florida?"

I shook my head. "Killed him in New York. Dismembered him. And then I drove to Florida to dispose of his parts."

"No one drives that far with a mutilated and rotting corpse. Unless they are stupid, and I'll admit that's one thing you're not."

I sighed aloud; people like him should know better. "I put Alex on ice. That's Body Disposal 101. Come on, Bob, you're telling me you've never moved a body?"

"Of course, I have. But driving through multiple states, now that shows some serious balls." He nodded his approval; I assumed.

"It's a good thing you're learning so much from Morgan and me. Do yourself a favour and never underestimate a woman. We are born multi-taskers and problem-solvers. And it's clear, some of us are born with bigger balls than most men."

Bob laughed. "It's not often that I enjoy the company of my targets. Again, you're not wrong. I've taken out far too many spineless, ball-less little pricks. It gets old after a while."

"I'm not saying this in an attempt to negotiate my freedom. I accept my fate. However, you're wasting your time working for Bing. I've got connections. If you get my phone, I'll give you their numbers. Remember to drop my name when you contact them. I've solved a lot of problems for many people over the years. All I've ever wanted was to give families closure. Not my fault Alex Bing walked out of court a free man after his first victim came forward to lay charges. If I didn't stop him, nothing would have. Not with his daddy's money and influence to buy his freedom."

There was no point in trying to establish a relationship with Bob. People like him – hitmen – weren't easy to befriend or persuade not to kill once they received the order.

Him working for some of my contacts might prove helpful, and continue my legacy without him realising it.

To Bob, and those like him, a kill is a kill, no matter what the person did or didn't do. Criminal, innocent bystander, eyewitness, a problem which needed to be taken care of – all the same.

"Your friend wants to pay me off. And you think I'm dumb enough to switch on your phone so that someone can track your location? I'm not an idiot. I've allowed you to make your jokes, even brought you coffee as a sign of goodwill. This isn't my first time, Allysa. I know how to do this job better than you do. I'm not a bored housewife turned vigilante or murderer, depending on how you want to spin it. To me, you're nothing but a job."

"Your talents are wasted on the likes of Bing. You enjoy taking your time to break people down. My connections have enemies who will challenge you. We both crave the challenge more than anything. Am I right?"

Bob nodded. "I've destroyed your phones. No one will find you here. Your tricks might've worked on the dead guy, but I freelance. I'm my own boss."

The freelancers, or guns for hire, were the ones you needed to be most weary of.

They're loose cannons in a world where people still fight with bows and arrows.

I rambled off a list of names; his left eyebrow raised. "Just use my name."

"I'm impressed."

Two words followed by eight seconds of excruciating pain. And wet pants.

Agony, I never thought possible.

I prayed for death.

Sixty-five

Morgan

Unlike Allysa, I didn't lose consciousness. I may have looked and felt like road-kill, but I heard their entire conversation. It took all my willpower not to open my eyes when Allysa screamed as her body burned from the inside out. *I know the feeling.*

I never expected her to pass out from the electricity pulsing through her, but emotional exhaustion took its toll on her. Allysa deserved to die with an answer. We both did.

Every muscle ached. My torso burned. Blood trickled from the cuts. One thing I was certain about – I didn't want Bob to press the button a second time.

"Hey, blondie, you can open your eyes. I've used these things enough to know when someone fakes being asleep."

I lifted my head and found his dark eyes. I forced the corners of my mouth towards my ears. "Oops. Busted."

"What's your deal? I can't place you." Bob lowered himself to the ground, crossing his legs.

"We are more alike than you think. In another life, and if your face looked less zombie-like, we could've been lovers. Partners even." Bob wasn't unattractive, but the sound of his laughter and his career choice made it impossible to consider going on a date with him. I preferred my men a little less homicidal.

Bob pushed his fingers through his dark hair all the way to the back of his neck. "Are all authors like you?"

"It depends what you're referring to. Another factor is the genre or genres they prefer to write. A thriller author is a different breed compared to say, a fantasy author. At the end of the day, we give life to our imaginary friends and their worlds. You need to ask specific questions if you want direct answers."

Bob's smile reached his eyes. "Definitely lovers. There is something special and different about you, Morgan Wright. I can't put my finger on it. With your money, why didn't you hire a team of private investigators and experts to solve the serial killer case?"

"First, you won't put a finger on me. Don't try to figure me out. Some mysteries are not meant to be solved. Allysa's hunt for The Skull Keeper is a personal matter. I'm just along for shits and giggles. May I ask you a favour?"

Bob chuckled. "You're at my mercy and you want to ask a favour? I've already brought you coffee. More than one cup a day keeps the sandman away."

He couldn't be more wrong. I drank more than my fair share of double espressos at night and never struggled to fall asleep. After brushing my teeth. Nothing repulsed me more than caffeine-stained teeth.

"Before she dies, Allysa deserves the truth about what happened to her brother. The least I can do is tell her the name of the person who killed him."

He studied my face. My facial muscles too sore to express any emotion. "What do you want in return? No one asks for favours if there isn't something in it for them."

All I wanted? To get back to the room and then out of this house. With or without Allysa. "Okay, could've-been-lover, I want to alter the game. You give Allysa the remote to my belt, and I'll take the remote to hers. We get to ask each other questions. That's all. Oh, wait, one more thing. I want to sleep one last time. In the room upstairs. Tomorrow morning you can kill us. I don't have children, so I'll leave my entire estate to you. You'll only need the offshore bank account details and those I keep in my head. Not a bribe. Just imagine how handsome you can be with some reconstructive surgery to correct your deviated septum and skin grafts to remove the scars on your face. Some more wisdom coming your way. Are you ready? Lay off the steroids. How small are your balls? Please *do not* show me."

More chuckles from the man sitting at my feet. "You're a sadistic bitch. I like it. You weren't involved in Alex Bing's murder. How do you know where she dumped his body?"

"I know Allysa better than anyone. And you have no idea what I'm capable of. Chopping up a rapist isn't rocket science, neither is disposing of a body."

Bob tried to read me. "Sometimes it's best to leave the body to be found."

Agreed. "What will you do with ours? I'm curious."

"Don't you worry about that. Here's a fun fact for you, seeing as you like to play teacher – female skulls are thicker than that of males." He grinned.

Sixty-six

Allysa

Sandpaper brushed against my skin. A tugging sensation around my waist. Warm air on my cheek and chest. I tried to pull away, but the restraints cut into my wrists and ankles. My inner voice screamed at my eyes to open. Every part of my body ached, including my eyelids. I didn't know how long I'd been out cold. For years I believed childbirth to be the most painful experience I've ever had, that was, until the damn stun belt tried to fry me like Old Sparky.

"Hello sunshine," Bob said.

I managed to glare at him. His head blocked my view of Morgan. *Is she still alive?*

"It's time for the final round." A straw pushed past my lips and I sucked at it, hoping it was fit for human consumption. "Water. You need to stay hydrated."

Bob removed the straw and stepped away; Morgan's smile was pitiful.

"You'll be glad to hear I made some modifications to your belts. None of this passing out bullshit. It's still going to hurt like a mother—"

"Get to the point." Morgan kept her eyes on mine.

Dread washed over me as I tried to flex my fingers and toes. The muscles not yet reacting to the cues from my brain. Despite the certainty of death staring me in the face, I made a promise to myself to sleep more. Pointless as it seemed.

We were going to die in this basement unless a miracle happened. I never believed in miracles when the cold, hard facts of life stared you in the face. Sometimes I wished I lived a different life, wondering what kind of person I may have become.

But I was a pragmatist. Life is shit for some of us. We're not all destined for happy or long lives. More often than not, the victims I sought retribution for barely made it past their thirtieth birthday. We're not entitled to anything when so many are denied the basics we take for granted.

Life sucks.

Bob turned to me with a grin. "Are you a lefty or a righty?" He didn't give me time to answer and pushed something between my joined hands. "Figure it out for yourself."

I glanced down at the remote in my hand. When I looked at Morgan, I noticed she clutched a matching one. Tears rolled down her cheeks. She mouthed, "I'm sorry."

"You came to Wild Bay looking for answers. What does it say about you, Allysa, that the one cold case you failed to solve is that of your own brother's murder? Ironic, don't you think?"

Bob turned to Morgan with his arms crossed over his chest. "You write stories for a living about murderers and other criminals who get caught in the end. Yet, here you are, unable to predict what will happen before your end. You're going to die. That's a fact. How and when isn't in your hands."

Bob started pacing the space between the two chairs. "Maybe I am The Skull Keeper. People think some serial killers decide to go dormant or end up in prison for unrelated crimes. Have either of you considered that sometimes we find another way to feed the beasts inside us? Killing is fun, but making money from it is better."

Morgan's tongue flicked over the cut on her lip. "Yay, I don't buy it. Most serial murderers stick to a specific victim type, because of who or what the victim represents to them. No way did you go from butchering young women to whoever your clients paid you to murder. Once you've tasted the level of sadism TSK showed, you can't just hide it. A single bullet to the head, execution style, won't give you the same rush."

My neck muscles responded and moved my head up and

down. "Morgan is right. I'll consider the plausibility of your argument if you can back it up with proof. Where are the skulls?"

Midstride, Bob opened his mouth. I cut him off. "Yes, there are serials that don't have a specific victim type. Some even experiment with different weapons, but TSK knew before the first kill what he wanted. Victim. Torture methods. He even planned where he left the victims and the positioning of their bodies."

"Bob, did you remove the tracking device from our rental car?" Morgan grinned.

"Shit." Bob marched to the door, reaching for it he laughed. The sound bounced from the walls and hammered into my eardrums. "Listen ladies, playtime is over. Let's get this party started."

Bob disappeared into a dark corner of the room and returned with a chair similar to the ones Morgan and I sat on. He positioned it to have a clear view of both of us, then found a bucket. After sitting down, he turned the bucket upside down, rested his feet on it, and placed his hands behind his head. "Wait, I need one more thing."

He rummaged through the duffel bag and returned to his chair, placing a small black bag on his lap. With the same gentleness one uses to hold a newborn baby, Bob unfolded it and lifted a shiny metal object. I swallowed hard. "Shurikens." Bob smiled like a new father.

"Awesome. You've got a thing for unconventional weapons. Maybe I'll take those ninja stars for myself. Allysa, do you want to split them? We never got the matching tattoos I suggested, so we might as well take those as a keepsake from our trip. Don't know how we're going to get them through airport security, but that's a later problem and not a now problem."

Bob's stomach growled. "Let's wrap this up. *Light up* might be a better word choice. The rules are easy: you each get to ask the other a question. If you're unhappy with the answer or think your *bestie* is lying to you, press the buzzer. If I'm unhappy with the questions, for whatever reason, I'll gift you one of these."

The overhead light glistened on the stainless-steel star as Bob played with it between his fingers. The rhythmic movement reminded me of the way my father had played with a coin when deep in thought. He stopped soon after Rachel and her spawn moved in; it had worked on Rachel's nerves.

Bob studied the object in his hand. "Morgan, seeing as you didn't pass out, you get to go first."

Sixty-seven

Morgan

Allysa and I were in the final moments of our lives. I could talk my way out of anything or into whatever I wanted. Not once did I choose this. At least Bob was sadistic enough to listen to my plan. The beast in him spoke a wordless language to my own.

Perhaps one day, I'd think back to this brief chapter in my life and about Bob. I might even contemplate what had happened to him to unleash the beast inside him.

The beast lives in all of us. It remains dormant, in a state of constant hibernation, until circumstances wake it up. Once awake, it will never sleep again, only retreating to its corner of your psyche when fed what it craves.

"If you don't ask Allysa a question within the next three seconds it will be her turn and you're left breast will have more in it than silicone." The shuriken glistened in Bob's outstretched palm. *How many lives have those hands ended?*

"Lysa, please tell me the truth. I don't want to hurt you more than he already has."

Allysa pursed her lips, shutting her eyes.

I continued, "Your father didn't receive a life sentence for drug trafficking, not as a first-time offender. Why did he take the fall for you? A double homicide? That's more than my father ever did for me."

Allysa's eyes opened and narrowed; her face turning red. "Who are you? Who the hell gave you the right to dig into my past?"

"Allie, I knew before meeting you in Marcel. It changes

nothing between us." I smiled; the words spoken from my heart.

"No one but Jake calls me Allie." She tried to move, but the restraints held her.

I wondered whether, under less constrictive circumstances, she would attack me. Me? Her best friend. The person who kept her secrets. When she needed me, I always made time for her. No matter the time or my deadlines.

Time zones are a bitch; ask anyone with friends on different continents.

A silver streak passed between us. "Does this look like a therapy session to either of you? Last time I'll ever pull a double with two women. You're way too emotional and chatty. Allysa, answer the question or blondie is going to press the button. If she doesn't? Pop goes the boobie."

Allysa stared through me. Unfamiliar anger contorted her beautiful face. "Rachel had forced him to take the blame for what I did. Those two bastards raped Jen. You didn't see how badly they hurt her. For days, she couldn't walk or sit. I should've made them suffer, but I didn't know enough back then."

Bob turned to me. "Are you happy with that answer?"

I shook my head. "No. Allysa omitted the fact that she wanted to kill someone. Those two pieces of shit crossed her path at the right time. They gave her a reason to do what she had wanted to do for a long time. Kudos for ending two rapists. Sorry, bestie."

Allysa's body jerked as the current surged through her. I poked the beast inside her. Time to see how vicious it was.

Survival and betrayal stir the most primal of reactions in us.

Bob waited for Allysa to compose herself. "Your turn, *murderer.*"

Unfettered hatred stabbed at me from Allysa's eyes. The realisation that our friendship might not survive this, even if we did, hurt more than anything Bob did to me. It even made a day with Ray look like a stroll around the Colosseum in Rome.

"Who is The Skull Keeper?" Allysa repositioned the remote in her hand. "Who murdered my brother?"

I wondered if Bob hoped we would press the button when convulsing and shock each other at the same time.

Allysa's question wasn't something to ponder. It didn't surprise me. "My mother. Amanda York. Wild Bay's resident crazy."

Allysa dropped her head forward and shook it. "You're lying, because your mother is dead and Jen was murdered the same way as Sebastian."

"Who is the one person who knows as much about the murders as the killer? A person who is still alive? Think, Allysa. The answers have been right in front of you this entire time. And before you jump on your mountain bike – because you hate horses – you thrive on the rush of hunting criminals. I didn't want to deny you that. Even though you were hunting a ghost."

She refused to meet my eyes. I connected the dots for her. "Detective Will Boyle."

"It still doesn't explain why your mother murdered Sebastian. What reason did Boyle have to kill Jen?"

Connecting the dots wasn't enough. I needed to colour the picture in as well. Not a big deal. I had done Holly's homework for her.

Unspoken words died on my lips. My muscles contracted.

A blue fire spread through me, scorching everything in its path.

Sixty-eight

Allysa

Morgan's body twitched. The sight of her in horrendous pain amused me more than I thought it would. We spent days together, talking about the murders. She had more than enough opportunities to tell me the truth. Why protect a woman she hated? "Sorry, *bestie*, I don't believe you."

"Whether or not you believe it, I'm telling you that my mother was The Skull Keeper."

Bob snorted a laugh. "I'm trying not to choose sides, but I agree with Allysa. No way did a woman murder seventeen people."

Morgan and I spoke at the same time. Her words uttered a little slower than mine. "Never underestimate a woman."

Sebastian overpowered and murdered by a woman? I doubted it. Unless she had drugged or surprised him. "Okay, I'll bite. Let's say your mother murdered my brother. A question remains – why? All the victims were young women. And most were from out of town. What reason did Amanda have to kill him?"

The realisation struck me again how little time I spent studying the case files. The brutality of the crimes, knowing my flesh and blood had met a similar end, were all too much for me.

I never made a timeline of the murders to see where Amanda York's death fit in. Morgan had a very good reason for keeping the files locked in her room.

"Mother set fire to the house and buildings on the farm the same day Terry was murdered. I believe he went to the house to find out where I had gone. I had told him I was leaving town, but never gave him any specifics. This all happened about a month after I left Wild Bay. Terry had known about my mother's schizophrenia. Maybe he hoped to talk to her on one of her better days." Morgan tried to shrug. "I never introduced them, not once in the five years we were together. I didn't want him to see her on a bad day and wonder if, one day, I would turn into her."

I wanted to ask about her reasoning that Boyle killed Jen, but Bob cut me off. "And here I thought my childhood was messed up. No serial killer in my family, or any crazies."

Laughter erupted from my belly; my stomach muscles protested. "I find that hard to believe. Psychopathy tends to run in families."

Bob closed his eyes and lifted his arm. The silver blade spun through the air. Instinct be damned. I didn't close my eyes. Nothing could hurt more than Morgan's betrayal. The shuriken grazed my left tricep and embedded itself into the chair.

"Morgan's turn to ask a question."

"Thank you, Bob. I have two questions, but I will keep the other one until it's my turn again." My former friend kept her face devoid of emotion. "How did you kill Rachel?"

Impossible. Morgan was fishing. She couldn't know I had sat next to the queen of evil-stepmothers as she drew her last breath. I glanced towards Bob, who held a star in each hand. *Screw it.*

"I made it look like a myocardial infarction. Bob, that's a heart attack if you're not familiar with the correct terminology."

Morgan didn't press the button, instead, she nodded and grinned. "I approve. Not only did you rid the world of her, but it brought us together. I will always love you more."

It didn't surprise me that Morgan approved, seeing as she already knew what I'd been capable of as a teenager. Love and hate battled in my heart. I desperately wanted to hope our friendship might survive, but she lied to me by omission.

And I doubted a day would come when I saw her face and her eyes didn't remind me her mother had murdered my brother.

Did I have the right to feel this way when I ended brothers, sisters, fathers, and mothers?

If Morgan had cut off Sebastian's head, I'd kill her. *My turn.* "Back up your conclusion that Boyle murdered Jen."

Morgan stared at me as if looking at the dumbest person in the world. "Will wanted us out of town because he's worried what I'll do with the evidence I have that proves he was the last person to see Holly alive. Who better to get rid of a body without leaving a single trace of evidence than a police officer? Will always bragged about the forensics courses he'd attended in Marcel. He probably thought killing Jen, making it look like The Skull Keeper's work, would send us running out of town. No one wants a serial killer hunting them, especially when you're hunting him. Or her. Or her ghost. You get what I'm trying to say. Will never connected the dots between my mother and the murders ending after Amanda had walked into the flames."

Bob opened his mouth and stared at Morgan. He leaned forward, elbows resting on his knees. His smile predatory. Morgan returned his gaze, lifting an eyebrow. "Now, isn't that interesting? Little Mandy York."

Sixty-nine

Morgan

Bob didn't allow either of us to ask another question before returning the stun belts' voltage back to the original setting, after yanking the remotes from our hands. He laughed as he pressed the buttons and I prayed for death. Not mine. His.

With the black pillowcase over my head, he carried me back to the room and chained my wrists and ankles. I wanted to fight him, but my body refused. Multiple electric shocks must've damaged my nerve receptors and short circuited my fight and flight response, leaving only freeze. If I weren't in better shape, I would've worried.

Allysa ran every day. *She's got more stamina than I do.* I reminded myself of this, listening to Bob carry Allysa up the stairs. The sound of chains and locks clicking into place drifted towards me through the air vent in the bathroom and from underneath the bedroom door.

Every cell in my body screamed, pleading with me to close my eyes and rest. Rest isn't for the wicked, an author on a deadline, or a woman who refused to die in this place.

The fact that I lay on a bed, a comfortable pillow supporting my head, didn't help much to keep sleep at bay. Desperate to stay awake, I focused on Bob and tried to place his face.

Him referring to me as *Mandy* York caught me off guard. I didn't remember him, and I estimated him to be at least ten years older than me. With all the work that had been done to my face over the years, Will was the only person other than Doctor Linetti to recognise me. The possibility existed that Will told Jessica my identity.

In the end it didn't matter, she died.

I willed my limbs to move, testing my strength. Determination and street smarts will take you further than any tertiary education.

Underneath the duvet, I fidgeted with the hem of my tank top until salvation stabbed my middle finger. A blood drop formed, and I sucked it out of habit.

From experience, I knew the locks wouldn't be much of a challenge. The duvet muffled the sound as I worked to free my wrists and ankles.

The deadbolts on the bedroom door were my second biggest obstacle.

I stuffed all my belongings back into the suitcase and double-checked to see that my passport was still in my handbag. My leg muscles didn't move as fast as my brain willed them to; giving me a little more stealth.

I pressed my ear against the wood, hard enough my temple ached. No sound came from the other side of the door.

Years earlier, I'd written a book about a serial killer who gained entry to his victims' homes by picking the deadbolt on the front or backdoors. A locksmith had shown me countless times how to do it. And as part of my research, he expected me to open a few myself. Write what you know people keep saying, as if fantasy and sci-fi authors don't use their imaginations.

People are idiots and should keep their silly mouths shut unless they've written a book and published it. It's hard work. I shook my head, refusing to dwell on an internal argument I've had for years with faceless dumbasses. Do they expect a thriller author to have a basement full of criminals to torture in order to add credibility to a scene? It was at the top of my author wish list to have such a room one day; filled with paedophiles and rapists.

Contrary to what Allysa might've believed, I still had a shred of decency left, despite not giving her an answer sooner.

With shaking hands, I bent the thin, rigid piece of metal into a 90-degree curve, creating a tension wrench. Inserting the short end of the wrench into the keyhole, I maintained the tension while picking with the pick itself. A time-consuming activity for those who've never done it before. I heard the locksmith's voice as if he was standing next to me until I reached the last pin. This one proved much harder to lift. I kept the tension on the wrench and lifted the pin with the pick. The slight movement of the barrel made me smile. The pin couldn't fall back. The pin kept moving deeper into the lock until I was sure I lifted them all. Using the DIY wrench, I turned the lock. One down, two to go.

From the hems of my other tops, I retrieved what I needed and got to work.

A faint light illuminated the short hallway. It came from downstairs. Three other doors on this floor. I paused outside the room next to mine. If I killed Bob and freed Allysa, she had to forgive me. I'd be the one to ensure she returned to her family and lived to fight another day solving cold cases.

When I had rummaged through my suitcase, I grabbed a pair of socks and pulled them over my feet. One chance was all I had. A split second all I needed.

The house remained quiet, except for the sporadic hum of what sounded like the refrigerator, which had stood in my mother's kitchen. Carpet on the stairs silenced my careful steps.

I kept expecting Bob to come charging at me; my senses in overdrive. *Adrenaline is a wonderful thing.* The anticipation of what would happen next forced my aching muscles to move.

I wasn't in fighting form, but I refused to die without putting up a fight.

Allysa deserved a grand act to prove my love for her.

I stepped onto the landing, glancing around the bare living space, except for the curtains covering the windows. To my right, the hum started again. I moved towards a sound from my childhood.

Bob sat with his back to the doorway, feet propped on a table, which was in desperate need of a fresh coat of paint. A trace of brown liquid remained in the bottle of Jack Daniels next to Bob's shoe. My hand shot to my mouth. The sound coming from the man in front of me, both frightening and funny.

To my left, a knife block stood on a weathered wooden counter. It didn't matter if the blades were sharp or dull. My fingers closed around the biggest handle. Holding my breath, I pulled it out.

"Never underestimate a woman." I jumped towards Bob's back, thrusting the knife forward.

I stepped around the table.

The tip of the blade protruded from Bob's neck. Nothing but gurgles and blood came from his mouth. He stared at me.

A clumsy attempt to stand sent him falling onto the Formica covered floor.

Before I lowered myself to sit on his chest, I grabbed another knife. Bob's head was propped up at an awkward angle due to the knife's handle in his neck.

"Silly man, I warned you. *We* warned you. But you didn't listen."

Weak hands grabbed at my waist.

"You shouldn't have called me Mandy. I'm not my mother." I sliced his neck from ear to ear. My smile was as big as the gaping wound across his throat.

Pushing to my feet, I scanned the room for signs Bob wasn't working alone. I found nothing except his phone, two handguns and the bag containing the shurikens. I switched the phone off, removed the battery and crushed it all into tiny pieces. Not before emailing myself a couple of screenshots of his text messages.

I grabbed the rest and headed upstairs.

You never know when you'll need a deadlier weapon than a seductive smile or friendship.

Seventy

Allysa

Movement in the air yanked me out of sleep and threw me against the wall of reality. The same feeling as when you're on the verge of slipping into sleep and experience the sensation of falling. I failed to calm my breathing.

The chains brushed across my lacerated stomach as I rubbed my arms and pulled the duvet up to my neck.

I never believed in ghosts or a sixth sense, but I could feel something was wrong.

My stomach growled. Hunger tried to keep me awake, while my exhausted body and mind fought to pull me back into sleep. Nightmares would keep me company until daylight came and Bob did what he was paid for.

I'd been a fool to trust Scully's employer. Underestimating Bing's reach was a grave mistake. One I'd pay for by ending up in one, *if* Bob went to the trouble of burying us. He struck me as someone who didn't care about leaving evidence. Bing would want to see proof. If only reading about it in online newspapers.

The double homicide of two women in a quiet town such as Wild Bay, when one of the female victims was a bestselling author? Our names were bound to end up on the evening news.

Jake and Daniel deserved better than the life I chose. Death ensures the living ends up paying the highest price.

Movement outside the bedroom door.

My heart beat in my throat, I swallowed hard, trying to accept what awaited me once Bob stepped into the room.

Unable to breathe, I clutched the duvet and stared as light spilled into the room.

Blood covered Morgan's face, chest, and hands.

I tried to jump from the bed, but my aching muscles made it harder than when I was pregnant.

"Are you okay?" After everything, I still cared about her.

Morgan gave a brief nod. "Sit down so that I can remove the chains." She pulled a set of keys from her back pocket and kneeled to free my legs.

I reached for the lamp on the bedside table and inspected her for new wounds. "What did Bob do to you?"

"Nothing." Morgan kept her focus on the locks. "I killed him. The sooner we get out of Wild Bay, the better. You know Bing better than I do, but I suspect he'll want an update from Bob soon."

Morgan rose as I rubbed my wrists. "I'm going to shower, scrub him off me, and then we're heading to Marcel International Airport. It's time you get back to your family. Pack your stuff."

I stared at her back as she exited the room. Next door, the shower started running, but I remained frozen to the spot. *Morgan killed Bob.*

I grabbed my suitcase and handbag, making my way down the stairs. The suitcase slipped from my hand; it hit the landing with a thud. The sound echoed throughout the house.

Familiar smells pulled my attention from the suitcase at my feet. *Whiskey mixed with copper.*

A fresh surge of adrenaline made it easier to move. I hoped it lasted until I got home and walked into Jake's arms. With my luck, I would crash on the aeroplane, which meant I could sleep all the way home. *Screw finishing my current read.*

Blood pooled around Bob's body; one eye stared at the ceiling. The tip of a blade protruded from his neck, close to his Adam's apple. The gaping wound above it looked like a grotesque smile. A broken shard of glass stuck out of his other eye socket.

"Allysa, let's go. Now." Morgan touched my shoulder.

I turned to her. "You killed him."

"Yes. Now we can leave this horrible place. You can go home to your family and I'll head back to Edinburgh." She tucked damp hair behind her ears.

I shook my head. "We need to contact Boyle. The Skull Keeper is dead."

Why did I want to cover for Amanda York? The victims' families deserved closure. To hear a schizophrenic, who had committed suicide years before was responsible, wouldn't be the same as hearing how our investigation led to The Skull Keeper's gruesome end. Too many questions would be asked.

"Little Mandy York won't be remembered as a joke, or a drug dealer. Morgan Wright will be this town's hero," I said.

Morgan hugged me and we both winced. "Sorry, but my breasts are tender after Bob ripped off the duct tape. I'm just grateful he didn't tear off a nipple because it felt like he did."

In time, our wounds would heal, but her saving my life was a debt I couldn't repay.

"Morgan, we need to find a phone and get our story straight before Boyle arrives." No doubt Bing would send someone else after me, but as long as my name remained in the newspapers, he couldn't risk it.

As soon as I got home, I had work to do. Time to take out the contact who stabbed me in the back and annihilate Bing before he sent another hitman to finish the job.

Seventy-one

Morgan

The rental car's headlights illuminated the trees on both sides of the road. I knew these roads like the tattoo on my wrist, but gripped the steering wheel until my hands ached.

Allysa forgot I understand her better than anyone, including her husband. She didn't want to frame Bob for The Skull Keeper's murders to bring closure to the victims' families or to protect my family's name. Allysa wanted to cover up the fact that Scully had worked for one of her contacts. Our abduction and subsequent captivity were orchestrated. And then things took a turn for the worse.

It didn't take a developmental editor to see the plot holes in her story. With Will, we couldn't risk making a single mistake.

Allysa kept her focus on Scully's phone, ensuring he followed both of us on Instagram to make it plausible that he was a fan of CJ Green. Not a difficult task, as he had downloaded several of my books to his phone.

"Bob isn't the first person you've killed."

Unsure whether Allysa phrased it as a statement or question, I answered with an eloquent, "Huh?"

"How did your husband die, Morgan?" Allysa switched off Scully's phone, removed the battery and told me to stop the car. She climbed out, walked through the field, and tossed the phone and battery into a pond. Lucky for her, the pond was fed by an underground spring. The chances of anyone discovering it was slim.

The farmer had chased Corey and me away more than once when we wanted to swim in it as children. People in town always said it was too deep to swim to the bottom on a single breath. Corey and I wanted to prove them wrong, despite neither of us being the best swimmers. Ironic, as we both were the sperm who had won.

I shut my eyes, gripping the steering wheel so hard I expected to hear it crack. Images of Corey's mangled and headless body flashed through my mind. My childhood friend had deserved better than the horrible hand life dealt him from the moment of his conception.

I still hated Amanda for forcing me to make friends with a girl. According to my mother, it wasn't healthy that Corey and I had spent so much time together. *Mother knows best.* Rich coming from a person whose only friend had been the area's ME. Jessica Linetti. The one person who had understood my mother's personality disorder as she was a medical professional and not an asshole, like most of the people in town.

I never meant to kill Jessica. Although, I didn't go to her house unprepared. *I'm not stupid.* Neither was Jessica. She had mentioned her suspicion about my mother, and her theory regarding Jen Burke's murder. I couldn't risk her digging into the past.

Allysa shut the passenger door harder than needed. I told her the closest house was that of the fun-killing farmer. She said I should keep driving, but then realised Boyle might ask why we didn't stop at the first house we came across.

"How did your husband die?" Allysa asked for the second time.

A well-rehearsed speech I knew by heart. "A lot of people knew about Ray's controlled drug addiction. That's how we met, when he came to Wild Bay for holidays. He came here because fewer people recognised him. His closest friends knew he liked to party hard when not in London or travelling for business. Our honeymoon hadn't been an exception. Whatever he took that night made him hallucinate, and he jumped overboard. Weird, when he was high, he wasn't the monster I married."

"Did you have anything to do with his bad trip?" Allysa looked at me, the console casting a blueish glow on the side of her face.

I returned my focus to keeping the car away from the trees, driving slower than necessary down the gravel road. "It was the only way to end the abuse. Our pre-nuptial agreement had very specific clauses regarding divorce or in the event that I cheated. No clause prohibiting *him* from cheating, though."

"You could've just left him." Judgement dripped from her words.

Taking a deep breath, I tried to control the bubbling rage in my veins. "What exactly is your problem? You've murdered … who knows how many people. He abused me, Allysa. Ray battered me so bad once, his friend, a plastic surgeon, had to undo the damage Ray's fists caused. Not all the work done to my face was by choice. Elective surgery, my ass. I didn't want to live in this shithole town, where everyone had whispered behind my back all of my life. Or hear the jokes they made to my face. Where would I have gone? A twenty-three-year-old waitress who specialised in selling drugs on the side to pay off her long-dead father's debt? I didn't have many options. Wait, I didn't have *any* options. I grabbed hold of the golden carrot Ray had dangled in front of me, and believe me, I paid for it."

"You had my brother." Allysa placed her hands on the dashboard.

"I married Ray for us. In my stupidity, I thought I could marry him, steal some things from his various homes, and pawn them off later. I had even saved some of the monthly allowances he gave me. Mrs Ray Wright needed to look and act like a trophy wife. Not long after I left Wild Bay, I couldn't get hold of Terry. His phone was always off. I contacted Donna, and she told me he had skipped town. She lied to me, because I checked the date in his file. He didn't leave. He was murdered."

The farmhouse came into view. Allysa rolled her hoodie around her left hand. "Stop the car."

I hit the brake.

Allysa's fist connected with my nose.

"My turn," I said, tears rolling down my cheeks. Blood streamed from my nose and into my mouth.

I punched my best friend. Twice.

Allysa cursed.

I shrugged and told her our injuries wouldn't look realistic if we both had broken noses. "For our next trip, we should go on one of those plastic surgery safaris in South Africa. I can't walk around with whatever my nose will look like once the swelling goes down. As long as you haven't pissed off anyone there. I don't want a repeat of this little adventure. Are you in?"

Allysa held the hoodie to her nose. "Just drive. It's show time."

Seventy-two

Allysa

The farmer stood in the doorway with his arms folded over his chest. He wasn't the good Samaritan type. Lucky for Morgan and me, his wife believed in helping two bleeding and hysterical women.

Mrs Farmer (their actual surname) forced us to eat. Not a punishment considering we were starving and our bodies craved sustenance, but we were convincing in our act of being terrified. I forced myself to sip the coffee Mrs Farmer made for us. The emotional and physical toll of the past few days' events clawed at my insides.

Since we fake stumbled out of the car, I kept an eye on Morgan. Did I have the right to judge her when we had something else in common? Healthy friendships aren't forged in the pits of death. Then again, serial killers make pen pals while on death row. Perhaps our friendship would be stronger than ever. Our secrets were out in the open. No one knew me better than Morgan, even if it wasn't my decision. Sometimes you can't control circumstances.

Boyle took a seat across from us and listened as we told him what happened. He didn't say a word, ushering in the paramedics as soon as they arrived. Mr Farmer appeared even more furious.

"What's his deal?" I asked Morgan when we were alone.

"Two of The Skull Keeper's victims were found on his farm. He started drinking more than the occasional beer after discovering the first woman. The discovery of the second sent him over the edge. He spent some time in one of those mental hospitals which go by a less stigmatising name. Last I heard, he gave up the booze while there, but needs his daily anxiety pills."

I nodded. "He's part of our unspoken club."

Boyle returned from escorting the paramedics to the door. "You refused medical treatment. Big surprise." He sat down harder than necessary and apologised to Mrs Farmer.

"Will, chill. We'll go to the hospital as soon as we've taken you to the house." Morgan scooted closer to me and grabbed hold of my hands. "It's him, Will. The Skull Keeper."

Tears rolled down her cheeks; Mrs Farmer placed a box of tissues on the coffee table. Morgan was a far better actress than me. I went for too in shock to speak full sentences. Morgan for hysterics. Our psychology degrees and interaction with real-life victims were being utilised for the wrong reasons. Not that either of the two men who'd held us captive deserved to live.

I made a mental note to ask Morgan when she had learned to pick locks, then remembered the first book in her Sabine series. Sabine had hunted a serial killer who broke into his victims' homes.

There were many things I could still learn from my best friend.

Boyle drove us back to that house. Morgan and I sat in the back, huddled together.

The brutality with which she murdered Bob stayed with me. It was one thing to slip something extra into someone's drugs or spike their drink. There were no words to describe what she did to him, except – overkill.

The knife through his neck did the job. Unless Morgan slit his throat to stop his suffering. The piece of broken glass she jammed into his eye proved she enjoyed it.

I didn't know how we were going to explain that to Detective Boyle.

Morgan leaned forward, positioning her head between the

two front seats. She moaned in pain. "Will, we haven't shown you our other wounds. I didn't want Mr Farmer to be triggered by the damage inflicted to our bodies."

"Let me guess, you also didn't show them to the paramedics either?"

"No. We need answers as much as you do. We all know that once Morgan and I are admitted to hospital, you'll start treating us like victims and not survivors." I placed a hand on Morgan's back. She glanced at me as she moved backwards.

We weren't friends anymore. We were sisters.

Blood fused our bond.

The blood we lost in that basement, and the blood she spilled to save us.

I rested my head against hers and whispered, "I love you."

Morgan squeezed my hand when Boyle asked what I said. We were at the mercy of the very person Morgan suspected of murdering Jen. She didn't appear to be phased by it.

Boyle ordered us to wait outside while the crime scene investigators processed the house.

I didn't want to stand there in the cold waiting for the sun to rise. It would take them days to gather all the evidence.

Morgan stepped away from Boyle's car without saying a word. She spoke to one of the officers keeping an eye on us and returned with two Styrofoam cups. "Police coffee is disgusting. Trust me, you'll appreciate your morning coffee for the rest of your life. And every cup after the first one will remind you how lucky we are to be alive."

I sniffed at the brown liquid in the non-recyclable cup. You'd think the police would be environmentally friendly. I guess no one cared as long as they caught the bad guys and protected the innocent.

By the time the last drop of the vile coffee passed my lips, Boyle walked out of the house. He stopped, lifted his head to the stars and smiled when he looked at Morgan and me huddled together next to his car.

We both clutched the cups as if they couldn't break from a

mere squeeze. Neither of us had the energy to talk, let alone litter a crime scene.

"It's him, that's for sure." Boyle pulled Morgan to him, releasing her when she cursed.

Morgan told Boyle to grab his flashlight and lifted her shirt, instructing me to do the same.

I placed the cup on the roof of Boyle's car and showed him the damage left by the a whip and stun belt. Gashes and welts told the story for us.

Boyle dragged his hands down his face. "It doesn't make sense that he deviated from his preferred torture methods."

Morgan reached for my hand. "Killers are complex creatures and you know he changed course. First with Terry and then with Jen. He wanted us to suffer because we hunted him. The exact type of woman he hated. He didn't ask about our childhoods. His focus remained on who and what we are now. I told you before, I suspected TSK had an accomplice. Did you find the other one's body?"

She handed me my hoodie and pulled her matching one over her head. Morgan had sent it to me the previous Christmas. The words printed on the front were an inside joke. 'I love you. I won't kill you.'

"We found more than his helper's body. Did he take either of you into the last room down the passage on the second floor?"

We both shook our heads.

"What's in there?" I asked.

Boyle stared at the ground. "Eighteen human skulls."

"That doesn't make sense. Whose is missing?" Morgan hugged herself.

Seventy-three

Morgan

Eighteen skulls instead of nineteen had been a huge oversight by whoever created the display. *Amateur.*

Allysa's contact followed her instructions, but she got it wrong.

I had the screenshots to prove it.

"It's possible the killer didn't keep Sebastian's skull, as he wasn't a woman," Allysa offered.

The skulls were in a perfect line on a single shelf. Their exposed teeth looked like overeager smiles.

The shelves above and below were empty. Nothing else in the room, not even curtains or the black paint which coated the bedroom windows in which Allysa and I were held.

I asked Boyle who the current owner of the farm was.

He said the house had been vacant for a few years. People didn't want to buy the property next to one where a crazy woman had lived and killed herself. Not forgetting her husband had done the same. According to the locals, the place was cursed.

Little did they know how true their superstitions were.

I studied the skulls as if they were paintings exhibited in the Louvre. "*Detective*, you won't be getting much sleep in the next few months. You have more than nineteen cases."

"What are you talking about?" Will asked.

I rolled my eyes, despite him and Allysa standing behind me. "Has your photographer taken photos of these?"

"Yes."

"Please hand me a pair of gloves. It seems all those forensic seminars you attended years ago were not very detailed, or you weren't paying attention in class." I bent my arm at the elbow, palm up, and angled over my right shoulder.

Will handed me a pair of gloves. With latex-covered hands I reached for two of the skulls. "There are a few differences between male and female skulls. My, not completely uneducated guess – eight male and ten female skulls."

"Since when are you a forensic anthropologist?" Will smirked and repositioned his glasses.

"I've consulted with a forensic anthropologist in Virginia more than once when conducting research for my novels."

Will removed his tie and pushed it into his jacket pocket. "Enlighten me with your brilliance, *CJ Green*."

I stopped myself from smashing the skull in my right hand into his condescending face. Time to teach him a lesson. "In my left hand is a male skull, and a female in my right. Look at them, do you see any differences?"

Allysa's eyes answered, but she held her tongue. Will shrugged.

"I'll dumb it down for you, *Detective*. The rounded forehead indicates this is a female skull." I held my right hand out towards them and then added the left, ensuring they saw the skulls from a side view. "Male skulls aren't as round and slope backwards at a gentler angle. Now look at the eye sockets. Males have more square sockets, whereas females have round ones."

I turned my hands again to give them a view of where the victims' ears would've been. "Square jawline indicates male; the female jaw has a gentler slope towards the ear. I can continue, but whoever is standing in for Doctor Linetti will tell you the same."

"She's right, Detective." A voice said from the door. "I'm Doctor Chandler. My apologies for being late. I was on the way down from Marcel when I received the call about your crime scene. I haven't even had time to check into the hotel."

Doctor Chandler explained he was assigned to take over

from Doctor Linetti until they appointed a new Medical Examiner for the area.

My stomach knotted as I turned to place the skulls back on the shelf. The last thing I needed was a fresh pair of eyes on the investigation. Allysa and I both tried our best to hide our faces from him.

"Will, may Allysa and I leave? We weren't guests in this house. You've seen the basement, our injuries, the two men's bodies." I turned around as Allysa lifted her head. To his credit, Doctor Chandler didn't show any reaction to our facial injuries.

Will nodded and lifted his hand towards the door. "You can spend the night at the guesthouse. I might have some more questions for you. On the way there, you can tell me when you learned to pick locks. Let me guess, research for one of your books?"

I nodded. In the acknowledgements of every one of my books, I thanked the people who gave up their valuable time to assist me with research. I didn't pull ideas out of my butt and hoped readers wouldn't call me out on it. My reputation meant everything to me. Will didn't say a word when I dropped this information on him.

"Who are you?" Doctor Chandler asked.

"CJ Green is my pen name."

The ME turned to me and smiled; it reached his blue eyes. "I've read all of your books. I'm a huge fan. How surreal is this? Meeting my favourite author at a crime scene. Are you here for research?"

He shifted his focus to Will. "She thanks everyone that helps with her books in the acknowledgements. The first book in the Sabine series is the one where she would've learned about picking locks. It's rather scary how easy it is. If you ever need a consulting ME, I'll give you my number."

I forced my feet to remain on the carpet. A fan might overlook any inconsistencies in my and Allysa's testimony. Not that there were any.

We had plotted our story out. The opposite of the way I wrote. I wrote stories as they came to me; a pantser instead of a plotter. But mistakes creep into books, whether it be a spelling, grammar or punctuation error.

Allysa and I didn't have beta readers to check for any plot holes.

Will stepped towards the beaming Doctor Chandler. "They held these women captive in this house, and subjected them to horrific physical and psychological torture. Whoever contacted you, forgot to give you the details about this case. Can you not see they were beaten?"

"Detective, I rarely arrive at a crime scene where there are breathing victims. Do you not think these women deserve to leave this place with one memory other than the tremendous suffering they endured? If I can lift their moods by telling Miss Green I'm a fan of her work, then why not? What harm is there in treating them as actual human beings and not just victims?" He smiled, glancing between Allysa and me. "Has a doctor assessed your injuries yet?"

"Not a doctor, but paramedics came out to the farm from where we contacted the detective." I offered a sad smile.

Doctor Chandler glared at Will, who said, "Doctor, you don't know these two women. They're not the type to listen to anyone, including me, a homicide detective."

Allysa took my hand in hers. "I'm a qualified paramedic. If I suspect Morgan or I need any further medical care, I promise to call an ambulance. You have a lot of work to do here, Detective, and our rental car is standing outside the Farmer's house."

Doctor Chandler cleared his throat. "We need to take your clothes as evidence."

"Okay," Allysa and I said at the same time and undressed. The detective, ME and skulls all staring at us.

"Underwear as well?" I asked.

Both men's eyes roamed over our bodies. Lust didn't spark in their eyes. Our wounds would only excite a sadist.

Will called for an officer to bring us clothes and waited for it at the door.

Allysa took hold of my hand again. "My apologies. Morgan and I went through hell and we're still in shock. We could've asked you to leave the room, but there's evidence here. We know how these things work."

"You're both surviving. That's most important." Doctor Chandler smiled the way physicians do when they give you good news.

Will handed us each an oversized jacket. It smelled like the duvet in the room next door.

"You won't find much of his blood on my clothes. I'm sorry, but I needed a shower to wash him off of me. Ask Allysa, I was in a catatonic state. I've never killed anyone before." I gagged and forced tears from my eyes. "The clothes are in the shower. I just stepped inside, opened the water and started scrubbing as I undressed."

Allysa pulled me against her side. "You saved our lives. I'm sure they'll find enough evidence to prove he was The Skull Keeper. I have the utmost confidence in everyone working this case that you'll bring closure to all the victims' families. Including the male victims no one knew about."

I squeezed my friend's hand. Our bond stronger than ever.
Sisters by blood.

Seventy-four

Allysa

A lesson I learned a long time ago became even more important. If you want something done right, do it yourself. Circumstances forced me to trust my contact's ability to follow a few very basic instructions. It couldn't be that difficult to get your hands on eighteen female skulls. Graveyards are full of them. They just needed to look at the name on the tombstone. *Idiots.*

Boyle pointed towards our rental car as we approached the guesthouse. "The car is here. As for your clothes and other personal items, someone removed them from your rooms and the owner doesn't know when this happened. I'm sorry you lost your belongings. I'll ask a female officer to go shopping for you tomorrow morning first thing. There are basic personal care items in the room. I took the liberty of booking you into one room. If it's a problem, we can get you another one."

"No, one room is perfect. Allysa and I won't rest if we're not together." Morgan reached forward and placed a hand on Boyle's shoulder. "Thank you for everything, Will. I'm glad you are here tonight, despite the horrible circumstances."

Morgan's voice lowered. "Do I need an attorney? Are you going to charge me for what I did to get us out of that house?"

Boyle switched the engine off and turned to face her. "No. Once I have your official statements and you've recovered from your injuries, you'll be free to leave town in a few days. I might have some follow-up questions after the crime scene investigators finish processing the house. If you want, I can keep your names out of the newspapers?"

I looked at Morgan. She gave a half-hearted shrug. "I don't care. The people in this town don't know who Morgan Wright is, or Allysa Ross' name. It might help the victims' families when they learn that two women are responsible for ending the man who tortured and butchered their daughters."

Sometimes Morgan surprised me. This wasn't one of those times. Her words were an extension to our carefully plotted story. I thanked Detective Boyle and opened the car door. He handed me the keys to the rental car and left once Morgan and I were settled in our room.

"This is my room." Morgan grinned like a woman having the best sex of her life.

Without another word, she walked to the closet and opened the safe. She turned around, holding a stack of files in her hands. "A trick I learned years ago. There's a way to bypass anyone overriding the password you choose for a safe like this. They're pretty standard in hotel rooms and I'm surprised the new owners forked out the money. I'll burn it."

No argument from me. I wanted to leave Wild Bay as soon as possible. Bing could send someone else to take me out at any moment.

I was a sitting duck, and Morgan moved in and out of the crosshairs.

We slept better than either of us expected. Boyle arranged for breakfast to be brought to our room and made us each a cup of coffee before taking our official statements. This time, he brought another police officer with him.

An hour before his arrival, a female officer delivered two brand new sets of clothes and shoes for both of us. It made sense that Boyle knew Morgan's sizes, and I gave him full access to my body the night before when we stripped off our clothes in the room with the wrong skulls.

It still grated on my nerves that such a simple instruction couldn't be followed. More than ever, I wanted to get as far away from this place as possible. Morgan and I should've done a thorough search of the house to ensure there wasn't any incriminating evidence for the police to find.

With nothing left to ask for the time being, Boyle and the other officer left. He asked us to stay at the guesthouse. The moment the door closed behind him, Morgan and I grinned. Our eyes mirrored each other's anxiety and decision.

We waited fifteen minutes, climbed into the rental car, after checking that our suitcases were still in the trunk, and left Wild Bay behind us.

I drove while Morgan booked us flight tickets. She paid for mine, saying it was the least she could do, seeing as her mother had murdered my brother. I didn't respond. Too exhausted and desperate to reach Marcel International Airport. Home to the one place Bing couldn't get to me.

It wasn't easy to track someone down when they lived under a different surname.

Morgan and I passed the time waiting for my flight's departure sitting in a coffee shop. We drank more coffee than anyone should when not within walking distance of a lavatory. I ate a big slice of peanut butter and chocolate cake. Morgan opted for a ham and cheese croissant.

"Have you flown first-class before?" Morgan asked.

The fork froze half-way to my mouth. "No, you didn't?"

"Of course, I did. I love you. Do you think we'll ever see each other again?"

I shook my head and slipped the fork into my mouth. "Never like this. I've aged ten years since you walked into the Marcella Hotel's lobby."

We ignored the people staring at us; our broken noses and the dark blue circles under our eyes to blame. I considered lifting my shirt, but didn't want to get arrested for indecent exposure. *Been there, done that.*

"I have that effect on people. Why do you think I need so

many fillers, nips and tucks? I live with my squirrel brain. It's freakin exhausting. On a good day I make myself old."

A robotic female voice announced that my flight was boarding. Morgan's flight didn't leave for another two hours. She walked with me to the boarding gate.

I held her as tight as either of us could endure. The pain dulled by painkillers and anti-inflammatories we bought at a pharmacy in the airport building when we first arrived. Morgan proposed we split them and think of each other whenever we swallowed one.

The line cleared behind me and I hugged Morgan one last time. Fewer people in first-class, so there wasn't much of a line to begin with. It would be easy to get used to a life of luxury.

Morgan lifted her mouth to my ear. "I have screenshots of the communication sent between Bing and Bob, implicating you in Alex's murder. Scully also sent Bob text messages saying where we were being held. He even forwarded your requirements for our abduction and captivity. I love you more than anything in the world, Allysa Ross. Sorry, Allysa *Santiago*. Your secrets will always be safe with me."

I swallowed hard as my hands trembled. The woman at the counter politely ordered me to hurry. I turned to her; she held the door with a smile, but her eyes failed to hide her level of irritation.

Morgan eased back and smiled up at me. "The police and everyone else got it wrong. I didn't keep the skulls."

She walked away, glancing over her shoulder. "Please let me know when you arrive home. It's a sign of love. And I love you the most, *bestie*."

Seventy-five

Morgan

Right from the beginning, our friendship was special. It had started with our shared love of books, but little did either of us realise we would find a piece of ourselves in each other.

Allysa and I? An odd pair.

A vigilante and a serial killer.

I stood at the window and looked on as Allysa's flight departed. It would be a few days before I heard from her. She needed time to process my parting words.

I grinned at my reflection in the glass, remembering the first time I'd erased someone from my life.

Holly's skull never joined the others at the bottom of Mr Farmer's pond. She left town with hers intact, but without me. I had begged her to give me time to save up enough money to run away with her. Holly disappeared, but no one other than her overbearing parents were to blame. They'd wanted their precious daughter to stay in Wild Bay. Forever.

Holly wanted to see the world and make her own decisions regarding meals, clothes, and her future. There wasn't an aspect of her life her parents hadn't controlled.

I hated her for leaving me.

The last time I saw Holly, she had sat at a café in Paris, her laughter carried across the street. I remembered that day and every emotion I felt as if it happened now. Holly Green, my childhood best friend, happier than I'd ever seen her. In that moment, I stopped hating her, but didn't dare approach her.

Holly deserved so much more than reminders of Wild Bay.

I've murdered nineteen people. The only one who hadn't deserved it; my heart would always belong to – Terry.

He had gone to my mother's house more than once, desperate to get hold of me. Her carer told me about the handsome young man who kept stopping by the house, asking about my whereabouts.

I went to Wild Bay and asked Terry to meet me at the farm. He waited in our special place – the barn. If those wooden planks could talk, they'd need serious therapy after witnessing us going at it countless times, like rabbits who were desperately in love.

The Skull Keeper had fascinated him from the day the first victim was found. He became obsessed after Will interviewed him. Terry didn't want to go to prison for crimes he didn't commit. Now I wondered if he knew the truth about what his father had done for Allysa.

On one of the many days Terry stopped by the farm my mother had wandered around without the nurse Ray paid for. Amanda told him about the sounds she heard coming from the barn at all hours of the night. She never understood why I used a drill, but when she went to see what I spent so much time doing in there, she had found nothing.

Saw dust and hay made for amazing ground cover. In case the plastic sheets I placed around the despicable women didn't catch every drop of their vile blood.

Terry suspected my mother was The Skull Keeper. He even showed me a bloodstain I'd missed. I didn't suffer at Ray's hands just to lose it all when I was close to having the life I deserved. Our wedding took place a week after I murdered the man I loved … will always love.

I murdered seventeen women who thought they could steal Terry away from me.

Who gave them the right to flirt with him?

Did money make them better than me?

I hadn't gone through all that trouble teaching them, even giving them back to their families, for nothing.

Terry didn't understand. No matter how hard I tried to explain. Everything I'd ever done was for us. He gave me no choice.

When he turned his back to me, I had a split second to decide my future. A hammer lay within reach; the angle grinder I put to use later.

Survival and self-preservation. I killed both of us that night.

The carer had come to the barn to inspect the noise the grinder made. A proper hammer-smack to the head and she fell to the floor. I dragged her back to the house, lied to my mother for the umpteenth time, and crushed sleeping pills into a cup of tea. Good daughters make their mommy a cup of tea. Even more so when you planned to burn her alive.

I didn't want her to suffer; I had suffered enough for the both of us.

The same robotic female voice announced my flight was boarding. I headed towards the gate. Wyatt would meet me in Bora Bora. After Allysa's flight left, I pulled my laptop from my carry-on and sent him an email with a brief explanation of why I couldn't return his calls. I promised to tell him everything once we lay naked in each other's arms.

The ocean was visible from where I stood, waiting for my turn to board. A new day dawned on the horizon. It sounded like a cliché, but watching the sunrise, I realised my life would never be the same.

No one would take the life I had fought and killed for from me.

Not Detective Will Boyle.

Not even Allysa. From friends to enemies to sisters.

Two different predators.

Will I kill her, or will Allysa kill me?

Acknowledgements

To thank everyone who played a role in helping me publish The Skull Keeper might amount to a novel on its own. If it takes a village to raise a child, an author needs the support of the entire tribe to release a single novel.

I used the names of several real and very awesome individuals and can't stress enough that they in no way resemble their namesake characters.

In no particular order, a heartfelt thank you to:

Alicia Rideout, words will never be enough to thank you or describe our friendship. It, and you, means the world to me (even though we live on opposite sides of the globe). Only those who truly know us will realise you are the Allysa to my Morgan. Despite us being less 'murdery'.

Sgt. Will Dodds, Forensic Specialist. You shaped the serial killer's torture methods and took my ideas to the next level. (Read darker). Thank you for your time, patience, and most of all for the work that you do to make the world a better place and get justice for the victims. I'll be sure to remain on your good side.

Jessica Huntley, my writing buddy and friend. Thank you for holding me as accountable to writing every day as I did you. And for being the last pair of eyes on this book.

To the wonderful friends I've made in the bookstagram community. Those whose names I used, and those I didn't. You know who you are. You've been my rocks throughout one of the hardest years of my life. If not for your support, The Skull Keeper might not have been written.

Everyone who allowed me to use their names without knowing what the characters would be like – having read my other books that took serious guts. Allysa Myles. Amanda Jaeger. Corey Reynolds. Donna Scuvotti. Holly Wisniewski. Jen Peterson. Sara Ennis. Sébastien Haté.

Nicolina Pieterse, for helping to ensure my medical information is correct and encouraging me to ask even more questions. Thank you for all the lives you saved during the years you worked as an ER nurse and for the difference you still make in the medical field.

My beta readers: Jean, Jen, Nicolina, Sara, Tania and Yolanda. Without your feedback, this novel won't be what it is.

Jana and Marc Barclay, for the exceptional cover and artwork. You're real-life angels.

To my editor, Marcel Koortzen. As always, thank you for allowing me to continue using your name for the city of Marcel, and for improving my writing.

Every ARC reader, I know your time is valuable and your to be read list never ending. Thank you for making time to read and review The Skull Keeper.

More than ever to my family and friends for their continued support and belief in me. My mother deserves a special mention. Not only did she at times help around the house and took care of my daughter, she also shook her head when inspiration struck with a new torture method. It isn't easy being the parent of a thriller author.

I will be forever grateful to everyone who supported me in pushing through and finishing this book, in order to get it in to your hands – the reader. Thank you for allowing me to share my imaginary friends with you and making my dream a reality. Nothing gives me more joy than reading your reviews, because everyone takes away something else from a story. May The Skull Keeper be no different and not make you suspicious of your bookstagram friends.

Most of all, to God. No matter what, I won't bury the talent You gave me.

All mistakes are my own.

About the author

Mariëtte Whitcomb studied Criminology and Psychology at the University of Pretoria. Writing allows her to pursue her childhood dream to hunt criminals, albeit fictional and born in the darkest corners of her imagination.

When Mariëtte isn't writing, she loves reading psychological thrillers and true crime books or spends time with her family, friends, and two miniature schnauzers.

Connect with Mariëtte:
Sign up for her newsletter on her website:
https://mariettewhitcomb.com
Email: mariette@mariettewhitcomb.com
Facebook: https://www.facebook.com/mariettewhitcombauthor
Instagram: https://www.instagram.com/mariettewhitcomb/
Goodreads: https://www.goodreads.com/goodsreadscommariettewhitcomb
Bookbub: https://www.bookbub.com/authors/mariette-whitcomb

Also by Mariëtte Whitcomb

FINLEY SERIES

Orca / Book One

Deception / Book Two

Binding Lies / Book Three

Fortius / Book Four

Ingram Content Group UK Ltd.
Milton Keynes UK
UKHW040713210323
418905UK00005B/560